TO LOVE AND DIE IN DALLAS

TO LOVE AND DIE IN DALLAS

MARY ELIZABETH GOLDMAN

A TOM DOHERTY ASSOCIATES BOOK
NEW YORK

This is a work of fiction. All of the characters, organizations, and events portrayed in this novel are either products of the author's imagination or are used fictitiously.

TO LOVE AND DIE IN DALLAS

Copyright © 2007 by Mary Elizabeth Goldman

This book is printed on acid-free paper.

A Forge Book
Published by Tom Doherty Associates, LLC
175 Fifth Avenue
New York, NY 10010

www.tor-forge.com

Forge® is a registered trademark of Tom Doherty Associates, LLC.

Library of Congress Cataloging-in-Publication Data

Goldman, Mary Elizabeth Sue.
    To love and die in Dallas / Mary Elizabeth Goldman.
        p. cm.
    ISBN-13: 978-0-7653-0934-1
    ISBN-10: 0-7653-0934-3
    1. Legislators' spouses—Crimes against—Fiction. 2. Friendship in adolescence—Fiction. 3. Reunions—Fiction. 4. Diaries—Fiction. 5. Dallas (Tex.)—Fiction. I. Title.
    PS3607.O4545T6 2007
    813'.6—dc22

                                                      2007008188

First Edition: July 2007

Printed in the United States of America

0 9 8 7 6 5 4 3 2 1

This story is dedicated to Lindsey, may she rest in peace.

ACKNOWLEDGMENTS

I've heard it said that writing is a lonely task but the truth is no writer works alone and because of that, because of the people that were there to support me, this book was possible. *To Love and Die in Dallas* is a story of multilayered relationships, serious relationships that were not always pleasant, and the characters, some more amiable than others, portrayed here have evolved from both personal experiences and my active imagination.

There are a few people whom I want to acknowledge for their influence, their talents, their unselfishness, their friendships, and their guidance. Without them, this story could not be told, and I am grateful to them on many levels.

My gratitude extends far and wide, but first to Tom Doherty at Forge Publishing, for his willingness to take a gamble on this novel and on this writer; a large share of thanks goes to all the talented people at Forge who routinely sort through the reams and reams of paper, and in my case paper dripping with red ink, in an endless effort to make projects such as this, and this writer, look good; and to Eric Raab, whose professional and likable mannerisms were huge in reassuring me on those rare occasions I had a tendency to be stressed. And while he may not want me to, I want to single out Robert Gleason, because it was Bob who made critical suggestions, read and re-read time and time again, and it was Bob who, without questioning, cut me slack from time to time when I fell behind schedule. Thank you, Bob, for your encouragement, your sage advice, and your loyalty.

And thanks to my visiting Canadian friend, Kathy Wrath, who may never understand the power behind the Texas mystique but loves us in spite of it or, more likely, because of it, and who encouraged me in her own special way by laughing out loud as she read the manuscript in the shade while keeping me company as I painted the barn during the hottest Texas summer in decades. Thanks also to my lifetime friend Bunny Mogilnicki, who grew up on the same street as my family on a hill overlooking White Rock Lake and who faithfully read the manuscript for grammar (Bunny is an English teacher) and who swears, or at least as close to swearing as Bunny can do, she knows the real identity of these fictitious characters. She is *so wrong!* Thanks also to Dr. Lola Jackson for her unfailing encouragement.

For their support and advice along the way, and especially for their friendship, a double share of "thanks" goes to Win and Meredith Blevins. Thanks also to college professor Bill Waggoner for his early encouragement and comments on the story, to literary agent Susan Gleason for liking my story and for patiently working out the bid'ness details of the bid'ness, and a special tip of the hat to good ol' boy Mike Blakely who not only walks the walk but also sings the talk and who embodies the Texas swagger like few other cowboys! Thanks for the inspiration!

And as for the ultimate in encouraging and never-ending support and enthusiasm, I owe a special acknowledgment to both my parents. To my father, who walked the downtown beat from 1931 and for more than forty years after that, and who knew more about the ins and outs of the dynamic city than any man alive at the time, who was in the basement when Oswald was shot, who eventually had words with Jack Ruby while he was being held in the Dallas jail, and who knew everything about every bar, restaurant, office/courthouse/public building in town. And to my mother who proudly and diligently kept endless scrapbooks on the events, the tragedies, and the celebrations that took place in Dallas for over seventy-five years and loved to tell the history of the colorful city by the banks of the Trinity River.

In November 2002 I had the opportunity to be in the court room when Vincent DiMaio, M. D., Chief Medical Examiner for Bexar County, testified in a gruesome murder trial. During that same trial two Texas Rangers also gave vivid testimony about the manner and cause of death, the crime scene, as well as the firing mechanism of the lethal weapon and the trajectory of the bullet. I found this experience helpful to recall when writing this story. I also want to thank the Dallas Police Department for the tedious work their investigators tackle every day, and a thanks to the fingerprinting specialist for showing me the various methods they use when collecting evidence.

I especially want to acknowledge the dedicated men and women in the Emergency Medical Services for their role in not only saving lives but for their importance in controlling and preserving crime scenes. During my training with the Houston Public Health Department and as an active member of a Houston area EMS team as well as a first responder, I had experience in preserving crime scenes and developed a respect for CSI teams early on.

I'm always in awe, and a little intimidated, by library staffs but in this case I am indebted to the staff at the Dallas Public Library who enthusiastically assisted me even though I knew that they knew I was asking too much. I also want to acknowledge other resource material made available to me and other writers. Specifically to Larenda Roberts for her guide book *Dallas Uncovered,* to Keith Wilson, M.D., for his writer's guide *Cause of Death,* and to Russell Bintliff for his guide

Police Procedural. These resource books were helpful to me in substantiating or correcting me in what I either knew or *thought* I knew about the Dallas scene, police investigative work, and the order and role of autopsies in solving crimes.

On the lighter side, for the choicest of teenage memories, thanks to my graduating class of Bryan Adams High School in Dallas, Texas. Thanks also to the security guard at the Old Red Courthouse in Dallas who, by looking the other way, allowed me time to explore the many dark and musty hallways beneath the huge building prior to renovations and to climb to the top of the uppermost chambers to the old hanging gallows. A special thanks to the fireman who came to talk me down and help me off that old and swaying wooden staircase that daring afternoon as dozens of pigeons swooped by me while I hung out in a precarious position in that same airy loft.

Sincere thanks go to Janet Goldman for giving up her weekends to assist me and for the hours she spent driving me numerous times around Dallas and eventually for learning to be a "street walker" as together we explored the avenues and alleyways of downtown during incredibly heavy spring rains and who, along with me, sought refuge from one particular storm in the lobby at the Adolphus Hotel. And thanks also to the hotel's doorman who may have thought we were street walkers of another kind but who took pity on us and graciously offered us towels to dry off with before having hot coffee and a little slice of cheese to go along with our whining at the hotel's magnificent bar that afternoon.

And last, but as far from least as one can get least, to the guy from back East, the guy in the yellow Bonneville convertible, the guy in the black leather jacket, the tough guy, the one real deal—forever—thanks.

From the beginning *To Love and Die in Dallas* was a joy for me to write and through this writer's wonderful world of *selective recall* it was possible for me not only to revisit the past but to reinvent history and create the cast of characters in this story.

Still, these characters, the good, the bad, the beauty, and the uglies, like everything else in life, have undergone several transformations and while some of them with their unique traits and personalities may *seem* real, and I hoped that they would, they are not and, except for a glimpse back to the sock-hop era and a chance to briefly recall a few isolated political and special events such as the assassination of President John F. Kennedy, the Cotton Bowl game, and the Texas State Fair and popular places like Brownie's, The Pig Stand, Winfrey Point, and other landmarks around White Rock Lake, this is entirely a work of "inspired" fiction.

The inspiration started like this: The very week after high school graduation I left home, I left Dallas, and I left Texas. In the soaring '60s, Las Vegas was a small windy town in the middle of the desert where the wealthy, the desperate, the naïve, and the notorious came to play, catch good lounge shows featuring top industry names, enjoy free call drinks, and roll the dice. Clark County, Nevada, was the last frontier of the fast and furious, where gamblers and mobsters and lawmen rubbed elbows, and I was underage in a city that looked the other way. Politicians freely moved about the casinos with high-profile celebrities and scantily clad starlets, and all cameras were strictly forbidden. In those days, what happened in Vegas really did stay in Vegas. There was too much at stake for it to be otherwise, consequences were swift and exact and I was paying attention to those who introduced me to the glitzy lights of a darker world.

A few years later, I left Vegas and thought I was prepared for anything. I returned to Dallas, Big D, where women had big hair and men didn't walk, they strutted! It was an era where wildcatters were as comfortable climbing the rigs as they were buying furs for their "gals" downtown at Neiman Marcus. No writer has ever had more colorful history to draw upon than Texas and Texans, a treasure trove of inspiration.

Years went by quickly and one day in the early spring I received a notice of my upcoming high school class reunion. Early on I had resolved, and up until then had managed, to avoid such events but apparently time had softened me, and now I was curious to discover what had become of my classmates at the school "near the city's eastern borders underneath the Texas sky."

Were the football players still popular? Did the ROTC cadets continue to stand at attention? Did the class personalities become as successful as I imagined? Did the cheerleaders continue to exude bubbly encouragement? Did the preacher's daughter ever learn to behave, and was homecoming queen still the most enviable girl alive? Sadly, there were several, too many, missing from this one-time hopeful group of wide-eyed wonders, but Vietnam, the drug culture, and the sexual revolution had that effect on many graduating classes in the sixth decade of the twentieth century. I wanted to bring them back, to remember them in an imaginary world, and as a result, I created a handful of eager young people found here in the pages of To Love and Die in Dallas. I hope you enjoy reading the mystery, perhaps solving it as you go, and *almost* recognizing the characters portrayed.

And, the answers to my questions are absolutely yes, in every case!

PART ONE

THE DECEPTION

1

From the beginning, there was something more than any schoolgirl friendship between them and while neither of them had the experience to recognize the attraction, in retrospect, they were both aware that something exceptional had occurred from the beginning.

———

When Lindsey and I met in the ninth grade I thought she was the prettiest girl in Gaston Junior High School. With dark brown eyes and delicate features, she had a natural beauty that didn't need her freshly applied makeup, the subtle brushing of mascara, and the cherry-red lipstick.

We met because we were assigned desks alphabetically, and because her last name was Wilson and mine was Williams she sat behind me in sour-faced Mrs. Dobson's homeroom class. This seating arrangement allowed Lindsey to speak nonstop to the back of my head and each weekday morning she managed to maintain a whispered commentary about the other students in our school— what they were wearing, what they did over the weekend, what happened last night, who was dozing at their desks, who was playing with himself, and who was smoking in the girls' room.

Everybody liked Lindsey and everybody wanted to be her friend. But that first day in class she made it clear we were going to be friends, best friends—me, a skinny, shy, and bespectacled girl wearing my sister's hand-me-down clothes.

I was the youngest of four girls and lived with my family in Lake Highlands on the then easternmost border of Dallas at the edge of White Rock Lake. We had outgrown our old house, close to downtown near the railroad tracks on the frugal side of Turtle Creek, and we moved to the lake the summer I turned six years old.

A large two-story house on a hill, our new home with dormer windows trimmed in white had a basement game room finished with knotty pine paneling lacquered with a glossy finish. A small white picket fence thickly entwined with red climbing roses enclosed the front yard.

The lake was at the bottom of the hill. In the summer we could walk—or in my case run—down to the bathhouse, pull the chain for the mandatory outdoor shower, and swim "free" from 9:00 to 11:00 each weekday morning from Memorial Day through Labor Day.

That first summer at the lake I broke my arm and then one of the kids at the end of our street came down with polio. Our parents and every parent on that side of the lake was terrified of the crippling disease and my sisters and I were confined to the house during the hottest hours of those summer days. Each afternoon, after lunch, Caroline, Letty, Maggie Louise, and I made pallets on the floor in the living room in front of the fan and used our cooling-off time reading aloud to each other.

As the cicadas shrilled at fever pitch and the outside heat spiraled up from the sidewalk, we read of *Call of the Wild's* great dog Buck, stolen from his master, delivered into bondage, and whipped into pulling a heavy sled through the frozen Klondike. We shuddered at the fierceness of Kazan, the wolf-dog. We laughed when our mother imitated Aunt Polly calling Tom out over some prank and we felt sticky from the spray of sea salt when Melville's whale did battle with Ahab and his deadly harpoon. We cried over *Black Beauty* and careened around dusty back roads in a green coupe with the Hardy boys, hiding in eerie night shadows as their mysteries unfolded one page at a time.

In spite of the plastered arm and the threat of a disease a six-year-old cannot understand, it was still an idyllic summer by the lake.

Lindsey, on the other hand, lived alone with her mother, Dena, in a small rented house on Centerville Road in Casa View, a planned community with row after row of cracker box houses and miles from the serenity of the lake. Lindsey spent that summer—and every summer—watching her mother leave for work, watching her struggle to make ends meet, watching her ever-changing parade of friends, boyfriends, and bill collectors.

But now we were teenagers and we'd become "best" friends and I was spending the night with Lindsey. Her mother had a date and had already left when my father dropped me off curbside at her house. I knocked on the door and when there was no answer I opened it and called out as I stepped inside. I found Lindsey in the kitchen, searching the pantry shelves for something to eat.

Another knock from the front porch and there was Butter at the door, her overnight case in hand. Before the door closed, I could see her father's car pulling out of the driveway. Like me, she'd been dropped off.

I was jealous of Butter. Categorized as one of the "cute" girls in our school I feared she might take my place and become Lindsey's best friend and that I would be forgotten.

Smiling and confident, Butter walked straight into Lindsey's bedroom and returned with two pillows. She tossed one to each of us and threw a couple of the sofa cushions on the floor for herself.

"Did you get it?" Butter asked as she folded her legs under her and fluffed and stuffed another cushion into her lap.

Lindsey ducked around the corner into her room and quickly returned, fanning the pages of the paperback novel.

Banned throughout the Bible Belt as well as Dallas, Lindsey had nevertheless obtained a copy of Peyton Place. With the good parts underscored and the pages flagged with little shreds of paper, Lindsey plopped on a sofa cushion on the floor and Butter passed out the cigarettes. Shoulder to shoulder with me, Lindsey began to read "the best parts" from the forbidden book.

Until that night, I had masked my sexual ignorance with silence, but that evening, filled with revelation and laughter, I lost my inhibitions. Every time we reached an erotic passage, my friends explicated it for me—then expanded on it with scandalous gossip and lascivious speculation. They looked forward to elaboration, and I was ecstatic with this carnal edification.

Lindsey's mother didn't come home that night and I volunteered to fix the three of us breakfast that next morning. Standing in front of the opened fridge I reached for the cold new pack of Winstons, tapped the unopened cigarettes and calmly pulled that thin red strip. Taking out the first new cigarette, I rapped the filtered tip against the back of my hand, placed the unlit Winston loosely in the corner of my mouth, and stared indifferently into the almost empty refrigerator. It was useless. I closed the fridge door and walked into the living room, retrieved the lighter from the sofa table, and for the first time with one hand, flicked the lighter to a flame and took a long drag on that first delicious cigarette of the morning.

What was left of that spring semester in the ninth grade dragged. Since that portentous night at Lindsey's, I had learned to like Butter, but vague uncertainties and not-so-vague insecurities kept me from feeling completely comfortable with her.

By the end of May, Lindsey was taller, leggier, and tittier. And now she had a boyfriend, Tommy Lee Horton, older by two years and with a car of his own. Her life was perfect, and I was a spectator living my early teens vicariously through this very real Dallas beauty.

The beginning of summer was marked by one event—the last day of school. Most of the silliness we'd gone through at Gaston Junior High was behind us. We were maturing, some of us more than others, and we were desperately trying to keep from being bored while being "good girls."

And so it was a guileless and virginal summer.

Dena had settled down with one regular friend, a Dallas cop, but was still seldom home. With her frequent absences we had the house on Centerville Road to ourselves.

Lindsey was a free spirit that summer and that translated to no curfews—day or night. She and Tommy Lee spent a good deal of the summer cruising around the lake in his white convertible with the top down. "See and be seen" was the objective. Most nights they'd swing by my house and I'd crowd into the front seat of the Chevy and the three of us would drive to the Hi-D-Ho on Garland Road and share an order of curly fries served by carhops at the drive-in diner.

Secure against the door and happy to be included, I maintained my third-wheel position. Since there were no exceptions to my curfew they would drop me off in front of my house on Peninsula Drive at ten o'clock.

But even with the imposed and inflexible deadlines, I was content with my peer standing. There was satisfaction knowing that Butter didn't have a boyfriend either. I could wish and I could dream—and I wrote it all down.

Every thought, every fantasy, every desire I recorded in my diary. I hypothesized these private journals were in the same sacred category as the United States mail, the ark that preserved the tablets of stone, or the tag sewn onto the seam of mattresses and pillows and sofa cushions that warns against removal and promises penalty of imprisonment for such an arrogant deed. No one would ever dare to violate those sanctified passages written in my book.

I got a job as a clerk at Mott's five-and-dime in Casa Linda, an early shopping center with its distinguishing Spanish tile roof connecting all the shops and the landmark flying Red Horse on top of the Mobil station at the intersection of Garland Road and Buckner. All day friends from school would come in and out of the five-and-dime and whether they bought anything or not was of little consequence to me. It was my turn to "see and be seen."

Until Skillern's Drugs opened on the corner, Mott's was the best place to shop for most anything—cosmetics, fabrics, notions, toys, goldfish, small appliances, school supplies, Christmas decorations—it was all there. Mott's didn't sell major appliances, those could be bought next door at the Western Auto or at Sears and Roebuck on Ross Avenue, but that's the only thing that couldn't be found at the five-and-dime.

On the other side of the street Tommy Lee worked at Ashburn's Ice Cream Shop. I worked flexible shifts, sometimes split shifts, but he came into Mott's every day while I was working just to say hey. Lindsey, on the other hand, rarely came by and when she did, she bought something.

Saturday nights were the best nights of the week. Monday

through Friday Mott's closed at 9:00 P.M, but on Saturday the store closed at 6:00 P.M. and was never open on Sunday. Sunday was the Sabbath and, for the most part, the community kept it holy. After all, the Texas blue laws were there to remind us of our ancient covenant.

A courtyard separated Mott's and the record shop and in the middle of the brick pavement was a small Spanish fountain and several iron benches. Concrete planters, filled with blooming annuals in the spring and summer months, marked the corners of the outdoor retreat.

Sequestered behind this shopper's cloister but still part of the complex were a few professional offices, the optometrist's center, the barbershop, and the second most popular establishment in all of White Rock—Teen Timers.

Home of the original dirty dancing, the birthplace of the Casa Linda Low Life, Teen Timers was so full of smoke, noise, and packed bodies, that we could barely see, hear, or breathe. Amateur bands imitating Jerry Lee Lewis, Jimmy Reed, and Buddy Holly played nonstop for the dancers and listeners alike. It was a blissful sanctuary where rumors not only circulated wildly, but originated right there in the girl's room. In short, Teen Timers was a dimly lit haven with parental blessing.

That September we were high school students and while we were the low dogs, according to our school pecking order, Lindsey and I had a certain advantage. Tommy Lee was a senior and by now he and Lindsey were going steady.

Santa Clara Drive was not close to Peninsula Drive, it wasn't even on my side of the lake, but Tommy Lee and I had become friends that summer and he drove from his house on Santa Clara to my house every morning to give me a ride to school. I thought he would have given me a ride anyway, but Lindsey had a way of making it clear that Tommy Lee was doing her the favor by giving *me a lift.* We had to pass the high school to pick up Lindsey where we inevitably waited in the kitchen. We'd help ourselves to coffee and sit at the drop leaf table arranged next to the back window while she finished getting dressed.

The tardy bell rang as we took the steps two at a time into the school, and I spent a good deal of time in detention, but considered it a small price to pay for being part of the entourage.

Traditionally the Texas State Fair is held each October in Dallas and one day has always been designated as Dallas Student Day at the fair, and every student in the city is given a holiday from class and a complimentary gate pass for that weekday event.

Lindsey and I rode the city bus to the fairgrounds that afternoon. Tommy Lee had intended to meet us there later. Even without a rendezvous point, it was assumed that running into one another that night would be easy among thousands of milling people.

But while we were waiting in line by Fletcher's corn dog stand, Tommy Lee and a friend of his—a tall guy with dark hair combed back into a ducktail, a tough-looking stranger in a black leather jacket—walked up behind us. Lindsey and Tommy Lee exchanged cool greetings and for the first time, I caught myself paying more attention to the "other" guy.

I watched the unlit cigarette that dangled from his lips. Never once taking his eyes off me, he flipped the hinged lid of his Zippo and brought the end of the Lucky Strike into a bright glow. With a flick of the wrist he slipped the lighter back into his jacket pocket.

That's all it took. A Zippo lighter, a near smile, and the course of my life had suddenly changed.

Lindsey and Tommy Lee were soon arguing. Maybe he was late—maybe we were late—nobody ever knew why they fought, but by that time they fought more often than not.

I was still fixated on the stranger when Lindsey grabbed my arm, broke my trance, and pulled me away. When I turned around I saw Tommy Lee and his buddy laughing, dodging mock jabs at each other, and making their way through the crowd toward the midway, in the opposite direction.

After that, Lindsey and Tommy Lee became an on-again off-again kind of couple. From that first summer of young love, their relationship was now in a state of deterioration. Like a game between them, they fought about anything and everything. I was caught in the middle. Then one night just minutes after I'd hung up the phone listening to Lindsey declare the relationship was over, Tommy Lee called and asked me to ride down to the Hi-D-Ho with him.

This was the moment I had dreamed about for a hundred lifetimes. There couldn't be anything wrong with me going out with Tommy Lee, just two good friends out to get a Coke. What was the harm?

I couldn't go I told him. I'd already promised Butter I would be right over. Then he offered to fix her up with this friend of his who'd just moved into the neighborhood from back East. The four of us could go.

Butter's dad nixed our plans. As promised I went to her house but spent the evening sulking about my ill-fortune.

Before long Lindsey and Tommy Lee were back together again and the next time Tommy Lee called me he suggested I go out with them and this same friend of his. I would not be sitting next to Tommy Lee but was happy to be included.

It was early spring and Tommy Lee had the top down when he and Lindsey picked me up. We drove by Ashburn's and picked up my date, the same guy I'd seen with Tommy Lee at the State Fair, who was getting off from work. From there we cruised through the parking lot of the Hi-D-Ho, checking to see who was there. We didn't stop, but drove down Garland Road just past the spillway—that marks the line between wet and dry—to the Pig Stand, another choice hangout where an older crowd gathered.

On that end of Garland Road—where East Grand picks up, past Tennison Park, past the old Brownies restaurant—neon signs glow or flicker above several liquor stores. Carhops at the Pig Stand stayed the busiest, serving beer and burgers two hours after the Hi-D-Ho closed on Saturday nights.

Still not stopping, we turned around and headed back up Garland Road past Casa Linda and Lochwood, turned right, and crossed the railroad tracks on Barnes Bridge Road. Everybody that was somebody in our limited world was there. Dozens of cars were already pulled over, lining a path on undeveloped land, and more were still arriving.

Tommy Lee was there to race and my date and I got out of the backseat. Lindsey took the scarf draped above the rearview mirror and placed it on her head, wrapping the ends around her neck and tying it snug in the back. She smoothed her blond bangs to the side and tucked them into the edges of the scarf.

With engines revving, headlights on high beam, the night vibrated with high-pitched excitement. Silhouettes were outlined among the thick dust. Shadowy forms darted out of harm's way and joined together in rows. The race was about to start and we stood on the hoods of the parked cars with our friends to get as good a view as possible.

The finish line was at the far end of the caliche road and as the two cars sped past, the crowd rushed in behind them only to be covered with dirt and dust. Nobody could see, but when the cars swung around and came back to the start, Tommy Lee was happy and had his arm around Lindsey.

We didn't stick around, but drove back to the lake and out to Winfrey Point, the pavilion set high on a hill that overlooks White

Rock Lake. Tommy Lee and Lindsey changed seats with us. We got out and walked around and as we did they scrambled over the seat to the back.

The twisting and rocking, the giggles and sighs, the inevitable gasp in the backseat were intensified in the dark night. At once, I was reminded of the "good parts," the really good parts, in "the" book.

Sitting next to the door on the shotgun side, I was nervous. My "boyfriend" slid in close. He had his arm across my shoulders and with his other hand he turned my face to his and gently kissed me on the lips. Again and again until those sweet gentle kisses got harder and harder.

He whispered for me to open my mouth. Surprised at the spoken words, I was nevertheless compliant as he slipped his tongue into my mouth. Years earlier my friend Davy had pinned me down while wrestling in the backyard and kissed me, but until that night out by the lake, that playful smack somewhere between my lips and right cheek had been the sum total of my sexual encounters.

Mother was waiting on the porch when Tommy Lee pulled into the driveway. We were late and it was one of life's most embarrassing moments. I was humiliated in front of my dearest friends.

Another summer came and passed and I continued to work at the five-and-dime. I didn't date but when the Christmas holidays came, Tommy Lee's friend asked me out again. But this time, we wouldn't be double-dating.

Curfew was the last thing on my mind and once I climbed in the yellow Bonneville, slid over to sit close to my date, I never gave it a thought—until we pulled back into the driveway a little past midnight.

I knew then *exactly* what time it was because there was Mother standing under the porch light in her chenille robe, asking me if I knew what time it was. I glanced at my watch and when I looked up, my whole body felt flushed. As I walked past her she followed me in the house, never stopping the verbal assault. I never said good-bye to my date and that was the last time I went out with the handsome tough guy in the black leather jacket.

I was being mothered to death.

2

The office was cool and dimly lit. Dark paneling, plush Oriental rugs over parquet floors, and drapes with a hint of gilded threads woven into heavy tapestry were drawn shut across the window, keeping it that way summer and winter, day and night. Cove lighting hidden behind ornate crown molding cast a lustrous opulence to the private office. A spotlight from the ceiling focused on a massive bronze sculpture displayed on the credenza behind the oversized desk. Teakwood tables, each adorned with a unique piece of Lalique crystal, flanked the leather couch and matching chairs. The office was categorically ostentatious and David Matthews's reputation as a criminal trial lawyer was as outrageous as the office trappings. But neither prosperity nor the respect and attention he craved had come easy.

David's mother had died in an auto accident when he was a young boy. After her death, his dad, a machinist at Texas

Instruments, added a second work shift to his schedule, and David had grown up alone in the house by the park at White Rock Lake.

He was called Davy back then and back then Davy spent most of his days barefoot and outside, either up a tree or fishing down by the lake. There were usually boats tied up along the shoreline at White Rock and he had no compunction about borrowing them when the fish were biting.

That's where he'd met Annie. With her arm in a cast, she was sitting alone one morning in one of those wooden rowboats tied to an old willow by the lake while her sisters were swimming at the public beach.

"Hey . . . whaddya think you're doing . . . ?" Annie was surprised, she hadn't heard him come up behind her and now this troublemaker was starting to deliberately rock the boat. "Quit it," she demanded, trying to stand.

"Says who?" The smart-aleck kid laughed. "Who's gonna make me—you? Ha, fat chance, kiddo."

Adversaries and friends from the beginning; when those two strong-willed minds met head-on, the feathers were bound to fly. For the years that followed Davy found reasons to hang around Annie and Annie kept up the effort to be irritated by him.

But Davy was a troublemaker in many ways and by the time he turned seventeen he was on probation from *juvie* court. It could have been worse than probation, but he'd managed to get away with other, more daring crimes. After graduating from high school a year behind the rest of his class he began working full time in the garage at the Texaco on the corner of Lake Highlands Drive and Buckner Boulevard.

Four years later those few classmates who remembered Davy and those neighbors that used full service at the Texaco were surprised to learn he'd applied and been accepted for college admission at North Texas State in Denton.

Nobody knew what motivated Davy and, except for Annie, nobody cared. In all respects, Davy distanced himself from family and friends. Two years later he'd transferred to Baylor University and after graduating with honors he was accepted into Baylor's College of Law.

Throughout law school he continued to work, first as a clerk with a prestigious firm in Waco. Impressed with his ability to think on his feet, his quick recall of prior dispositions, the respect he garnered from colleagues, and his near charismatic appeal to women, the Old Guard offered him an unprecedented associate partnership upon passing the bar. It was a generous offer, but Dean Walters, who had considerable sway in these matters, offered another option.

He recommended that Davy, now David, work as an assistant district attorney in the Dallas County court system. The compensation was considerably less than the firm's offer, but the dean believed that in the long run, given David's competitive nature, the overwhelming caseloads of the large and diverse county would better prepare David for a career in litigation. In time his experience in the D.A.'s office would become invaluable to his success in private practice. So from the prosecuted to the prosecutor, David's expertise in criminal law had come full circle.

———

David Matthews stood from the chair behind his desk and crossed the room to the closet where he'd carefully hung his sports coat on the brass hanger. He felt for the breast pocket and pulled out a pack of cigarettes.

Why in God's name did she have to write everything down?

Late yesterday the courier had delivered the package marked PERSONAL. Liz Jamison left it unopened on the desk so that her boss would find it first thing in the morning.

The handwritten note enclosed read simply:

D.
Thought this would interest you.
Love, B.

He hadn't smoked much since he was a teenager, but any-time he thought about her, he felt the need for the damn things.

David sat down behind the desk, opened the drawer, fished out an old matchbook and again went over the unexpected late-evening phone conversation.

"Hello."

"David?"

"Yes?"

"David, this is Anne—Annie."

"Where are you—are you in Dallas? It's Annie"—she could hear him speak to Taylor in the background—"Taylor says hi. How are you?"

"I'm fine."

"You don't sound so fine—what's the matter?"

"I have a favor to ask."

"You got it."

"Don't be so agreeable."

"Okay, you don't have it—is that better?"

"How do you put up with me off and on all these years?"

"It's been hell!" He laughed a little as he lit a stale cigarette.

"Are you still smoking?"

"Is that what you called about?"

"Of course not—it's none of my business. David, I need to know if I could get some information from the police—if it would be available to me and—or maybe—if you could get it for me. . . . "

"Like what? What's this all about, Annie?"

"Look, David, this is a mistake—I shouldn't have called—I don't want to cause trouble between you and Taylor."

"Hey, kiddo, that's not going to happen."

"Good—because that's the last thing I want—you sound happy."

"I am."

"I'm really glad for you. Okay, here goes—this is still nothing more than a gut feeling, oh, call it intuition, if you will, but I've done a little research at the library in Austin and also here in Dallas last summer at the Morning News—old newspaper clippings, society page, election news—"

"Why?"

"And I've done a little snooping around—well, not snooping—but I've been thinking—and I've put a lot of things together—and I think I've come up with some interesting conclusions."

"Damn it, I wish you wouldn't do that. . . ."

"I know, but listen, David, I have all her letters and now, more than ever, I'm convinced we're dealing with a man capable of—"

"Hold it. Stop right there. What's this 'we' business? Is there a 'we' now? What? Did hell freeze over? Did I miss something? What?"

"No, of course not—and you're absolutely right. It's me—I'm dealing with a man that I'm certain is more than capable of committing a horrible crime, and I think we—I think I knew that years ago. It's more than that though, David, it's . . ."

"It's what, Annie? You never liked the guy and nobody, but nobody ever thought for a minute that you did. If it's a vendetta you're after, I'm not gonna help you. Every time you get messed up with Lindsey, every goddamn time, things go to hell and I'm not

*gonna be a part of it. Let it go, damn it, she's dead and to be per-
fectly honest about it, I can't say I'm gonna shed any tears over her
demise!"*

It would have been Annie-like to quietly replace the receiver, simply hang up, and let him rant and rave. But this
time, she stayed on and somehow he knew she wasn't going
to leave him with a ringing in his ears. Not this time—not
yet.

"*I know everything you're saying is true—has been true—but
don't you see it's more than just a personality issue. I'm scared,
David—I'm really scared. And I need you to help me get a copy of
the autopsy report. If I can find out where . . .*"

"*Annie, you know, you're too damn naïve—and I shouldn't
have snapped at you like that—it's just that—*"

"*Please, David, I shouldn't be calling this late at night. I didn't
really want to get you involved, but please I need to talk to you.*"

"*It's okay, Annie.*"

"*David, if you were my attorney, wouldn't everything I told
you be confidential—nothing could come back to hurt either one
of us?*"

"*That's right—if I represent you.*"

"*Then will you?*"

"*I thought you'd never ask.*"

"*This is serious, David, I need your help—will you?*"

"*You don't need to ask—you know that.*"

"*Okay.*"

"*Now, what the hell's this all about and what exactly are you
mixed up in?*"

No answer.

"*Annie, you've gotta be straight with me.*"

"I know and I will—but it's hard—it's about Lindsey."

"You're here for the funeral, aren't you? I guess I should have been expecting you to call."

"Yes and no. I did come in this afternoon for the service, but I didn't plan to see you—or talk to you."

"Thanks."

"You know what I mean, David. I doubt Taylor . . ."

"When do you want to meet?"

———

David finished another cigarette and closed the cover on the red leather-bound notebook. He couldn't imagine how Butter came by this journal, but this was Annie's work and he would return it today.

3

David was waiting on the sidewalk. He glanced at his watch. A quarter past one and the lunch crowd had come and gone. She was late, but he figured she would be. She always was and he had long ago stopped getting twisted over fifteen or twenty minutes. It wasn't worth it.

He didn't have to wonder how long it had been since he last saw her. He knew exactly. Four years ago next month—on the fifteenth. He was having dinner with a client at the Petroleum Club and when she walked into the private dining room he looked up. As the maître d' greeted them, her friend slipped the black wrap from her shoulders and handed it to an attendant. They were seated at a choice table by the window overlooking the Dallas skyline. David was envious of the man who was so taken with his companion; Annie never knew David was at the club that evening.

Since that night David had married again for the third

time. From her first marriage his new wife had one child, now grown and married, living in Atlanta, and expecting her first child.

A grandbaby, even a stepgrandbaby, should place him comfortably in the folds of a family, a place he'd been trying to settle into for most of his life. Marrying Taylor had been the most sensible thing he'd ever done—the right thing—he was sure of it.

─────────

From the middle lane of the one-way street the taxi took a sharp right and slid in next to the curb, coming to an abrupt stop. It wasn't the screeching brakes that got David's attention. It was Annie; she still had that effect on him. David went to open the cab door for her.

She stepped out smiling, reached up, and gave David a brushing kiss on the cheek. It was yesterday all over—he really wanted a cigarette.

"Hungry?" he asked.

"Always," she answered.

The entrance to the café was around the corner and set back at the end of a series of connecting office buildings in the core of downtown Dallas. In that same set of buildings is a local bar where chrome barstools with faded red vinyl cushions stand facing the worn bar. The glare from outside veils those few patrons who feel comfortable or lack concern with the bleak setting. On all days and most nights any air circulating comes from a draft through the door, propped open with a short stack of the *Dallas Morning News*. When the outside air doesn't stir, an oscillating fan whirs back and forth behind the bar, a luxury for the bartender and not the customer. To the right of the open bar door in that same alcove

is the eating part of this choice piece of downtown real estate. The bar is just called "the bar" and all of it is owned by
Francis Zacchoias.

Without a recommendation, coupled with a good deal of
faith, only those with a knowledge of the ins and outs of
downtown Dallas, a fool, a drunk, or a combination of all
would venture around that corner for the first time—even at
high noon. As far as anyone knows, the dismal bar above is
and was unofficially off-limits for the working lunch crowd,
as the bar seemed to cater only to the downtown riffraff. Occasionally a down-on-his-lucker was found sleeping off a ben-
der against the brick wall in the alley, but cops on the beat
who ate at the café, and many did, were careful to keep
drunks off the stairs—and Dallas cops never reached into
their own pockets for their meals at the café. That was the
understanding—from the beginning.

As skyscrapers rose to greater heights on the outskirts of
town and downtown grew older and shabbier, eager young
professionals became more sophisticated than those just
ahead of them on the executive rung. A smart new generation was emerging and the zealous Dallas corporate world was
at a pivotal point.

But the café had its own brand of ambience and it wasn't
going to change. The food alone was good enough and priced
so that the line of regulars began backing up and onto the
sidewalk during the early part of any given weekday lunch
hour. For a time Annie and her best friend Lindsey were regulars for lunch at the small café hidden around the corner.

———

Washed trays, hot and still dripping with moisture, were
stacked high at the beginning of the buffet line. David

reached and brought two down and placed them side by side on the stainless parallel rails.

The double doors to the kitchen swung open wide as the large man backed out. He wrapped the white apron strings around his back and tied them with a quick slipknot at his waist in front. "Whata can I getcha?" he asked without looking up, but waiting now behind the counter to serve.

"The steak, please," Annie answered.

"As if we had a choice," David leaned down and whispered into her ear.

The man peered over the top of his wire rims, balanced almost to the end of his nose, and stopped still.

"Annie! Is thata you? Of course, it's ah you." Francis Zacchoias started to smile and quickly plopped a second scoop of the cabbage on the next plate. He picked up both plates and carried them around the end of the serving line and firmly set them on the trays. Untying the apron strings, he wiped his hands and draped the apron over the cash register. Before she could brace herself, he grabbed Annie in an enormous, joyful hug and swung her off the ground.

"My goodness," he said with his heavy Greek inflection where r's rolled thick off the tongue and most words ended with a short ah. "I can'ta believe it's ah really you—look ata you. You don'ta change ata all—still ah my little Annie—so young ah, so pretty, what's ita been—five—six ah years, maybe eh?"

"More like *ten* years, Francis," Annie answered as the big man held her now at arm's length.

"Nah, couldn'ta be." Francis took a good look at David, turned Annie loose, and grabbed David in an equally enormous hug.

"Bring us ah pitcher of beer," Francis called out in the direction of the kitchen.

Francis released David and returned all his attention back to Annie. Crossing his arms across his large barrel chest, he stood there smiling and shaking his head. He pointed to her and looked at David. "Just as pretty as ever, eh? My little Texas friend. Sit, sit," he instructed, sliding into the booth next to Annie.

The waitress brought a tray with a pitcher of beer and three frosty mugs. "Ten ah years," Francis said beneath his breath, tsking his tongue against the roof of his mouth, and shaking his head in disbelief. "How have ah you been? You ah married aren'ta ya? Of course you ah married—the two ah you meanta for each other. So how's ah Lindsey? You seen ah her lately?"

"Francis . . ." Annie was hesitant. "Francis, Lindsey's dead."

Francis withdrew his arm with a jerk from behind Annie. "No," he pleaded in a raspy low voice, "don'ta talka like ah that."

"Oh, Francis, I'm sorry. I'd thought you would have known—heard about it or read about it in the newspaper or something."

"Francis, when was the last time you saw Lindsey?" David asked, more out of curiosity than concern.

Francis did not speak right away and David and Annie both waited anxiously for the answer.

"About ah six months ago," Francis began quietly. "I ran into her one day on the way to the bank with the afternoon deposits. She was in ah big hurry and she didn't see me ata all. I called to her ah two, ah maybe three times before she turn around and saw me."

"How did she seem? I mean, was she okay—how'd she look?" Annie asked.

"Kinda strange. Like ah she had her mind on ah something real important. At first, I don'ta think she knew it was ah me—right here in front of the café and all. Imagine that—she almost didn't even know where she was. But she sure was ah in a mighty big hurry. How did she die—what happened?"

"Francis," David spoke, "did you talk to her?"

Francis nodded.

"What happened after she saw it was you?"

"She was justa real jittery." Francis imitated the shakes with his hands. "I caught up with her on the sidewalk and started to give her a hug. She stopped me. Put her hand righta here," he said, placing his open hand on his chest over his heart. "I coulda feel right then she wasa trembling. I wanted her to come down and have a talk ah with me, but she said she woulda some other time and then she justa walked on down the street to the corner and crossed ata the light. I thought ata the time she was ah like ah trying to stay away from ah me. Maybe she wasa embarrassed to see me again and I hated to think ah she mighta feel thata way abouta me after all we'd gonna through."

David and Annie looked at each other and David picked up the mug and took a long drink.

David motioned for the waitress to remove the untouched plates. Annie put her arm around Francis's shoulder and gently rubbed the back of his neck with her fingers.

"Thata son of a bitch," Francis said as he worked his handkerchief from his back pocket.

"Who?" David wanted to know.

"That creep ah she was a married to—the lawyer fella. That son of a bitch. He used to come in here and threaten me to leave her alone and he wasa the one that shoulda have left her alone. It wasn't enough he send her boys away from her. He had her beat up and now he kill her too. I oughta kill thata son of a bitch."

"Francis, you don't know what you're saying. Everybody's upset here but don't go talking like that," Annie said.

But David saw an open window and he had no intention of letting it close. "What makes you think he killed her?" He pressed for the answers before Francis could clear his thoughts.

"He's a crazy man that'sa why. He don'ta deserve Lindsey. He use her justa like ah some kind ah toy. He got no respect for her and when he wasa done with her he toss her out the door like a piece ah trash. Embarrass her—humiliated in front of her friends and family. Son of a bitch. I shoulda have helped Lindsey when I coulda. I shoulda known."

"Known what, Francis?" Annie asked. "How could you have helped Lindsey?"

"Oh, Annie"—Francis reached for her hand—"there was a lot I coulda have ah done for Lindsey. I woulda have done anything for her." Francis spoke directly to Annie, "I loved her—I'd loved her for years. After you moved away, Lindsey woulda come in here almost every day after the lunch business. I'd sit and we'd visit for a long time—we coulda talk about anything. We were, how you say—easy—comfortable with ah each other. Sometimes she'd ah reach across the table and holda my hand—or just toucha my fingers. Those were special times. If she coulda, she'd ah wait for me to get the day's receipts ready and walk ah with me to the bank to make a deposit. I loved ah being with her and she loved ah being with ah me. She'd ah laugh ata my Texas jokes and when she'd ah hear a new one, I'd ah be the first person she'd ah tell. She thought it was a great thing that a poor Greek boy like ah me loved ah Texas as much as she did. A real Texas beauty she was a—a fine girl.

"Ya know," he went on, "when Ismini and I were first married, I wanted us to be so happy, to be ina love, to be ah lovers, but Ismini loved only whata I give her—things, she loved *things*. Now, we have understanding. She gave me three fine sons and I leave her alone. Ismini hated Lindsey, but Ismini never wanted me—not the man—only things." Francis stopped his story and waited for a response, but David and Annie could only look at each other for reaction.

Annie was the first to speak. "I can't believe what you're telling us, Francis. Were you and Lindsey having an affair . . . ?"

"Go on," David urged.

"An affair? Yes, it was an affair. But I loved her and she loved ah me back. She was ah kind and gentle and she loved ah loving me.

"Ismini never wanted me to toucha her. But Lindsey—ah, sweet, beautiful Lindsey . . ." Francis talked softly now and, for the moment, seemed to forget David and Annie were listening to this great remembrance of love. Francis dropped his head, his chin almost touching his chest. He was quiet.

"Francis," Annie spoke softly. "Francis, I'm sorry, I never knew, not once—not a clue. Lindsey and I shared so many secrets, but never ever did she let on about her relationship with you. I'm so sorry."

"Francis," David said, sliding out of the booth, "I'm sorry we broke the news to you like this—we had no idea about you and Lindsey. Are you going to be okay?"

Francis nodded, slid from the booth, and held his hand to help Annie out.

"Look," David continued, "the funeral's tomorrow at two—at Oak Hill. You're more than welcome to ride out there with us. If you'd like, we can pick you up about one-fifteen."

"I don'ta know. No, I'll be there—but I'll drive ah myself out. I'll have to speak ah to Tomas," Francis said.

"We'll see you tomorrow then." Annie reached up and kissed Francis on the cheek. David offered his hand and when Francis took it he drew David close and hugged him like a brother.

Annie and David left the café but stopped on the sidewalk. Dark clouds were beginning to gather in the afternoon sky and David and Annie both took notice as the winds began to foretell of the impending storm. David said his car was parked a few blocks down and that he would give Annie a ride back to the hotel, and from there they walked in silence to the parking garage.

———

Like a man half his age, Francis hurried out of the café and entered the bar.

"Hey, old man," the barkeep said, "you could hurt yourself running like that." With a worn square cotton tablecloth tied around his waist for an apron, the unflappable, gray-haired bartender turned, reached for the bottle of ouzo, poured the Greek a double, and with a precision aim that comes only after years of practice, slid the shot glass down the length of the bar where it stopped next to Francis's hand.

"Ya know, Marcus, my friend, I don'ta feel like a old man today. Funny, sometimes things work outa like ah you don'ta expect." Francis swirled the anise-flavored liqueur in the shot glass and tossed it back.

Francis held onto the glass as Marcus refilled it. "Here's to you, my faithful friend," he said as he again tossed back the drink, squarely placing the empty glass on the laminated counter.

"What's got into you, old man?" Marcus asked, wiping down the bar, leaving streaks with the wet towel.

"Not a thing my friend, not a blessed thing." Francis slapped the counter with his open palm, stood, and as quickly as he'd arrived, returned to the café and hung the CLOSED sign on the door.

4

As they entered the parking garage, David removed his sports coat and when he opened the car door he reached for the journal, tossed it on the backseat, and deliberately placed his coat over it.

They drove to the Adolphus Hotel in silence. David pulled under the porte cochere and stepped out as the valet greeted them. He left the engine running and walked to the passenger side. Annie was already stepping out, but he accompanied her to the revolving entry door. He didn't go in with her, but said he'd call later.

He returned to his offices and found that Liz had locked up and gone for the day.

The door to the office looked old and ornate, but looks were deceiving. The elaborate door was a facade and underneath the carving was a steel door fortified with a sophisticated security system. David passed the electronic key card through the slot and turned the brass knob.

The grand chamber seemed dreary and he carelessly flung his sports coat across the arm of the chair where it slid to the floor. "Ah, hell." He picked it up and the pack of cigarettes fell from the pocket. Loosening his tie, he walked to the desk where the dog-eared matchbook still lay.

She's doing it to me again. With the journal once again in hand, he sat down and turned on the table lamp in the otherwise dim room. He opened the book and stared at the neatly written epistle in his lap. *What am I getting myself into?*

Slipping on a pair of reading glasses, he began where he'd left off.

———

But by now there was too much happening in the world. There was too much happening in Texas and there was especially too much happening in Dallas.

What had meant the world to me a few months earlier no longer seemed that important. It was a time of incredible change and I made up my mind I was going to be a part of the changes.

Lindsey and Tommy Lee were still squaring off on a regular basis, but I was convinced I no longer cared about their petty wars.

Jack Kennedy opened my eyes. I likened him to Moses of ancient times and now getting Kennedy into the Oval Office was the single most important challenge in my life.

Butter was also captivated by the Kennedy mystique, and together, early one Saturday morning, we rode the bus downtown to Democratic Election Headquarters and proudly pinned on Young Democrat buttons, donned pseudo-Panama hats with the red, white, and blue-striped hatbands, and armed ourselves with information leaflets to distribute. We were "official" election volunteers.

When the votes were tallied in November, I was surprised that not everybody in the country could see the real issues as clearly as I. It was a close election and could have gone either way. But, for me, the choice was not Democrat or Republican. This was a matter of good and evil and the outcome of the election was either salvation or perdition.

And then quickly it became yesterday's news. Americans quit asking what our country was going to do for us—or what we were going to do for the country—and the Republicans and Democrats alike went back to squandering money with little regard for the country.

The soaring sixties took flight and prosperity was unprecedented. Wages were rising faster than prices and leisure time was predicted to be a problem both Republicans and Democrats would have to reckon with. What would Americans do with all their idle time and with all that money?

We didn't have that problem in my family. Money, or the shortage of it, was a real problem. Even attending a state college, I would need a job.

Lindsey, on the other hand, had other problems. She and Tommy Lee had finally called it quits. Now a junior at North Texas State he was transferring to the University of Oklahoma at Norman just south of Oklahoma City. He would be leaving Dallas at the end of the summer, and Lindsey was about to enter her second trimester.

So Lindsey got knocked up. He looked at his watch. Almost seven P.M. That morning he'd told Taylor he'd be home early. He hadn't mentioned whom he was having lunch with—just that it was a late lunch and he'd be home shortly afterward. He felt the well-known guilt, picked up the phone, and dialed.

When there was no answer in Annie's room at the Adolphus, he called home.

"Hello," Taylor answered.

"Hi, honey," he tried sounding blameless, but it came across like what it was. "I'm late, I know, but something came up and I'm still at the office. I apologize, I know I should have called earlier—"

"It's okay," Taylor interrupted. "Are you on your way home?"

"As soon as I hang up."

"Good," she said, "I'll wait till you get here to start supper. I'll have you a cold beer waiting."

"Sounds good."

"Oh, yes, I almost forgot, Annie called—just a little while ago. Said she didn't get a chance to get into something or the other with you at lunch today. Wants you to call her— sounded important, but you *know* how Annie can get. She left a number—said she was at Dena's."

"I'll give her a call right now."

"David—don't be long."

"I won't and, Taylor . . ."

"Yes . . . ?"

"I'll fill you in when I get there."

Flipping through the Rolodex, he pulled out the card with Lindsey's name. Her mother's number was penciled in with all the other numbers that had belonged to Lindsey in the past. Most had been scratched out and replaced, but Dena's had been the same now for many years.

David had no idea how old Dena was, but until that moment when she answered the phone she'd been ageless, resilient. Now she sounded worn and fragile, even feeble. He identified himself and expressed how sorry he was to learn that

Lindsey had died so unexpectedly. He said he hated to bother her, but explained he had a message that Annie wanted to speak to him. Was she there? Dena thanked him for the kind words and said she would put Annie on.

"David?" Annie presumed predictably.

"Taylor said you'd called." He ran his fingers through his thick hair and slumped back into the desk chair. "I tried calling at the hotel a little while ago. I can pick you up tomorrow afternoon, say at one, or earlier if you want—we could grab a bite of lunch—"

"Actually, David, I think I prefer just to catch a cab and go on out alone tomorrow. There are some things I have to do in the morning and it might be best if I met you there a little before the service. Is that okay?"

"Whatever you want, Annie. Are you sure you want me to come to the funeral?"

"Yes, you have to, I really need you, to talk to you—tomorrow, after the service."

Her pleading words and her desperate tone took David by surprise. "But you know how Annie can get," the instant replay of Taylor's warning served to remind him to be cautious of the woman who was so drawn to melodrama.

"Okay, then, tomorrow—at the funeral home."

He slipped the journal in his briefcase, snapped the lid shut, picked it up along with his crumpled coat, shut off the lights as he walked through the office, and left for the night.

5

Ismini was not in her private bedroom, but the maid had turned the feather duvet back for Francis in the adjoining master suite. The Greek sat alone on the edge of his bed and pulled off his shoes, leaving them on the floor where they fell. He stood, crossed the room, removed his shirt as he walked, and tossed it in the direction of the hamper in the master bathroom. He returned to the bedroom and lay alone in the massive postered bed. He needed time to think. Time alone—time to put all he'd heard and done in order. No more mistakes, no more regrets. And when a restless sleep finally came to Francis, it brought back all the memories.

————

The Greyhound bus, covered with black grime from fumes, pulled under the station canopy on Lamar and Commerce. As the engine idled and noxious black smoke filled the garage the driver opened the door and a lanky, dark curly haired boy effortlessly took the half-empty and battered valise from the overhead compartment and stepped onto the pavement in Dallas, Texas.

With only immigration papers in his worn wallet, hardly more than loose change in his pants pocket, and wearing or carrying everything he possessed, the fifteen-year-old son of a Greek fisherman was ready to take Dallas by storm. He had come to America to make his fortune and nothing short of his own death could keep him from achieving his dream.

Within six months, Tomas, Francis's younger brother by a year, followed. At first the boys lived in the dormitory at the downtown YMCA. Each of them held down two jobs at four different diners, all on a downtown city bus route.

They saved their wages in the empty valise stored under the bed and every Monday morning, Francis deposited it into a savings account at a downtown bank.

Five years quickly passed and when the fifth summer came it was the same summer that six-year-old Annie broke her arm, the same summer she met Davy by the lake, and it was the same summer Lindsey began staying home alone while her mother came downtown to work. It was 1951 and Francis signed a twenty-year lease for space in the old Chamberlet Building on Akard Street where he and his brother opened their business in the heart of downtown Dallas.

It was the beginning of an era when odd was in. Peeling plaster, bare floors, and poorly lit halls were soon to be trademarks of instant success.

There were very little changes to be made. Tomas cooked and Francis had the shrewd business mind, as well as the friendliness and graciousness, to successfully operate the new café on the busy street corner.

In a matter of months, the popular little eatery proudly named Stellar Café became known on the street as just the café.

Francis and Tomas continued to live like paupers, saving all their money and spending only for the bare necessities.

Francis tossed in his sleep and his mind raced back to those early years when the business was starting and when life was exciting.

He saw himself as the proud young man standing in the crowded courtroom before the judge administering the Oath of Allegiance. He could remember every word, every pause— even in his sleep. He would never forget what had meant so much to him—to be a citizen of the United States of America.

Tomas, however, did not apply for naturalization but instead remained in the United States working as an immigrant. That was the year Senator Estes Kefauver led a Senate investigation into organized crime and the year before John Fitzgerald Kennedy won a seat in the U.S. Senate.

The intersection of Main and Akard were the crossroads of downtown and the busiest pedestrian intersection in Dallas and every day at noon the hurried office crowds found their way to the little café on Akard. One needed only to figure out what day of the week it was to know what they were going to have for lunch. Monday was sausage links and rice and beans. Tuesday was shrimp Creole and rice and beans. Wednesday it was smothered steak and rice and beans and so forth. Entrees came with a thick slice of crusty sourdough bread and a vinegary limp green salad. The choices were few—with or without rice and beans.

And all the while they were serving lunch to the white-collar crowd, Francis had secured loans from unknown sources sufficient to buy the entire building from a now aging and ailing landlord. With down-to-earth management, a vision, and very little renovation, the shrewd new proprietor kept the offices in the building above the café leased to capacity. And each weekday at noon, Francis, wearing a clean white apron and boosting an affable smile, greeted his faithful patrons at the cash register and methodically, quietly, and steadily began increasing his holdings.

The Democrats, now with Kennedy as the newly elected president, were running the country and were determined to set all the wrongs in the world right. And even though an invasion force of anti-Castro Cubans, trained and directed by the CIA, failed to establish the beachhead at the Bay of Pigs in Cuba, they did manage, with the Cuban missile crisis, to successfully force the Soviet Union to remove nuclear weapons from Cuba. America was a safer place.

And at home, while satellites orbited and the space program was being developed, the nation's youngest elected president forced the steel industry to rescind price increases, backed civil rights, and proposed expanded medical care for the aged. At the same time, Lee Harvey Oswald married the daughter of a KGB colonel and, a few blocks from the café, Jack Ruby continued to operate his bawdy Carousel Club where stripper Candy Barr appeared on stage nightly and a standing-room-only crowd gathered each Friday for popular amateur night in the smoke-filled establishment.

But as the new sharper Dallas developed at warp speeds, the war in Southeast Asia also intensified. Kennedy now had 16,000 so-called military advisers in South Vietnam at the same time he started the Peace Corps and pressed for racial integration in the South.

Dallas was about to explode, and Francis continued to quietly acquire more and more concrete real estate. He knew somebody would want those old buildings if for no other reason but to tear them down and build again.

Downtown was getting a face-lift and everybody was eating rice and beans.

Francis Zacchoias, hard-working immigrant boy, had declared Dallas home in 1946 because it felt "right." He was a Texan by choice, a Greek by birth, and a good Catholic by the grace of God.

Then Mama Zacchoias came to the United States. Francis had to personally escort her from Greece, but once she arrived she stayed forever. Until Mama Z came to Dallas Francis had lived a spartan life. But for Mama he built a mansion that was the envy of Dallas society. Courtyards filled with terra-cotta planters, marble fountains, statues, and lush topiaries could be glimpsed through the estate's surrounding wrought-iron fencing. Though she never spoke a word of English, Mama adopted the foreign country and at once assumed her rightful place as palatial matriarch.

The year before Francis went to accompany Mama to the United States, Tomas had returned to the islands for a visit. While he was there he met and fell in love with Rhoda, a young woman in the village. In a matter of months they were married and he was content to remain in Greece with his new wife and the old ways. For a modest but fair sum of money Francis bought out his brother's interest in the café and it wasn't until Francis decided to return to Greece for Mama that he was able to convince Tomas to come back to Dallas. Tomas's bride was Francis's ally in persuading his brother to listen to his older and much wiser and now much richer brother. Tomas would work for Francis and the new arrangement between the brothers was never shared with anyone, not even Mama.

––––––

President John Fitzgerald Kennedy was assassinated on November 22, 1963, within earshot of the café. And on April 4, 1968, the Reverend Martin Luther King, Jr., was assassinated outside his motel room in Memphis, Tennessee. Two months later the country would reel again when the president's brother, Senator Robert F. Kennedy, was shot to death in Los Angeles. And on the last day of October of that same deadly year President Lyndon Johnson would order a halt to all bombing of North Vietnam.

While the country waited to exhale, Francis made a rare and unexpected trip back to his native Greece. Now in his late thirties, Francis was thinking of marriage. He wanted a son. Several sons, maybe even a few daughters to spoil, to adore. Francis needed a Greek Orthodox girl to marry. The family there arranged to celebrate his arrival and it was then that Francis was introduced to Ismini, a suitable young girl from a respected family in a neighboring village.

While still on the plane to New York, Francis began writing his little Ismini. In a matter of weeks a marriage proposal was mailed to her father and preparations were initiated.

Ismini, barely fifteen years old, accompanied by her watchful duenna, would travel to Dallas at the beginning of summer. Francis would make all the arrangements, and take care of all the expenses.

––––––

When she arrived at the airport with her aunt, Francis was waiting at the gate with a lavish bouquet of yellow roses. As he approached them he drew a single rose from the bunch, handed it to the shy girl, and presented the bundle to the old duenna, who nodded her head and smiled knowingly at the thoughtful, handsome, and clever man.

Even more beautiful than he had remembered, Ismini's long dark hair was pulled back from her face and tied neatly with a slender white ribbon. Protected from the sun, her skin was fair and the contrast of her dark bright eyes and long lashes was striking. Her cheeks were bright with the pink of innocence and added a delicate glow to her exquisite features. The pale yellow batiste dress with a white battenburg lace collar hung loosely from her shoulders and draped the swells of her small and recently maturing breasts.

Francis couldn't stop smiling and for those next hours with Ismini he thought only of his misspent youth. He chastised himself for ignoring his manhood all those years. On the long drive to the house, his obvious discomfort reminded him of the opportunity he now had to revive his neglected virility with this beautiful, young, Catholic girl—a virgin.

The wedding date remained to be set, but a nuptial agreement and a suitable dowry was agreed upon at once. For now, Ismini and the duenna lived in the guest cottage on the estate. Francis arranged for private tutoring so that his betrothed could learn to speak English quickly.

Since Francis still opened the café every morning, he provided Ismini with a car and driver. She was fifteen and enjoying unlimited freedom.

After her initial visit to the prestigious store bounded by Main, Commerce, and Ervay, the career salesladies at Neiman Marcus recognized Ismini on sight and catered to her every whim. Whenever the ladies from Greece were in town, they enjoyed a lingering lunch at the Zodiac Room while wispy models, wearing the latest Paris fashions, paraded for the elite patrons, kibitzing over bouillon, popovers, watercress salads, and mint tea at the linen-draped tables.

Ismini soon began wearing subtle eye shadows, lip glosses, and blush across her high cheekbones. She spent hours by the Grecian pool on the estate. Under the Texas summer sun, her fair skin darkened to a glistening bronze.

By the time she turned seventeen, she dressed and acted like the prima donna she had become—an enfant terrible— temperamental, assertive, and very spoiled.

Francis was growing impatient now to set a date for the wedding, but Ismini had learned to avoid answering his direct questions. She was especially quick to sidestep any physical contact with the Greek.

But Francis yearned to hold his young beautiful Catholic girl; he doubted he could refrain much longer. Night and day he dreamed of lying next to her on the bed and making love to her. He wanted to feel her firm young breasts in his power-ful hands and trace her slender hips with his fingers. He was consumed with making love to her and he wanted her to de-sire him as much as he wanted her.

More and more whenever he approached her she would evade his attentions, preferring instead the company of Tomas and his wife, but never Mama—the eminence grise.

Each night when Francis would escort Ismini and her aunt back to the cottage after the late suppers, he would attempt to hold her hand, and occasionally to kiss her good night. Dutifully she would present her cheek, but never once al-lowed him to kiss her on the lips. Each time he drew her close to him she could feel his protruding manhood press against her. He would embrace her tightly and breathe the sweet perfumes in her hair. He was tortured. Ismini was bored.

When Ismini became homesick for her family, Francis generously arranged to fly her two younger sisters to America for the holidays. They arrived as scheduled with the expected chaperone— another duenna. Though lavishly appointed, the little guest cottage was not large enough for the five ladies so Ismini moved into a suite in the mansion and both duennas stayed in the guest cottage with the sisters.

During those last few months before the wedding, Ismini created for herself a secret world. Every morning after a leisurely late breakfast, she would summon her car and driver and leave the estate without the chaperone. Exhausted, she would return in the middle of the afternoon, draw the drapes on her bedroom window, and nap for several hours. If it were a warm day, she would lie out by the pool. Each evening she would shower and dress elegantly for supper with Francis, Tomas and Rhoda, the two younger sisters, the two duennas, and, of course, Mama.

Ismini would have been content to have this arrangement go on for the rest of her life, but by now Francis had had enough excuses. If he couldn't have his Ismini's affection, the very least he expected was a son.

Mama took control, breaking the news to Ismini at the supper table that April evening. On Saturday afternoon, on the thirteenth of June, Francis and Ismini, on the day of her eighteenth birthday, would be married. Ismini left the dining room and walked alone to the familiar and safe cottage. Francis did not attempt to follow her, but remained seated opposite Mama at the end of the long dining-hall table. In two months Ismini would be his wife. He would have his sons.

————

Francis put his feet on the floor and sat on the edge of the bed. The time for remembering the past was gone. There were things to be done.

6

A streak of lightning sliced the blackness as two crouched figures darted across the cemetery, freeze-framing the ghoulish pair in motion.

"Shit," the raspy voice muttered as he stumbled across the slippery grass. "This be the last time you call me for these 'favors' you and your friends dream up. Ain't *nobody* in their right mind gonna come out here in this here graveyard and dig up no body for nobody. I must be outa my fuckin' head thinkin' I need this kinda work."

"Shut your bellyachin', Earl, you sorry tub of cow shit. The sooner we get to diggin' the sooner we git outa here. I don't like it any better than you but some things you gotta do. Sides, that fella done paid us cash money and we can probably git a little more outa him."

"Ah, shit, Lonny, you knows how I hate being round dead folk."

"It ain't the dead ones you gotta be scared of, you idiot, now git on up here and git to diggin'."

The body had been buried that morning and the loose dirt was easy enough to put a spade into. Two men wouldn't have to spend a lot of time reaching the top of the coffin, but the mud was making the task more than a little difficult. Another streak of lightning shot out of dark clouds and lit the cemetery with an eerie glow, silhouetting the grave robbers. The steady rain escalated now in blinding sheets.

"We damn sure shouldn't be doin' this, Lonny. It just ain't right. I think we oughta git the fuck outa here and forget the whole goddamn mess."

"Too damn late for that, bro, I done took that man's money and you know if 'n we don't have no money, we be the next poor suckers they'd be diggin' a hole fer."

The next jab with the shovel produced a sloppy *thud*. "There we musta hit the top of the vault. Let's clean it off and git the lid open."

"Open it? You don't mean we're ga-ga-ga-gonna *open* it?"

"Hell, yes, we're gonna open it. Go on now, git busy, use the damn cheater bar and git to pryin' that end. Hurry. I'm gittin' cold."

Together the two men pried open the vault with crowbars and once the lid was dragged out of the hole and laid on the mound of slush, they went to work prying open the coffin. The lid to the economy-line casket opened easily. The body was wrapped in a thick black vinyl bag and they struggled to pull it out of the metal box, filling now with rain and slush. The slippery bag and its contents now at last lay on the pile of mud next to the grave with Lonny and Earl sitting half buried in mud next to it.

"Who is he?" the smaller of the two wanted to know.

"How the hell would I know? Anyway, it might not even be a man."

"You mean this is a dead *woman?*"

"What the hell difference does it make whether it's a man or a woman? It's a fuckin' dead body, stupid, and that's all the fuck they asked us for. Now shut up."

Without further conversation they pushed the vault lid back into the hole, and hurriedly began to fill in the gaping hole with the sloppy mud.

"There, that oughta do, let's git outa here," Lonny instructed.

Lonny and his brother struggled with the dead weight, slipping and sliding with it down the wet hill to the truck parked by the curb at Peaceful Valley Cemetery.

"Throw it in the back."

"What? Shit man, have you lost your fuckin' mind? We can't go drivin' through Dallas with a goddamn fuckin' body in the back of the truck."

"So who the hell's gonna know what's back there?"

"Man, there ain't *nothin'* right about this."

"So, dick brain, maybe you want we should put the fuckin' corpse up here in the seat with us? Huh? Hell no, now do what I tell ya and, for the last time, shut the fuck up."

"Ah, shit."

An hour and a half later the truck pulled into the service driveway of the Dallas funeral home. Lonny cut the headlights as he pulled around to the back of the building. The double doors were open at the loading dock in the back and two men, one wearing a dark suit and the other wearing a heavy black rubber apron over dungarees, were waiting. Lonny backed the pickup into the bay with the cargo bundled tightly where it had been tossed aboard. It was a little after five A.M., still dark, and still raining.

"I was starting to worry about you boys," the man in the dark suit said.

"We came 'round the back way," Lonny said. "Didn't wanna take no highway so we come 'round through Grand Prairie."

"Here you go, boys," the man handed Lonny the envelope. "You both need to go somewhere and dry off. I hear it's not raining down in Mexico. Think about it. Here's two tickets for the nine o'clock flight this morning out of Love Field and a little extra cash that will help you make up your minds. And, by the way, boys, if you had any thoughts about getting more, if it ever crosses your mind, you may as well know right now, up-front, that would be a big mistake. Don't even think about it."

"No problemo, man, never gave it a thought," Lonny said.

"Adios, amigos," Earl said as he slammed the tailgate shut and got in the old truck.

By 7:00 A.M. the incinerator was turned off and six pounds of cremains were funneled into a small cobalt-blue glass urn and placed inside the cabinet. The black plastic bag lay in the middle of a puddle of muddy water on the concrete floor.

———

Earlier that afternoon, after David returned Annie to the Adolphus, she'd taken a cab to Dena's home in Oak Cliff on the west side of Dallas. Dena had married a Dallas police officer, and they bought a small 1930s stucco home near the municipal golf course. For the first time in her life Dena was completely happy, but the happiness she found in that marriage was brief as her husband was killed in a traffic accident the next year.

The visit with Dena had been emotionally difficult for Annie, more so than she had anticipated. Annie had not seen Dena in many years and the once beautiful Dena was now an old woman, bent and stooped. It had been several years since Dena lost her sight to macular degeneration and now she was completely homebound.

"Lindsey came by almost every day," Dena told Annie, "up until about two months ago. Then her visits became less frequent and after that there would be days without so much as a phone call. The last time I heard from Lindsey was the day before she died. She stopped by, brought a few groceries, and put them on the shelf.

"You know how I always like to sit outside, but it had been raining for days and then when the rain let up for a while that afternoon Lindsey unplugged the percolator from the kitchen wall and carried the coffeepot and two mugs out to the swing in the backyard.

"We never talked much, me and Lindsey, but there we sat, side by side, in that old squeaky glider, enjoying the sounds and smells and the cool breeze between rain showers.

"When Lindsey left she hugged me and when she did," Dena said, "she held me a little tighter and a little longer than usual. Like she knew that would be the last time.

"'I'll be fine, Dena, don't worry about me, don't worry about anything, I'll always take care of you,' Lindsey said. 'Hey, don't you go fretting none about your old Dena,' I told her. 'You're the one best to take care.'" Dena finished relating the conversation to Annie and said she patted Lindsey on the hand she held while they walked back into the house.

Dena couldn't have known how Lindsey grimaced at the

touch. Her hands were badly bruised and her right eye was discolored and tightly swollen. Dena could never know.

"'I love you, Mom,' she called back to me from the car when she was leaving. That was the first time in years Lindsey had called me 'Mom.' You know, Lindsey never called me 'Mom,' hardly ever, even as a little kid, she always called me 'Dena,'" she reminded Annie, "and when she said 'Mom' it sent a chill through me. Somehow I think I knew then, things were about to change."

———

There was a soft tapping at the door. Annie fumbled with the bedside lamp, almost knocking it on the floor. She squinted at the digital clock radio next to the bed.

It was seven A.M.

Another knock.

Annie slipped one arm into her robe and went to the door. "Yes?"

"Room service," she heard a quiet voice say on the other side and then remembered leaving the request hanging on the doorknob when she returned from Dena's that night.

She struggled to get her other arm in her robe sleeve and slid off the privacy latch. "Leave it over on the table." With one hand she pulled her hair away from her face, and with the other initialed the charge, and the boy left.

Annie stared at the insulated coffee carafe. She was tired. Her purse lay on the chair in the corner, she opened it and withdrew the piece of paper with the scrawled telephone number. She dialed and shakily poured the coffee as the phone began to ring.

The voice was deep and barely audible.

"Is everything ready?" Annie asked.

"Yes."

"You're sure?"

"Of course."

There was no way to turn back, not now. *What's done is done, after today, after the funeral, I'm completely on my own.* Annie sat holding the phone, the dial tone blaring.

7

A parade of black limousines lined the driveway outside the chapel at Oak Hill Cemetery that afternoon. One more limousine, more or less, wouldn't matter. No, one more limousine one way or the other would go unnoticed. But inside one long black car, obscured from view, the woman sat and waited. She looked at her watch. He was late.

Francis Zacchoias had not yet arrived, and Ismini wondered where her dear old husband was hiding out. She was sure he would be here. He wouldn't miss the chance to see his beloved Lindsey this one last time.

Ismini slipped a cigarette from the sterling case as a yellow cab drove by the car, slowed, and pulled under the awning to let the woman in the blue coat step out and enter through the front doors. Ismini barely noticed and her thoughts quickly returned to rage.

Where the hell was Francis?

By one-thirty p.m. the first person entered the chapel from the foyer. The lights behind the stained glass windows in the chapel were off and the room was dark. There were no floral arrangements. There was no body placed for viewing.

When the funeral director was ready to bring the casket into the room, several others were now seated and waiting in the dismal room. He apologized for the inconvenience and asked them to wait outside and ushered them to the vestibule with the others for a few more moments.

The press had turned out in full regalia—armed with flash, filters, roving cam team, and umbrellas. Senator James "Buddy" Mitchell's wife was dead and the party was well represented today.

Mitchell's popularity had dropped off in recent months and a sympathy vote might get him reelected to the Senate.

This time when the two attendants wearing dark suits and black ties opened the doors, soft incandescent lighting filled the chapel. Freestanding baskets, overflowing with lush fern laced with white roses, flanked both sides of the velvet-draped pedestal table. A spray of hundreds of miniature pink rose-buds draped across the bottom half of the ivory Byzantine casket where Lindsey's body rested in tufts of cream-colored satin. A pasticcio of piano etudes was piped through the ceiling's audio system—a little Mendelssohn, a bit of Bach, a Chopin nocturne—a classical touch.

It was two when Annie stepped from the cab and walked into the foyer of the funeral home. The attendant helped her with her raincoat and took the dripping umbrella from her. The service was about to begin and the director started to close the doors behind her just as David came through a side door into the vestibule and joined her.

"You okay?" he asked, placing both his hands squarely on her shoulders.

She nodded.

"It's almost time," he said. "What kept you? I was getting worried."

"I know," she whispered as she entered through the double doors to the chapel. Everyone was seated.

With eyes fixed ahead, Annie walked down the center aisle to the front of the room to the opened casket. David followed and stood behind her while she studied her friend. She found herself searching for tiny flaws in the smooth opaque skin. But no bruises, no discoloration, no scars were seen on the perfect porcelain face. Lindsey's hands with long fingers and manicured nails rested gracefully across the satin embroidered bodice of her dress.

Then Annie saw the rosary, woven between Lindsey's fingers. Annie leaned forward to look carefully.

Lindsey was a Protestant when she and Jimmy married. Now somebody had placed this rosary over her. Worse than that, not just slipped it inside the coffin or laid it by the table but actually positioned it in her hands. Twisted and wound it around her fingers.

Annie's temples throbbed. Her hands were hot and she turned them over and stared at the drops of sweat beading on her palms.

The music played louder and louder and the room began to spin.

David was there to catch her.

———————

There was no processional. The body was to be cremated, the ashes kept in the selected cobalt-blue urn, and sealed in the wall vault in the mausoleum area of the memorial gardens.

Ismini waited in the limousine and watched as the crowds left. When there were only a few guests left standing under the protection of the awning, the partially opened car window quietly hummed to a close and the driver pulled away.

"Where to, ma'am?"

"The café."

"You sure?"

Ismini reached for the silver case as she pressed the inner partition switch to separate herself from the chauffeur. Cigarette smoke swirled in the backseat as the car turned from Northwest Highway onto Central Expressway toward downtown.

While the car and driver waited on the curb on Akard Street, Ismini carefully made her way along the sidewalk and turned into the alcove. The café was locked and the handwritten note posted on the door read CLOSED TODAY COME BACK TOMORROW.

Ismini was muttering in perfect English as she left the café and entered the open bar.

"Where's Francis?" Ismini demanded.

"Ms. Mini? Is that you?" Marcus asked.

"Of course, it's me, you stupid old fool," she said, just loud enough for the barkeep to hear. "Where's my husband?" She hatefully spat the words.

Marcus wiped his hands on the towel, shoved it back under the bar, and walked around to meet Ismini, a woman he recognized from snapshots of her with the children that Francis kept tacked on a corkboard in the kitchen.

"Francis . . . he uh . . . he's closed today," he answered. "Said there was ah . . . somebody died. Somebody real special—was it Mama? Francis didn't have time to say. Just that he was closing and I should tell anybody asking to come back tomorrow. To-morrow he'd be open."

"Tomorrow?"

"Yeah, tomorrow, 'Business as usual,' that's what he said."

"Tell me something, Marcus—it is *Marcus,* isn't it?" Ismini brushed past him and came around behind the bar and started moving the bottles on the shelf. "Is there anything here that won't burn a hole in my stomach?"

"A nice glass of wine maybe—a chardonnay?" Marcus took a stemmed glass off the shelf and began rubbing off dried water spots with a paper napkin.

"Something stronger," she said, still rearranging the liquor bottles.

Marcus pulled a bottle of Jack Daniel's from under the bar, reached for a tumbler, and poured the whiskey for Ismini.

"How come Francis closed the café today?" he asked when he handed her the bourbon. "All the years I've worked up here, he ain't never closed for the lunch crowd. Who died? Mama?"

"The *Lindsey* died, that's who. You didn't know?"

"Lindsey? When?"

Ismini tossed back the shot of Jack Daniel's.

Marcus refilled Ismini's glass and poured himself a shot as well.

"Oh, come now, don't tell me this is the first you've heard of it? Surely dear old Francis has been up here drowning his sorrows in ouzo." She tossed down the second shot and took the bottle from Marcus's hand.

"No, ma'am, not a word. I saw him just yesterday. Oh, sure, he had a drink up here yesterday afternoon—just before closing—but he was a happy man. He couldn't have known about Lindsey then."

"You think?" Ismini slid off the stool and walked out, taking the whiskey bottle and the shot glass with her.

Marcus followed her out to the sidewalk and watched as the waiting limousine driver opened the car door for her.

———————

The highway diner was quiet. David helped Annie with her coat, shook the rain off, and hung it on the wall rack near the door. An elderly couple seated at a table by the door and two bearded men wearing Levi's and trucker hats and eating at the counter turned to watch as they started for the booth near the window. Armed with splattered menus the waitress in a pink uniform and white apron followed them.

David asked her to bring them coffee.

"Feeling better?" David asked.

"Funny, isn't it," Annie said, keeping her voice low. "I mean, the way things work out. You know Lindsey was the most remarkable woman I've ever known, smart and clever, fun—always laughing."

"Are we going to sit here and continue with the eulogy?"

"No." Annie shook her head and the waitress returned with the coffee.

"Annie, last night, when you were out at Dena's, did she say anything about Lindsey having problems?" David asked when the waitress left. "Had she been ill?"

"I don't think so, and Dena didn't say anything about her being sick. Besides, I think I would have known if she was sick."

"But when was the last time you actually *saw* her? Had a good visit? Besides on the phone, that is."

"Not too long ago, right after New Year's—but we didn't have a chance for a long visit, not then. I'd been in Dallas that day on some business for an art dealer in California and I called Lindsey that same morning I flew in from Austin. She told me to catch a cab later that day when I'd finished my business and come out to the house for supper. I wouldn't have accepted except she said Buddy was out of town. But when I got there, she wasn't home. She'd left a message with Lupe that the senator had returned unexpectedly and Lindsey wanted me to meet them both at some restaurant for supper. They'd gone on ahead to meet others for drinks. They'd be expecting me."

"So you met them?"

"No, as much as I wanted to see Lindsey, I sure didn't want to spend the evening with Buddy and their circle of *his* friends so I used the telephone from the house, called the restaurant and had Lindsey paged. I told her I'd had a long day and would have to beg off. I suggested that we could get together the next day for a late lunch. If not that, maybe she could meet me for a drink at the airport before I had to fly back to Austin early that evening."

"And who's Lupe?"

"Housekeeper," Annie answered, returning her cup to the saucer.

"Didn't that strike you as a bit strange?"

"Strange?"

"I mean her inviting you out and then not being there and all?" David asked.

"That's the way Lindsey was, not strange, spontaneous."

"In most peoples' book it's *rude*."

The rain that had started the night before was coming down harder now and Annie and David both turned to watch from the window.

"The next day I called Lindsey about noon when I finished

my business in Dallas," Annie said, picking up the conversation again. "We met at a restaurant down on Greenville. After that, Lindsey drove me out to Love Field to catch my plane. And *that's* what I wanted to talk to you about, David."

David looked up as the waitress, carrying the last remainders in the coffeepot, approached them for yet a third time. He waved her away.

"Doesn't look like we're going to have any privacy to talk here, Annie. Let's go, I'll drop you off."

David laid a five spot on the table while Annie slid out. He took her coat off the wall hook and held it for her while she slipped her arms into the sleeves. Straightening, she turned to face him.

"I'd like to get together with you later if you're up to it," David said. "About seven. I'll pick you up. Right now I've got to get back to the office."

8

David was frowning when he returned to town that afternoon.

"Everything okay?" Liz asked, handing him his phone messages.

David did not answer. He scanned the messages and tossed them on the desk, and started for his private office.

"One more thing, Boss," Liz said, following him into his office. "Now this *oughta* get your attention. There's somebody waiting in the conference room for you—a real knockout—said her name was Roberta Duplissey. I take it you two are friends? What I want to know is, is she for real?" Liz asked, referring to the guest in the next room.

"If it's the Roberta I know, she's for real all right, all too real—most of her anyway," David said as he gave Liz a quick wink and walked into the adjoining conference room.

"Butter?" Roberta turned to face him, slower and more

deliberately than necessary and when she looked at him David didn't think he had ever seen a more alluring smile. His own reaction to her surprised him.

"David," she said, crossing the room with her arms outstretched. She hugged him warmly, pressing her body, curves and all, the real and the almost real, to his own hard firm body. David found himself aware of holding her equally as tight for a few extra seconds before he held her away at arm's length and looked into her bright blue eyes.

"Butter, my God, girl, you look terrific."

"Thanks, you're looking pretty terrific yourself"—and her delicately lined red lips opened to allow a seductive smile. The petite blonde, known by her early classmates as Butter, stepped back and straightened the bodice of her blue silk dress, repositioning the string of blue-black iridescent crystals around her neck.

"I didn't get a chance to speak to you at the service this afternoon. Looked like you had your hands full, darling, what with Annie *swooning* like she did. What 'a shame. Is the poor little thing okay? The two of you rushed out of there so quick after the service I wasn't sure *what* was going on."

David gave her an appraising look, but said nothing.

Butter crossed the room and took the cigarette case and lighter from her purse. She slipped a cigarette out, looked at David, and offered him one as well.

David took the case and matching lighter from her hand and helped himself. He held the dainty lighter for Butter and then lit his own.

"What are you doing here, Butter?" he asked, exhaling.

"David, you and I go back real far and, as I recall, we had some pretty good times. I know *you* thought so that summer out by the lake—remember? Did Annie ever know about us?"

"Butter, just what the hell *are* you doing here?"

"Careful, David, *dear*," she said as she approached him. "You know how *badly* it makes me feel when you get so—"

"The point, Butter."

"The point is, *sweetie*, did you get the book?"

"The book?" *The book, of course, Annie's diary.* "Just how'd you get your claws on such a thing?" he asked.

"Doesn't really matter now, does it?" she answered, expecting more reaction from David than he was showing. Picking up her small handbag from the oversized table she arranged the thin strap on her shoulder and crossed the room.

"Read it, David"—she stopped, turned to look him in the eye—"read it and weep, darling."

Butter turned and with both hands swung open the matching doors that led to and from the conference room, ignored Liz at her desk, and left the office leaving a trail of cigarette smoke in her wake.

Liz sat still, but followed the woman's exit with her eyes. "Ladies and gentlemen, Elvira has left the building," she said when she saw David standing in the doorway.

David let out a big sigh of relief, shook his head in dismay, and returned to his office. Liz came in to say she was leaving and asked if there was anything else she could get for him before she left. David looked at his watch; already half past five.

"No, thanks, Liz, everything's fine—and anything that isn't can damn sure wait till tomorrow."

"Hey, you know what, Boss, I'm not really in any hurry to get out of here. Why don't we grab a couple of cold ones down at the Elm? The boys there have been asking about you, and you sure as hell look like you could use a beer about now. How 'bout it? Thirty minutes to lighten up and then we could get out of there, go somewhere else and get a bite to eat, and talk. Tell you the truth, there's a few things I'd like to hear about."

"Thanks, Liz, but no, you go on. We'll talk later. Maybe tomorrow."

"Well, if you're sure . . ."

"Oh, Liz, one thing—lock the door on your way out."

"Sure thing, Boss. See ya in the morning."

David thought about his meeting with Annie. He used speed dial and the answering machine at home picked up on the third ring. He waited for the message to play through and what seemed to be the longer than normal beep to finish.

"Hi, honey"—he sounded contrite again—"looks like I'm going be tied up here till late. Don't worry about supper, I'll grab a bite before I get home. I'll call if I'm going to be too late." When he hung up, he had that old feeling, the one he knew all too well yet still piled on himself. No need to lie. All he had to say was, "I'm having supper with Annie" or "I have a meeting with Annie, why don't you meet us after that for supper" or "I asked Annie to meet us at the house for supper." Why did he feel he had to lie? To Taylor of all people— the love of his life.

David pulled his tie from under his collar and walked into the executive bathroom. There was a time he used the office shower often, but that was another time.

Since he and Taylor had married, he rarely had occasion to shower and shave before going home first. He wasn't about to fall back into old habits; that was the past, it needed to stay there—it had to.

Tonight was an exception.

He draped his tie on the brass rack behind the door, removed his shirt, and tossed it on the floor in the corner.

There were laundered shirts folded in the cabinet as the ever perfect Liz made certain her boss had what he needed for any occasion. She continued to rotate the clothes every week, regardless if they were worn or not.

David looked at himself in the cheval mirror. What he saw didn't surprise him. He was a good-looking man, a few years past forty, with a well-muscled chest showing through thick dark hair. Some gray. What did surprise him was the excitement he couldn't ignore, something he hadn't felt in a long time, a very long time. He unfastened his trousers and neatly folded and placed them on the wardrobe. He turned on the shower and stepped under the welcomed cool spray.

———

It was exactly seven P.M. when David picked up the house phone in the hotel lobby. Annie said she'd be right down and when he saw her step off the elevator into the glitzy lights of the mezzanine every part of his body stood at attention.

———

After the waiter cleared away the plates David reached for the wine, filled their glasses with the last of the Louis Latour, sat back, and smiled.

He'd long since lost count of the times he had wished to be seated like this, sharing the evening, sharing a bottle of French wine over candlelight, talking, smiling—hell, they were even laughing—and Annie seemed to be enjoying herself as well. David was fully aware he needed to keep his personal feelings aside.

He leaned in and spoke softly. "You know I've always been in love with you, don't you?" He couldn't stop himself and

Annie was visibly flustered by the sudden declaration and the change in tone.

"David, please don't say things like that—things you don't mean."

"That summer after graduation, at the lake . . ."

"David, there were some things you didn't know. That night—that night it was all so confusing—"

"Confusing?" David interrupted. "I loved you, Annie. I thought you loved me too."

"Of course I cared, David—but that was a long time ago—"

"You cared? You *cared?* I thought it was *more* than that. I thought we meant more to each other than *care.*"

"Look, David, I can't do this. Not now, not ever." Annie began to reach for her purse.

"Annie, Annie, look at me. Why did you leave Dallas like you did, without talking to me—without even saying good-bye?"

Annie stood from the table and cast an embarrassed glance around the room.

David tossed his napkin on the table and stood to leave with her.

The steady rain was intensifying and when they arrived back at the hotel David told the parking valet to "Keep it close." He walked Annie into the lobby.

"David," she said, "don't leave yet. Not like this . . . please, stay . . . let's have a drink here in the bar."

"It's been a long day, Annie, and I still have a phone call to make back at the office before I head home . . ."

"Of course, I understand."

"Do you?" David put his hands on her shoulders and brushed a light kiss across her cheek, turned, and walked away.

"David," she called after him. He hesitated, but did not turn around.

"Good night, Annie," he said with his back to her as he walked out the revolving door.

9

For the third time that evening Taylor picked up the phone and dialed the number but, like before, replaced the receiver when the recording started to play. This time, this message she'd deliver in person.

She pressed the electronic garage opener and as the door began to rise she slipped the gear into reverse and began backing out of the garage and into the street. Again Taylor touched the garage opener on the visor, and as she pulled away a slight figure dressed in black darted from behind the bushes, ducked under the closing door, and slipped unnoticed into the garage.

It was raining harder now and Taylor switched the wipers to full speed. The broadcast news on the car radio was warning of street flooding and urging listeners to stay indoors and off the streets tonight. She inserted a compact disc and as the music started she guided the small white Mercedes onto Central toward town.

As she accelerated she remembered the late-night office visits well—and she remembered the old David even better.

Red flashing lights in the rearview mirror caught her attention and she stepped hard on the brake. The rear of the car began to slide and in the next instant the car started to spin. The flashing red lights became a web of horizontal streaking blurs before the car came to a skidding stop on the far side of the exit ramp.

Taylor sat clutching the steering wheel, head against the seat with eyes closed, her foot still pressing hard on the brake. There was a tapping on the window.

"You all right in there? Ma'am? Would you put the window down? Should I radio for an ambulance? Ma'am? Ma'am, you okay?"

Taylor reached for the door handle and with her shoulder started to push the door open.

"Just sit there for now, ma'am," the officer said. "Don't get out—just put the window down."

Taylor nodded.

"You were going close to ninety when you passed me a few miles back. A night like this, nobody should be out unless they have to. Is something wrong?"

"No, Officer, I'm okay now—the brakes must have locked. . . ."

"If there's a problem, is there someone I could call for you?"

"No. I'll be fine."

Standing in the pelting rain on the southbound side of the expressway, the officer pulling traffic duty on the worst rainstorm in Dallas in more than a decade asked to see Taylor's license. She handed him her opened wallet and he asked her to remove the card from the transparent compartment. Her

hands no longer trembled and when he asked for the registra-
tion papers and proof of liability insurance she withdrew
them—without hesitation—from an envelope inside the
glove compartment.

"Please, Ms. Matthews," he said, handing the license and
insurance papers back, "take it easy tonight—for all our sakes."

Carl Jacob Malone had good instincts and going into police
work had been a calling he couldn't ignore—he'd tried. Now
a seasoned investigator, he'd experienced a fair share of the
good times and more than his share of the bad.

Barely out of his teens and straight from the academy he
had started his career as a rookie with the New Orleans P.D.
and after a quick five years in the traffic division advanced
out of the uniform and into the detective unit. He married
his high school sweetheart Charlene—those were the good
times.

The white sports car reminded him of his young wife's
white Mustang, a gift from her grandparents the summer
she'd graduated from Trinity College. Tonight's rainstorm
brought back a flood of memories, the night the good times
ended.

Charlene had an afternoon appointment and called to tell
Jake the good news. The doctor had confirmed it; they could
expect their first child in seven months. Jake promised to be
home as soon as possible, but because of the heavy rains that
seemed to never let up Malone would be on the streets,
pulling extra duty in traffic until after the evening's rush hour
in downtown New Orleans. They planned to celebrate as
soon as he could get home. Charlene would be waiting.

But Charlene wasn't waiting when he got home—she'd

never be waiting for him again. For years they'd made plans—plans that included backyards with shrubbery and swings, picnics in the park, teddy bears, blankets, and tiny pink and blue things, family things—they had a lifetime of plans. What they never planned on was a delivery truck driver who failed to yield for the classic car his wife was driving home from the marketplace that late afternoon. Malone's wife never saw it coming, never regained consciousness, and died three days later.

After the funeral Jake closed their modest bank account, left his notice on the sergeant's desk, and walked away. Jake Malone was a man destroyed.

For a few years he drifted. Unshaven and unkept he lived in roach-infested kitchenette motels, one after another, and always his empty bourbon bottles spilled over the trash can under the sink. In time he moved on to the next town but no town or any day was different or better than the one before and the empty bottles continued to pile up in a corner.

One day he woke up in Texas and through no conscious will of his own Malone began to sober up. The next week he picked up a *Fort Worth Star Telegram*, read the want ads, showered, shaved, drove his hammered truck to town, walked into the Tarrant County Courthouse and asked to speak with the sheriff. They offered him the deputy's job, conditionally at first, in a small town within the county just west of Fort Worth.

Four years later, with a sterling record, he petitioned for a detective's position with the Dallas P.D. From that time on he pursued the new position with vigorous intent. One year followed another and over the next fifteen years he became one of the most respected detectives in the division.

———

"Smiley" Johnny Johnson was asleep in his chair behind the security desk when Taylor walked into the lobby. An obliging man, he'd been the night watchman at the high-rise long before David moved his offices into the downtown building. He was an old man, but worked nights in order to augment his meager Social Security pay.

"Excuse me, Mr. Johnson—Smiley?"

Smiley awoke with a start and almost landed on the floor as the chair on coasters slid out from under him. Clearing his throat, he sat up straight and reached for the clipboard on the desk.

"Evenin', Ms. Matthews. Didn't hear you come in," he said, handing Taylor the clipboard with the after-hours sign-in sheet attached.

Taylor removed one of the leather gloves she was wearing and wrote eleven o'clock by her name. *Close enough,* she thought and handed the clipboard back to the smiling night watchman.

Like soldiers standing watch between the pink granite pillars, two pairs of stainless-steel elevators stood facing each other; all doors open to the lobby. Taylor stepped inside the first one on the left and touched the button for the tenth floor. When the elevator opened she hesitated before getting off and making her way to the law offices. She listened at the door and when she didn't hear anything, she tried turning the knob. It was locked. She began to fish for the electronic key card in her wallet.

The office was dark. Taylor ran her hand alongside the wall to locate the panel of switches. The first one turned on the cove lights and faintly illuminated the ceiling. Taylor carefully closed the door behind her so as not to make any noise and crossed the dim room to David's office. The door was locked and she had never asked for nor was ever given a key to this private room.

Taylor leaned her back against the door and took a deep breath. *Liz—of course, Liz has to have a key.* A letter opener was on the desk and Taylor easily jimmied the lock on the desk and picked up the small brass door key from the drawer.

Taylor's shadow was absorbed into the darkness of David's office and as she stood there she began to realize David had been telling her the truth all along, but, like a silly ripe schoolgirl, she'd been caught up in David's past.

Relieved and ashamed, she quietly closed the door and returned to Liz's desk, replaced the key in the drawer, picked up the phone, and dialed home. The machine answered the call.

As the message played through she saw the spots on the carpet in the far corner of the room. She could hear the beep as she hung up. Without taking her eyes off the spots, she crossed the room. She knelt and touched the carpet. It was wet. She glanced around the room. A few drops of water were beading on the seat of the leather chair. Taylor stood and returned to David's private office. She hesitated before she opened the door. This time she entered, crossed the dark room, stood in front of the desk, reached under the lamp shade, and placed her hand over the lightbulb. It was still warm, very warm. *Of course, I just missed him. He's on his way home.*

Smiley was sleeping in his chair as she hurried out of the building.

———

Jake Malone was standing by a late-model sedan on the shoulder of the northbound expressway when the white Mercedes sped by.

Taylor turned into the drive, touched the garage opener,

and the headlights revealed the harsh reality of an empty garage. She made a conscious decision to put off thinking about David. Right now she was wet and cold and starting to shiver.

The delayed shut-off of the headlamps continued to light the garage long enough for her to get to the top of the stairs, but before she got her key into the lock of the kitchen door they faded away and the garage went completely dark. She felt for the doorknob and realized that in her rush to confront David she had failed to lock the door behind her.

———————

The bathwater was hot enough to cause Taylor to lift her foot back out. She tried again, slowly this time. Standing now in the water, she reached for a bottle of lavender oil and generously poured it into the steamy water and lowered herself into the oversized tub. She turned on the cold water tap to a trickle, enough to make it tolerable—and just enough to muffle the faint sound of the bedroom door opening.

———————

Malone sat inside the patrol car in the parking lot outside the Kwik Stop, and was prying the plastic lid off a Styrofoam cup of hot coffee when the homicide report came over the police frequency.

PART TWO

THE UNEXPECTED

10

"Female Caucasian, late thirties, early forties . . ."

Malone exited northbound Central at Mockingbird Lane, crossed over the overpass, and reentered onto Central south toward town. The ambulance was stopped on the street with the emergency lights on, the rear loading doors open. Malone drove past and pulled to the curb just as a blue Ford Taurus passed him and came to an abrupt stop ahead of him.

The medical examiner, Dr. Benjamin James Pierce, wearing his vintage leather flight jacket over a white dress shirt and tie, stepped out of the car, onto the curb, and into the rain. Together he and Malone hurried under the canopy of the Main Street building, into the lobby, and took the waiting elevator to the tenth floor.

The office door to the outside hall was propped open with a side chair and the door to the executive office was ajar. Both rooms were flooded with light and from where he stood in the reception area, Malone could see a portion of the body on the floor, partially hidden behind the desk. She was lying on her back, her left leg twisted behind her. When he got closer he could see the blood smear on the bodice of the dress. Her eyes were fixed and staring at the ceiling. A chalk mark outlined the body on the floor.

Pierce spoke with the crime scene photographer, who continued to take pictures while they exchanged information Pierce collected trace scrapings from the victim's nails and picked up a few particles of carpet fabric from the floor near the victim. He rolled the torso, made a brief visual examination of the victim's backside, and after conferring with another member of the crime team, left as quietly and suddenly as he had arrived.

Once the photographer had finished, the victim was toe tagged, placed in a body bag, lifted onto the gurney, loaded in the ambulance, and taken to the morgue.

"Hate to lose a pretty one like that, huh, Sarg?" remarked one of the uniformed officers standing in the hall outside the office door when the attendants rolled the stretcher to the elevator.

"Detective," Malone corrected.

"Right, Detective, but she was a looker, wouldn't you say?"

"Anybody got a make on her yet?" Malone asked.

"Not yet, my boys are just getting started," another officer answered.

"Who found the body?" Malone asked.

"Old black man downstairs—security, that's a crock," the officer answered from the hall. "He says, he rides the elevator once or twice during his shift. Stops on every floor, sticks his head out to look and listen for anything unusual. That's when he noticed the door to the tenth floor office ajar and went to investigate.

Malone returned to the private office for another look before he left the office via the stairwell at the end of the hall, ten flights down and one more to the lower level parking. There were only a couple of cars in the underground garage. This time Malone waited for the elevator and when he stepped in he punched the tenth floor. But the elevator from the garage at that time of night was programmed to open into the lobby and Malone stepped off on the ground floor to join a group of uniformed police officers by the security desk.

"Ever see her before?" Malone heard a uniform ask the night watchman.

Smiley shook his head and the words fell out of his pocket-like cheeks, "No suh, no suhree, Officer, I sure nuff don't never sees her before."

"She signed in, didn't she?"

"It's likes I told you, Officer, suh, I ain't never sees her before—before I sees her lying up there ah . . . ah . . . dead on the floor in Mr. Matthews's office."

"Was she a tenant here in the building?"

"I told you—I ain't never laid eyes on her before. . . ."

"Doesn't every visitor, even tenants here, have to sign in after office hours?"

"They mostly do, yes, suh. The elevator stops right here and everybody has to sign in—right here on the clipboard"—Smiley fumbled for the clipboard on the desk—"and they puts the time they come into the building and time they leaves right there by their name," he explained, pointing with trembling fingers to the lines on the clipboard.

"But Johnny"—the officer took the clipboard from the guard's shaking hand and flipped through the handwritten pages—"the last person signed in here was Taylor Matthews."

"That's right. Mrs. Matthews was here tonight. I talked to her misself."

"I can see she signed in but she didn't sign out, did she?"

"No, suh." Smiley shook his head and cast his eyes down at the floor.

"Why is that, Johnny? I mean if everybody after eight P.M., tenant or visitor, has to sign in and everybody has to sign out, why didn't this Mrs. Matthews sign out? You're sure that's not the Matthews woman lying dead up there behind that desk? Or maybe Mrs. Matthews is still in the building. You don't suppose that's a possibility, do you?"

"No, suh, that's not her dead up there, I'm sure of that, but I don't think she's still here, Officer."

"And why is that, Johnny? Why do you think she's not here now? Have you checked around?"

"I dunno, but I think she must have left. You see, suh, I knows her and she's a fine lady, and uh I might have stepped away from the desk for just a minute and maybe didn't see her leave, that's all."

"But before that, before Mrs. Matthews, no one else was here and no one else signed in or out?"

Smiley nodded.

"Johnny, are you in the habit of stepping away from your desk during the evening or was it just a pretty quiet night and you thought you could take a little time away?"

"No, suh. I don't take no time aways from my job here."

"Mr. Johnson," Malone intervened, "nobody here is saying you weren't doing your job. The officer here's just pissed because he had to go out on such a nasty night." Malone gave the interrogator a look—a look that said back off, for now, Malone would be the good cop.

"No problem, I understands." Smiley nodded, responding to Malone's sympathetic manner.

"So, Mr. Johnson, what do *you* think happened? I mean if you were a guessing man, how could this woman have gotten past you without you knowing?" Malone asked.

"Well, I might have been resting my eyes a little. You see I was taking this here medicine for my allergy"—Smiley fumbled through the drawer and pulled out a package of over-the-counter antihistamines—"and sometimes it makes me real sleepylike—and I might have been resting my eyes for a bit."

"Did you hear anything, Mr. Johnson, I mean when you were resting your eyes—like the elevator maybe?"

"No, suh, I don't hear nothing."

Malone took the clipboard from the uniformed officer. Taylor Matthews 11:00. The name was familiar—the white Mercedes, around midnight, leaving town.

———

With her eyes closed Taylor relaxed with her shoulders covered in the hot bathwater. She was vaguely aware of the phone ringing from the other room. After a few more rings, unable to ignore the annoyance any longer, she stood, stepped out of the bath, loosely wrapped a towel around herself, and walked into the bedroom.

"Hello?"

"Taylor Matthews?"

"This is Taylor Matthews. . . . No, Mr. Matthews is not at home. . . . What's this about? . . . All right, I'll be expecting you."

Hurriedly Taylor dried off with the towel, tossed it on the bed, and walked naked across the room to the dresser to get a pair of fresh panties. She stepped into them and when she walked into the closet for her robe the intruder was standing there with a broad smile spread across his black face, revealing tobacco-stained teeth.

11

The squad car pulled alongside the curb in front of the Matthews's home. Malone rolled the car window down about halfway, surveying the house and yard as he came to a slow stop. The garage door was open and there was no sign of the white sports car.

The rain fell inside the car and Malone rolled the window shut, opened the door, hunkered down, and splashed his way along the pebblestone walkway to the front porch.

He rang the bell.

No answer.

He rang again. Again he listened as the chimes echoed throughout the large fashionable house. Stepping from under the porch and into the rain he squinted as he looked up at the second-story windows. He could see lights on somewhere on the second floor, but as far as he could tell, there were no lights on downstairs.

He pulled his collar up and walked around the side of the house, reached over the low gate, slipped the latch, and walked by the cabana, onto the pool deck, and to the back of the house. French doors opened to the patio from the roomy hall and Malone peered inside. Except for the light reflecting off the stairwell, it was dark on the ground floor. *So, the lovely lady is making a run for it.* He returned to the squad car and was calling for backup when David pulled his car into the driveway.

"What's wrong, Officer?" David asked as Malone approached.

"Are you David Matthews?"

"Yes, what's going on here?" David did not wait for an answer and Malone was right behind him when he unlocked the door.

David saw Taylor silhouetted at the top of the stairs.

"David," she said, clutching her robe shut and coming down. "David, thank God you're here. It was terrible—there was this man . . ."

"What man—did he touch you?" David asked.

"No, I'm okay, but there was this man—a black man—and he was hiding upstairs in the closet and when—"

"Wait outside on the porch." Malone drew his revolver and pushed ahead of them.

"He left," Taylor said, "grabbed my keys on the bed and ran downstairs. Oh, David, it was horrible, he just stood there staring at me and I didn't know what to do."

"Didn't you hear the doorbell, ma'am? Just now, I rang the bell several times? You didn't hear?" Malone asked.

"Yes, yes, I did," Taylor answered. "But I was afraid to come down—I wasn't sure he was really gone . . ."

"Well, the car isn't in the garage, so I suppose he used your car to get away. I've already put an APB on the vehicle so maybe he won't get far," Malone said as he slipped the revolver back in the shoulder holster.

"Detective Malone?" Two uniformed cops had arrived and were standing at the open front door.

Malone continued to watch Taylor. David had his arms around her.

"You boys take a look around outside," Malone instructed.

"Mrs. Matthews," Malone redirected his attention, "I came out here tonight to ask you some pretty serious questions. Do you feel up to talking to me?"

"Can't it wait, Officer? My wife isn't up for any questions and I'm here now, I'm sure your boys will—"

"I can appreciate all that, Matthews," Malone interrupted. "But you see it's like I just said, there's another reason I came here to the house tonight. I came out here to talk to your wife about a certain incident that happened earlier this evening and, no, it won't wait. I'm sorry, Mrs. Matthews, I'll make it brief. I'm not saying it is, but it could be somehow tied into this intruder here tonight."

Taylor nodded and as she and David sat down on the sofa Malone took a seat on the edge of a nearby chair.

"Mr. Matthews, Mrs. Matthews"—Malone began by looking at first one and then the other—"there was a murder in a downtown office building a few hours earlier this evening."

"A murder . . . ?" Taylor reacted.

"Murder happens every day in the city, Malone. Are you quite certain my wife needs to hear about this?"

"I wish she didn't, Mr. Matthews, but you see your wife wasn't here all evening. She's been out. Isn't that right, Mrs. Matthews?"

David bristled. "Just where did this alleged murder happen, Detective?"

"2010 Main Street, Matthews—on the tenth floor."

David revealed nothing by way of a response, but waited for Malone to continue.

"A woman was shot and the body was found in your office, Matthews, behind your desk."

"Who? What woman?" David asked.

"I can't tell you that just yet."

"Don't your boys have a make on her?"

"Not yet."

"So what do you need to talk to my wife about?"

"Your wife was there," he answered, but kept his eyes on Taylor. "Isn't that right, Mrs. Matthews, sometime after eleven o'clock and before midnight?"

"You're mistaken, Detective. My wife was right here this evening. I had to work late, I had a dinner meeting and Taylor was waiting here at home. I spoke with her on the phone."

"What time did you speak with your wife, Mr. Matthews?"

"Taylor, you didn't go out tonight, did you?" David turned and asked.

"I had to David. I was upset. I knew you were with her and I couldn't stand the thought of—"

"Taylor, don't say another word," he said, turning back to Malone.

"Detective, you can see my wife is upset. There was an intruder here tonight, a burglar most likely and God knows what could have happened if you hadn't arrived when you did. Under different circumstances," he said, standing, "I'd get back in the car right now and go down to my office with you. Believe me I'm as anxious as you to get to the bottom of this, but right now I need to be here with my wife.

"Look, I'm supposed to be in Judge Miller's chambers at

nine in the morning"—David looked at the clock on the mantel—"a few hours from now. No reason to wake the man at this hour, but I'll call him at home about six-thirty and reschedule that meeting. Do you want to meet me at my office at, say about, seven-thirty? We'll get to the bottom of this then and if you need to ask my wife some questions, and of course you do, she can meet us later at either my office or at the precinct, wherever you say."

Both David and Malone had influential and mutual friends on the bench and in the force yet neither David or Malone had crossed paths until now; but each man knew the other's reputation and already they were squaring off.

"Okay, Matthews, we'll do it your way. Let's all grab a few hours and I'll see you in the morning, seven-thirty, your office. By then we'll have a positive on the Jane."

12

The crime team stayed with the investigation in the Main Street building throughout the night and that morning when David got off the elevator on the tenth floor, he had to lift the yellow tape and duck under to continue down the hall.

The office door was still propped open with a chair from inside.

Dallas P.D. lab technicians were dusting the private office, the receptionist's area, and the conference room for fingerprints when the unsuspecting Liz walked in the office behind him and saw the chalk figure drawn on the floor. Blood had saturated the carpet, leaving a dark stain on the floor near the corner of David's desk.

"My God, what happened?"

"We don't know much yet, Liz."

"Excuse me, sir, Mr. Matthews, ma'am, can you tell if anything's missing?" a young uniformed officer asked.

"I don't know . . ." Liz answered while she glanced around the room, "I'll have to check things, but actually, Officer," she said, glancing around, "it doesn't look like the office files have been broken into at all."

David told her that her desk drawer had been forced open and Liz assured the officer she'd look through it and make him a list if anything was missing. It had already been dusted for prints.

From the doorway David could hear the elevator opening down the hall. Like David, Malone lifted the yellow tape and ducked under. David offered a handshake in the spirit of co-operation.

"How's your wife this morning, Matthews?" Malone asked, accepting the gesture.

"She'll be okay, Detective. Do you have a make on the woman yet?"

Malone pulled his notebook from the inside pocket of his jacket and flipped through several pages, searching through his notes. He read over the page carefully and when he spoke, he spoke deliberately.

"Here it is. Roberta Dianne Duplissey."

"Roberta?"

"One of your clients, Matthews?"

"No, Detective, not one of my clients, but I knew her. You're sure about the ID?"

David turned to speak to Liz. "Remember the woman that came by yesterday—the one waiting for me when I came back from the funeral?"

"You knew her, Ms. . . . ?"

"Liz Jamison, I've been Mr. Matthews's secretary for almost eight years," Liz answered Malone.

"Well, Ms. Jamison, you knew the woman—this Roberta Duplissey?"

"I didn't know her, Detective, but she came by yesterday afternoon to see Mr. Matthews."

"That's right, Malone, she was here, but not for long," David explained. "She stopped by after a funeral to say hello. We went to high school together, grew up in the same neighborhood, and we were both friends of the deceased—the woman whose funeral we attended yesterday."

"Did your wife know her, Mr. Matthews?"

"Who?"

"Ms. Duplissey."

"No. Well, yes, maybe she did."

"Of those three choices, Matthews, what's your best guess? Yes? No? Maybe? Did your wife know the late Ms. Duplissey or not?"

"They may have met once—but they weren't friends."

"And why is that?"

"Taylor and I haven't been married all that long. I've known Roberta for years, since we were teenagers back in high school."

"And you've stayed friends all these years?"

"Not exactly."

"What then, exactly?"

"Roberta Duplissey, was *not* an easy person to be friends with. She was what you might say conniving, dishonest— and deceitful. Not traits I want in any friend of mine. Added to that, she was greedy and near insanely jealous of most, if not all, of her acquaintances. And *those*, Detective, were her *good* points. In all likelihood she was a borderline schizophrenic—sociopath, at best. Bipolar, maybe. No, Detective, I wouldn't say Duplissey *had* any friends."

"Well, she must have thought you were her friend. Why else would she have stopped by to see you?"

"That's the way she is . . . was. I don't really know why she came here after the funeral, but knowing Roberta it wasn't just to say hello. I'd put money on it."

"So tell me, how long had it been since you'd seen her?"

"We didn't stay in touch."

"But yesterday somebody you don't consider a friend, somebody you obviously don't like even a little, just out of the blue stopped by to see you."

"Well, we both attended the funeral don't forget. She was probably in town on other occasions through the years and never gave a thought to calling me or stopping by. Like I said, Detective, that's the way Duplissey was and most likely, she had something else on her mind."

"Seems likely enough, and if that's the case, did you meet her here last night to go over some unfinished business?"

"No, I had other plans last night and after Liz left, which was *after* Ms. Duplissey left, I locked up and left."

"What time would that have been?"

"About six forty-five P.M."

"Are those your clothes in the bathroom?"

"Yes, Detective, they are. I showered, shaved, and changed before leaving, before seven, like I said."

"And you and Ms. Jamison left together?"

"No, Detective, Ms. Jamison left around five-thirty."

Liz was by the coffee bar behind her desk. "Detective?" she asked, holding up the fresh pot of coffee.

"Thanks, ma'am, I'd appreciate that. So, Matthews"—Malone redirected his attention to David—"what else do you know about Roberta Duplissey? Any family? A husband?"

"There's not much, Malone. Her husband is in a nursing

home in East Texas—Tyler, I think. He had a stroke about four years ago; there are no children that I'm aware of and Roberta was an only child herself and both her parents are deceased."

"So why do you suppose Ms. Duplissey was in your office last night?"

"Not a clue, Malone."

"You say you had other plans for the evening?"

"That's right, with a client. We had supper."

"Does the client have a name?"

"Anne Williams," David answered, resisting the obvious.

"Is Anne Williams also a friend?"

"What's the implication, Malone? Ms. Williams is a client and, yes, she is also a friend, an old friend. An old friend from high school and yes, there is a coincidence—two old friends from the old days, on the same day. There was a funeral yesterday—another old friend from days gone by. We were all friends at one time. This was years before I met my present wife and she is *not* involved in this in any way—"

"Not involved? You think your wife's not involved? No, Matthews, you're wrong, dead wrong on that score. Your wife, Taylor Matthews, is very much involved here. She may or, as you're so quick to point out, may not have known your girlfriends from the old days but she *was* here, Matthews, last night in your office at about the same time your old friend was murdered while you just *happened* to be having supper with another of your old girlfriends. I'd call that *involved*, what would you call it—another coincidence?"

"Look, Malone, I'm not trying to hide anything from you, but there are some things that while you may *think* they're relevant to all this, they are in fact, the same details that can keep you from finding out what really happened here last night." David glanced about his office. "Looks like your boys are finished, so let's go into my office and we can continue this conversation in private. Liz, bring the coffee in here."

"I'll ask you again, Matthews," Malone said, following David into his private office, "what do you think this Duplissey woman was doing here last night? Was there—"

"Was there something going on between us? No, Malone, not a chance in hell. Roberta was a hard one to figure out. Always was. She was a beautiful woman, smart, and could she ever turn on the charm—when it suited her. On one hand, she was perky and fun but, on the other, calculating, manipulative, and possessive."

David sat down behind his desk and motioned for Malone to sit on the sofa before continuing with the personality profile. "Like I told you, Duplissey was likely a sociopath, maybe worse. It was amazing how quick she could change her temperament."

"And you'd seen both sides of her?"

"More than that."

"You were lovers?" Instinct made him ask.

"For a short time, a few weeks at best, but that was a long time ago, Malone. My girlfriend and I had just broken it off after high school graduation when Roberta and I got involved."

"Who was the other girl?"

"Anne Williams."

"The same Anne Williams you had dinner with last night?"

"Yes," David answered, adding a nod.

"And did the late Roberta Duplissey know Ms. Williams?"

"From the beginning, wherever there was Annie and Lindsey, there was also Roberta Duplissey."

"And who's Lindsey?"

"Lindsey Rose Wilson. Eventually she married James Mitchell."

"You don't say, the *late* Mrs. Mitchell, Senator Jimmy Mitchell's wife?"

"One and the same. The funeral was yesterday."

"I know. Lots of VIPs there for that one and I pulled the extra duty. And you were there?"

"Yes. Ms. Williams was in town. Lindsey Mitchell was her best friend and she called me and asked me to go with her."

"To the funeral?"

"Yes, we were friends."

Liz walked in and both men fell silent. She set the tray on the credenza, handed each a mug of coffee, and left them to spar again in private.

"Go on," Malone said when the door shut.

"Well, Ms. Williams and I had lunch together the day before and I offered to pick her up and drive her to the funeral."

"So you met her before the funeral?"

"No, she changed her mind. Called me at home and left the message with my wife. I called her back and we decided to meet at the funeral home before the service. After that we had coffee and visited."

"And Duplissey?"

"No."

"But she was at the funeral with you, wasn't she?"

"Yes, she was there, however, I didn't see her at the time. But when she came by the office that afternoon she told me she'd been there."

"So you were still friends—even after you broke off your affair?"

"We hadn't seen each other in a long time. I was actually surprised she would stop by like she did."

"You mean just for old times' sake?"

"It's like I said, knowing Duplissey I doubt it was just for old times' sake. There had to be another reason. We visited a few minutes, she didn't stay long, it was late and I had some calls to make."

"Did your wife know about your relationships with your old girlfriends?"

"I suppose she did. After all, I haven't been married very long. Not to Taylor."

"But you've been married before?"

"Yes, Malone, I've been married before. Twice, but not to either Anne Williams or Duplissey if you're going to ask. My former wives don't live in Texas anymore. Both have remarried, there are no scars. I have no children. Check it out."

"Do you mind?" Malone asked as he walked to the coffee carafe on the credenza.

"Help yourself."

"Getting back to your wife," he said, refilling his mug, "you said you're not sure if she knew Duplissey or not?"

"They met here in the office—just once. Duplissey stopped by late last year. In September, I think. As I recall it was still hot weather so it was probably the first part of September. Taylor was in town to do some shopping. She came by the office on the off-chance we might have lunch together. If I wasn't here, she figured she and Liz would grab a bite—they were getting to be friends. Liz had already gone out and Duplissey was just leaving when Taylor came in. I introduced them on Duplissey's way out."

"Had she been a client of yours?"

"Never. For whatever reason she was in Dallas, it wasn't to see me. If I asked her why she was in town she didn't tell me or if she did, I don't recall. It was nothing and, to tell you the truth, I didn't think anything about it then one way or the other and I forgot about her visit and her the minute she left. It was—is, of no importance whatsoever."

"Okay, so let's get back to yesterday. Why do you suppose your wife came here last night?"

"My wife is a little insecure lately."

"Does she have reason?"

"There are things she doesn't understand."

"Like what?"

"Like my work for instance. For the better part of my life, work has been the only constant and reliable thing in my life. I've poured my heart and soul and all my energy into my business and now that we're married Taylor sometimes feels shortchanged of the time I have to spend in order to stay on top of things." David walked to the credenza and refilled his cup. "And you, Malone," he asked, "are you married?"

"I used to be—it was a long time ago. . . ." Malone's approach softened. "Did your wife tell you I stopped her on the expressway last night?"

"She told me, Detective."

"You know this doesn't look very good for her. She was a jealous woman and from the sounds of it, with good reason. What I can't figure out was what Duplissey was doing here in your office after you went to dinner with your girlfriend."

"She's not my girlfriend, Detective. She's my client and I've known her for a long time. We grew up together. Plain and simple."

"Did Mrs. Matthews know you were having dinner with her?"

"She knew I was out on business. I do not know if she knew it was with Ms. Williams. I may have mentioned her name."

"Okay then, plain and simple." Malone stood up and closed

his notebook. "I'm going to get out of your hair for a while. By now the lab probably has some answers for us. Also the M.E.'s prelims should be ready. I'll need to speak with your wife this afternoon. I suppose, you'll want to be there?"

"Count on it."

"Oh, by the way, your wife's car was found. Abandoned a few blocks from the house. I had it hauled into the police garage. We should be finished with it tomorrow."

"Good, the sooner we clear this up the better."

"One more thing, David," that was the first time Malone called him by his given name, "does your wife own a handgun?"

"No, Detective, but I do, a .38. It's registered in my name."

"Where do you keep this .38 you own, Matthews?"

"I'm sure you know the answer to that one already, Detective. I keep it in my desk drawer. Surely, your men have already bagged it, boxed it, and labeled it for evidence."

"If it was here, I'm sure they have it," Malone said. "I'll let you know."

13

Taylor arrived just before noon. The police were gone and the door no longer propped open, but yellow tape still stretched across the outside hall. Liz had left early for lunch, the phones were not ringing, and the office was eerily quiet.

David was waiting for her and together they walked across the street to the Main Street Coffee Shop.

Neither had an appetite and awkward silence fell between strained, but polite conversation. After lunch David hailed a cab on the street and from there they went to the police station. They were early, but Malone was waiting for them in his office.

David had expected the questioning to be demanding but Detective Malone was sensitive, even sympathetic, toward Taylor and, to David's relief, he steered clear of the subject of past lovers, girlfriends, and such.

When they left the police station and returned to the

Main Street building David walked Taylor to her rental car in the underground parking garage. He told her he wanted to check his messages and would call it a day and be home early. He took the garage elevator alone to the tenth floor.

It was almost four P.M. when he walked into the office and Liz had stepped away from her desk.

He thumbed through the appointment book lying open by the phone on her desk. Tomorrow would be catch-up as usual. He flipped through the pink slips of phone messages and walked into his private office. The D.A. had called twice, but David had already talked to him at the police station. A reporter at the *Morning News* had called for a statement and there was a call from Senator Mitchell with a message and phone number for him to return the call a.s.a.p.

"What the hell?" David said aloud to himself.

"Yep, the creep called all right," Liz said, walking by the inner office doorway. "What do you think he wants?"

"Beats me." David shrugged. "You'd think I'd be the last one on his hit list. Anything else?"

"Just this"—she reached in her sweater pocket and pulled out a message from Annie—"If you hurry, you might be able to catch her," Liz said.

David read the message: *Sorry about last night. Decided to fly back this afternoon. Will call soon. Regards to Taylor. Thanks for your help.*

"Try to get Annie back for me, Liz. She's at the Adolphus. Maybe she hasn't checked out yet."

Liz was dialing the number as Annie's cab pulled away from the hotel.

"1328 Thornton Place," she told the driver. "It's in Oak Cliff."

Annie could hear the television blaring from the porch. The doorbell wasn't working and she knocked on the front door. When Dena didn't answer, Annie tried the knob, found it unlocked, and walked inside the small house.

"Dena, Dena—it's me, Annie. Are you here?"

Dena was sitting in front of the television set. She had been crying, her eyes were swollen, and discarded Kleenex were tossed on the floor next to the recliner.

"Come on in, baby, come on over and give old Dena here a hug. I knew you'd come. You're the only girl I've got now and I want you to know some things." Annie kissed her on the cheek and kneeled on the floor next to the chair.

"You know, I've always thought of you like my little girl," Dena said. "You and Lindsey were as close as sisters and when you two were together I never worried about either one of you," she said, her voice trailing to a whisper. "You need to be careful."

"Careful? What do you mean? Careful about what?"

"Annie, things had changed for Lindsey. Buddy could be real moody and he had a real bad temper when anybody crossed him. Lindsey kept saying I was imagining things. You know he never came to see me. Not once in all these years. Not on Thanksgiving or Christmas, Mother's Day—never. Before he married Lindsey, he couldn't come around here enough, but the day he married my baby girl, things changed. He was the invisible man. At first she made excuses for him, but after a while she even stopped that. Eventually, I stopped asking. Then a few times, lately, I thought she was hurt. One time, I know she was hurt, had her arm in a sling. I didn't know it at first of course, but then one day when she was here

I lost my balance on my way to the backyard and grabbed for her arm. When I did, she couldn't help herself, she yelled. She was hurt real bad and I asked her why she didn't go to the doctor."

"So what did she tell you?"

"Said she didn't have time to spend at any doctor's office—that it was really nothing, a pulled muscle or something, she did it playing tennis and that I shouldn't worry. The next week, I made a point of hugging her when she left and her arm was in a cast. Not to worry? That was the second time her arm was in a cast—in less than a year."

"Some sprain," Annie said.

"Yeah, and there's more. The mailman came by one day while I was in the front yard and he asked me about Lindsey. That's okay, a lot of people ask about Lindsey, but he wanted to know if she was getting better—after her accident."

"What accident?"

"That's what I said," Dena went on. "So I asked him, 'What accident?' He said he'd seen her getting out of her car one day when she came by here for a visit and both her eyes were black as pitch. Said she had a cut on her cheek and it looked like two or three stitches. 'Real nasty-looking,' he said. So when she came out that next week, I asked her about her 'accident.' 'What accident?' she said. 'The one that gave you the two black eyes,' I told her, 'and probably a pretty little scar on your face to boot,' I said. But she walked right on in the kitchen and started putting groceries away, said I shouldn't be listening to that old postman. Said she didn't have any accident. Not the way he took it anyway. Just stumbled getting out of bed early one morning, too much of a hurry she figured. Said she was fine. 'Nothing's gonna happen to me,' she told me. Now look, she's dead. Just like that—*poof*. One day she's hugging me and driving away in that expensive little sports car and then I get a call from the police."

Dena started to cry again.

"The police told you?"

"Yep, I got to hear it from the police"—she reached for her box of Kleenex—"You'd think her husband would call but no, not him, not ole Buddy boy, I gotta hear about my baby's death from strangers."

"Dena, why don't I fix us a cup of coffee?" Annie asked as she stood up. "I could really use a cup and I think you could too."

"That'd be good," Dena agreed and started for the kitchen.

There was a knock at the door and Annie remembered she'd asked the cabby to wait. She opened the door, apologized, paid him the fare, tipped him well, and sent him away.

She'd stay with Dena a while longer.

———

David checked every waiting room at Love Field for every flight departing for Austin. It was after seven when he gave up and called Taylor from the car phone and told her he was on his way home.

14

It was a morning designed for sleeping late. The heavy rains had slacked to an on again, off again drizzle and by noon David decided to go downtown. Weekends at the office were not all that unusual. Saturday was the second best day of the week to work, Sunday being the best. Today Taylor didn't seem to mind.

David was wearing jeans and a stretched-out sweatshirt and carrying his briefcase when he walked into the dark office early that afternoon. Duplissey's death had no effect on David whatsoever. If it did, it was only that he realized he lacked any genuine emotion when it came to her. He felt nothing toward her now, alive or dead, and it was only the nothingness he felt that disturbed him.

He turned on the lamp, and took the red leather book from his briefcase.

What the hell was Butter doing here? Is this what she was after, did she have second thoughts?

He crossed the room with the book in hand and sat down comfortably on the sofa and began to read where he'd left off, and the events of the last few days began to fade.

————

Lindsey was in denial for a while but once she accepted the fact, she knew what she'd do about it.

There was no pro-choice issue back then. Back then the rule was "Bear the shame and bear the pain." If a girl was pregnant, she got married. If there was no marriage, she simply went away for a long visit with an "aunt" or other distant relative. After the baby was born she would return, without the baby, and without ever having to admit the shameful truth—or she got an illegal and risky abortion.

Abortions were performed in secret places, often with filthy and improvised instruments. Untwisted coat hangers, long hat pins, or an ice pick would quickly penetrate and cause the uterus to rupture. Performed without sanitation, without preparation for complications, abortion was a bloodletting of a lethal kind. It was innocence revisited and a young pregnant girl was entirely on her own—and completely in the dark.

It was risk versus reputation and legality was not an issue in the alley.

When Lindsey returned late that evening she was pale. That's when I learned she had been pregnant. By the next afternoon, the bleeding was so profuse we couldn't keep the sheets from being soaked.

Lindsey tried to convince me, tried to convince herself, that the pain was not getting worse, that the bootlegged pain pills were wearing off, that discomfort was to be expected. She pleaded with me not to call for help—but when she tried to get out of bed she passed out.

She didn't remember anything after that.

I managed to get her back into bed, propped her knees up with pillows, and frantically called the dorm mother. In minutes the woman was standing in the doorway and immediately assessed the bloody situation and called an ambulance.

I lied to the admitting nurse. Later when the doctor came out to let me know she would be all right, he asked me if I knew who had done the abortion. I could only shake my head. The police were waiting to ask the same question.

Tommy Lee never knew about the baby and a few days later Lindsey was released from the hospital and went back to be with her mom in Oak Cliff. She had to drop out of school before the first semester had barely begun, and now I was alone for the first time.

I didn't think I could be sicker.

Nausea took over my life. For six weeks, I threw up everything I swallowed. I gagged on the air I breathed. I began to lose weight. Attending classes was impossible. Cold washcloths were the only comfort I had as I stayed in bed night and day, dragging myself out only to sit on the bathroom floor in front of the toilet and retch.

I was going to have a baby and I wouldn't consider any alternative.

———

The word jumped off the page. *Baby.* Lindsey had an abortion, and now *Annie* was going to have a baby.

David crossed the room and found the pack of Winstons

in the desk drawer. He thought back about the one and only time they'd made love—out by the lake—that summer.

David crushed out the cigarette in the ashtray. If Annie was pregnant that September that would explain why she'd failed to come home for the holidays that year. It would also explain why she distanced herself from friends and family. Everyone but Lindsey.

What happened to the baby?

He paced the floor with the open book in his hands and looked for the answer.

For weeks I couldn't focus on anything except my pitiful condition. My grades were beginning to suffer and I would have to bring them up before it was too late. I called Lindsey and she drove in that weekend.

She had the perfect solution.

We rented a small garage apartment on Hickory Street several blocks from the campus but still within walking distance, and she moved back to Denton just before Thanksgiving. Officially I continued to live in the dorm and once the morning sickness had run its course, I began to catch up on my studies.

Lindsey got a job at the boutique on the west side of the Square, only a few short blocks from the apartment. She lived in the apartment and we spent our weekends together at the small retreat over the garage. After the baby was born, she would look after her— until we could figure out something else. Listening to her talk and make all the plans, it seemed simple. I knew it would work. Together we could do this and no one would have to know.

I made an appointment with the counselor and that next Monday began making arrangements to transfer to another college at the end of the spring semester. I needed to get out of state and as far away as possible to start a new life. I'd tell my parents it was because of a change in majors.

While I was trying to keep my weight down and not appear pregnant, my grades improved. In January I began making applications for financial assistance.

I went into labor on a Thursday afternoon that next April. The timing couldn't have been better. The reading on childbirth that Lindsey and I had done those weekends at the apartment paid off. It was an easy delivery.

I missed classes on Friday and by Saturday afternoon was feeling stronger. On Monday I made both my English and history classes, stopped by the chem lab and picked up an assignment, and went back to the apartment.

I was exhausted and slept the rest of that day and through the night. Tuesday, I skipped classes entirely and Wednesday went back to the regular schedule.

As planned, Lindsey stayed with the baby. We had the "how to" books and our little girl was taking the bottle without any difficulty.

We named her Lauren Rose and as soon as I took the final exams of the spring semester, we packed Lindsey's old car and headed for Fayetteville.

Lindsey and I spent a lot of time considering exactly how I had become a widow. Vietnam was on everyone's mind, the war was taking lots of lives and by now we all had friends there. A Marine's widow had possibilities. Sadly, the father of my child would be killed before we could be married. That was our story and while it was all a lie that's what I would tell my parents.

———

A girl, a baby daughter. Where was she now? How could Annie do this to me?

15

She heard the phone ringing as she fumbled with the key in the lock, but the answering machine picked up before she could get to it.

"Annie, this is David. I'm at the office. Call me—it's important—"

"David?" she interrupted his message. "Hi, I'm just walking in. What's up?"

"Look, I've got to see you right away. I'm going to catch the next flight out and—"

"Wait—hold on, David, I've got some things to do tonight. Can we get together tomorrow or maybe if it can wait, I'll be back in Dallas next week—"

"No, Annie, it cannot wait. Whatever you think you've got to do, cancel it. I'll be there, wait for me."

"Okay, I'll be here. I'll have supper for us—"

"Just be there."

When he pulled into the driveway David was still driving too fast. He slammed on the brake and stopped short of the back of the garage, but not before he'd run over a stack of clay pots, the yard rake, and the garbage cans. Taylor opened the kitchen door to investigate the commotion at the bottom of the stairs.

"What's the matter?" she asked as David put the car into reverse to free the garbage cans. "Been talking to Annie?"

"Not now, Taylor—not now."

She shrugged and went back into the kitchen. David took the stairs two at a time and caught her by the arm. "Look, Taylor, I'm sorry but something's come up. It's important— I've got to fly to Austin—"

"I thought we'd made plans—just the two of us, can't it wait?"

He walked past her and down the hall.

"How long will you be gone?" she asked, following him up the stairs.

"I don't know. Not long. A day, maybe two. I'll call you." David headed for the shower and Taylor pulled out a small piece of luggage from the bedroom closet and started gathering his things. "What do you need?"

"I'll do it."

"David?" Taylor opened the bathroom door.

"What?"

"What's this all about?"

When David didn't answer, Taylor went downstairs.

———

It was almost six P.M. and the rainstorms that had been deluging Dallas now extended southwest to the capital city and Austin was under flood warnings.

Annie was waiting on the front porch when the cab pulled up to the curb. David walked in, carrying the overnight bag.

"Are you staying?"

He walked by her into the living room, opened his bag, pulled out the red diary, and tossed it on the coffee table. "I need some answers, Annie, and I need them now."

"What are you doing with this?" She picked up her book.

"Tell me about Lauren, Annie. I think I have a right to know."

"Hold it right there, mister. You have no rights—no rights at all. Who do you think you are coming here, demanding *anything* of me?"

The doorbell rang. Annie ignored it. It rang again. A knock followed.

Pointing an accusing finger, Annie dared him not to speak while she backed into the foyer. She was still glaring at David when she opened the door.

When she turned, she faced two men standing on the porch and wearing damp rumpled suits.

"Ms. Williams?"

She stared at them and said nothing.

"Ms. Anne Williams?"

"Yes? What do you want—I'm in the middle of something."

David walked up behind her.

"I'm Detective Chavez. This is Detective Luce."

"Okay?" Anne said.

"Ms. Williams," Chavez said. "There are some questions we'd like to ask you. May we come in?"

"What's this about, Detective?" David intervened.

"Just a few questions, it shouldn't take long," he answered.

Annie stepped back into the room and David led the men to the living room.

"Weather's getting bad again," Luce remarked as he followed.

"Sorry to interrupt you folks like this." Chavez glanced at the overnight bag on the floor at the same time he took out a small notebook from his coat pocket. "We had a request from a detective"—he looked at his notes—"ah, here it is—a Detective Malone in Dallas. Just a few questions—it won't take long. You don't mind, do you? And then we'll be out of here."

"Go ahead, Detective, ask your questions."

"And you are . . . ?"

"Matthews, David Matthews—Ms. Williams's attorney."

Luce and Chavez exchanged a glance.

"And he's on his way out, so if you could just tell me what it is you want to know," Annie said.

Luce pointed at the suitcase next to the coffee table. "Going on a trip?"

"As a matter of fact, that's mine and I just came from the airport," David was quick to answer. "You want to get to the point, Detective?"

"Ms. Williams"—Chavez turned to Annie—"can you recall the last time you saw a Ms. Roberta Dianne Duplissey?"

"Butter?"

"If that's Roberta Dianne Duplissey." Chavez looked at his notes to double-check.

"It is, why do you ask, Detective?"

"Annie," David interrupted, "Butter's dead."

"What? When?"

"She was killed the day before yesterday—"

"Mr. Matthews, do you mind?" Luce interrupted.

"What happened?" Annie asked David, but turned toward Chavez and Luce.

"Where were you last Thursday, Ms. Williams?"

Annie was still processing the news.

"Ms. Williams?"

"I was in Dallas on Thursday for the funeral of a friend of mine."

"That would be"—Chavez looked at his notes—"Senator Mitchell's wife?"

"Yes."

"Then you are friends with the senator?"

"No, I am definitely *not* friends with the senator."

"But you were at the funeral?"

"Yes, his wife and I were friends."

"You were friends with the late Mrs. Mitchell?"

"We grew up together in Dallas."

"Annie," David stopped her, "all the detective wants to know is when you last saw Butter. Did you see her at the funeral?"

"I didn't even know she was at the funeral."

"She was," David gave up the information.

"Ms. Williams, how would you describe your relationship with this uh, Butter? Were you close friends?" Chavez asked.

"We know each other—we knew each other, that's all."

"So what you're saying is you had a falling-out?"

"No, that's not what I'm saying. Yes, we had been friends, but we grew apart through the years. It happens. We really didn't stay in touch with each other after high school. I saw Butter occasionally when I was in Dallas, and, coincidentally, Detective, she contacted me about two or three weeks ago here in Austin. We had not seen each other in maybe two or three years or even more than that, and then one morning she called me at the NIA where I keep a small office, said she wanted to have lunch. I was busy at the time and couldn't get away just then so I asked her to come out to my place for supper that night."

"So the two of you had patched up your differences then?"

"There was nothing to patch, Detective. Like I said, we'd grown apart through the years. Life does that to people, you know?" She glared at David.

"So did you have supper with her?"

"Yes, I was glad to hear from Butter that day and thought it would be good to catch up on what she had been doing the last few years. Butter had an exciting lifestyle and listening to her go on about her circle of friends was usually quite entertaining—in small doses, every few years or so."

"Annie, don't say anything more about this," David cautioned.

"So what you're saying is," Chavez went on, "you were not really friends anymore, but you must have wanted to see her because you invited her out to your place? Is that about the way it was?"

"That about sums it up," Annie replied.

"So the day of Senator Mitchell's wife's funeral you didn't see Ms. Duplissey even though you were back to being friends on that particular day, right?"

"You're quick, Detective."

"By the way, what's NIA?" Luce wanted to know.

"The National Institute of Antiquities—it's based in Philadelphia but has satellite offices, like the one here in Austin, throughout the United States. Anything else?"

"You know, I've been in this town for almost six years and I don't believe I've ever heard of the National Institute of Antiques," Chavez turned and commented to Luce.

"What a surprise," Annie added all too sincerely. "But it's *antiquities*, the National Institute of *Antiquities*."

"Oh, and one other thing," Chavez added, "this Detective Malone in Dallas says you were staying with the senator's wife the week before she died." He looked at his notebook. "Is that right?"

"Well, Detective, your man in Dallas is wrong. The last time I saw Ms. Mitchell was just after New Year's. I may have spoken to her since then, but I can assure you I have not seen her since. Can you pass that on to your crack ace detective in Dallas?"

Chavez jotted the information in his book. "Thanks, ma'am, we just needed to hear you say that. We'll be leaving now. I'll type this up and fax it on to our 'crack ace' in the morning and he can file it away. Sorry to hold the two of you up."

"There's one other thing," Chavez added as he walked to the door, "Malone wanted us to ask you. Seems there was this woman sitting all alone at the back of the chapel wearing these dark glasses. Malone wondered about the lady— wearing a long black or dark blue coat he said and a blue scarf. Yeah"—he checked his notes "definitely a blue scarf, he said—wanted us to ask you if you knew her name?"

"No, Officer, I can't help you there. I didn't see her."

"And what about you, Mr. Matthews, did you see her?"

"Sorry, fellows, I didn't notice the woman either, but I do know Detective Malone and I'm sure he's already figured it out."

"Well, that oughta do it," Luce said as David opened the door ahead of them.

It was raining harder now and neither Chavez nor Luce

had an umbrella or overcoat. Certainly not the first time those suits had been rained on. They turned up their collars, and made a run for the car parked on the curb marked as a fire lane.

Annie stood on the covered porch with the door open behind her until the unmarked car made the corner. David had gone into the kitchen and was looking in the cabinet for the coffee can.

"In the fridge," Annie told him without being asked. She walked to the glass patio doors and stared out at the wet darkness.

When the percolator began making plopping noises Annie went to get the cups from the cabinet. "You know, they never said what happened to Butter, did they?"

David walked up behind her, placed his hands on her shoulders, and turned her to face him. "Annie, Butter was murdered. She was at my office late that night—the night of the funeral when you and I had gone to dinner—sometime after I dropped you off at your hotel. I don't know why she was at my office or how she managed to get in there that night, but somebody was either with her or she encountered someone while she was in the office and they shot her."

"But why? Who?" Annie turned away.

"You're asking me who would shoot Butter and I don't know the answer to that one, but do you want to know what I think?" Annie turned back to face him and he went on. "I think you're covering for somebody, and I think you're somehow mixed up in this and way over your head *and* I think you're in real trouble—and I think *you* know it and I *know* you lied to Chavez tonight. Annie, what the hell's going on?"

Annie turned and walked into the living room, ignoring the barrage David had just wielded on her.

"Hard to believe it's April, feels more like November," she said quietly as she lit the gas logs in the fireplace.

"A blackberry winter," David answered, bringing in the coffee.

"What do you mean?" Annie asked as she tossed the sofa pillows on the floor and sat down.

"Some seasons, like some people, have trouble letting go. Now, Annie, tell me about my daughter, please."

———

Annie started from the beginning, when she and Lindsey had left for college, and told him most of what he already knew. He sat staring at the fire. He never dreamed he could hurt so bad or feel so helpless—or guilty.

"Annie, God, Annie, you should have told me. I'm sorry, I wish I could have been there for you—for Lauren, for Christ's sake."

"You didn't know and I never blamed you."

"Why didn't you tell me, didn't you think I'd want to know? You had to know how I felt about you, how I would have felt about *our* baby. How could you do this to me—to us? I don't know if I can ever forgive you for this."

"Why didn't I tell you? David, think back about that summer. By the time I knew I was pregnant, I was away at college, I'd heard you and Butter were together, and you were in some kind of trouble with the law again. What would you have expected me to do? I had to think first about the baby. We, you and I, we didn't have a future together. We never did."

"But later, you could have come to me with the truth. Butter meant nothing to me and I got myself through those hard times. You knew I'd straightened out and had a real future ahead of me. We saw each other after that, why not then?"

"I-I don't know. I'm sorry, a part of me wanted to—desperately wanted to—but I was still confused. I couldn't tell you back then but I couldn't forget it either. I'd think about that night at the lake and I'd remember the way I felt when you put your arms around me. I could remember the way you smelled, and the way you laughed, the way you'd tease me, and I knew as well as I knew anything in my life you loved me, but in your own way—and it wasn't enough. I also knew you had a wild streak in you—and I was sure I was not the first girl you'd made love to."

"Annie, *you* were the first girl I'd made love with." David got off the floor and walked to the fireplace.

"That was never the impression you gave." Annie sat with her chin resting on her arms folded across her raised knees. David turned and looked down at her.

"Annie, look at me. I have spent my entire adult life waking, sleeping, living with this huge empty void that you were meant to fill and you're telling me now that you weren't there because—because you were 'confused'? Well, I'm sorry, lady, but I cannot—I will not—accept that kind of excuse. You *chose* not to tell me. You *willfully chose* to stay away from me, to keep my daughter—*my* daughter—from me and for *that*, Annie Williams—for keeping my daughter from me—for *that*, I will never forgive you."

Annie looked back into the fire.

"Look at me damn it, who the hell do you think you are that you can take a man's child from him?"

"It can't make any difference now, I know," Annie spoke softly, "but I *wanted* to tell you." Annie stood to face him. "Not at first. At first, I was, like I said, confused. But then later, that first summer after Lauren was born when we were in Fayetteville, I wanted desperately to tell you. I was going to tell you but by then I thought you had forgotten all about me—and about what had happened out there at the lake. That it didn't really matter to you after all. That I was right about you all along."

"I never forgot." David picked up the cushions on the floor, tossed them back on the sofa, and sat down.

"As time went on we were doing fine," she continued. "I graduated, landed a good job and Lindsey and I both adored Lauren. We gave her everything and then one day I received a newspaper announcement in the mail that you had married and that put closure to that part of my life. Once and for all I never had to make that decision again. I thought that was the way it was meant to turn out—that you would get married and have a family of your own."

"You mean live happily ever after?"

"I suppose, but more like you didn't need us and that we had learned to get along on our own."

"What about your folks, Annie? Didn't they ever wonder about this mysterious grandchild? Or have you kept her from them as well?"

"No, they knew—but not about you. I was determined to make it on my own and transferred to another college, you knew that much, and Lindsey helped me through those first few years. It all fell into place and no one questioned me for details. Maybe they didn't want to ask questions because it was easier for everyone to accept my story and go on."

"Where is she now, Annie? Here in Austin? Is she a student?" David asked, surveying the room. "Obviously she doesn't live here with you—this place is far too neat, much too small for you and a daughter."

Annie stared into the fire.

"Annie? Where is she?"

"She died."

"Died?" With disbelief written all over his face, he turned to look at her.

"Yes—she was ten. We were living in Philadelphia, close to the elementary school. I dropped her off on my way to work in the mornings and in the afternoons she would walk home. She was a beautiful girl, and smart, and responsible. We had a small house in a nice quiet neighborhood and she had her own key. Our neighbor next door watched for her to come in after school and as soon as she was home, she'd call me. I didn't travel much, never overnight, and was usually home before five each day. Then one day the school nurse called and said Lauren wasn't feeling well. She had a low-grade fever and the nurse wanted to send her home. I called Mrs. Townsend, the lady next door, and she said she would walk up to the school, get Lauren, bring her back to our house, and stay with her until I could get home."

"She didn't drive, this Mrs. Townsend?"

"No, but like I said, we lived close to the school."

"Go on."

"I went right home and when I got there I found that Mrs. Townsend had put Lauren to bed in my bedroom. I took her temperature and it was just barely over one hundred, not so very much really. I fixed her a bowl of soup for supper and she ate a little and said she felt a lot better. But in the night, her stomach started cramping. I called the pediatrician and he told us to meet him at the emergency room. He was waiting for us when we arrived. They took her in for X rays and I stayed with her in the lab. She was real scared and in a lot of pain. Dr. Peterson examined her again and the blood work confirmed that her appendix was inflamed. Dr. Peterson wanted to operate as soon as he could assemble a team.

"They prepped her for surgery right away. I stayed with her in preop and the last thing she told me when they took her into the operating room was not to be afraid—that we'd be home for church that weekend." Annie cleared her throat and wiped away her tears with the back of her hand. "Anyway, Dr. Peterson said the appendix ruptured before they could remove it and the infection spread into her body. She lapsed into a coma and never woke up. She died three days later."

Annie stopped her story for a few minutes and David sat motionless, blindly staring into the fireplace.

"When Lauren went in for surgery," she began again, "I called Lindsey and she flew to Philadelphia that night. She was with us at the hospital during those last days. Then she made the arrangements for the funeral. What was the point in contacting you then, what was the point of anything anymore? I wanted to give up. Lauren was my entire reason for being.

"Lindsey stayed on and eventually she talked me into coming back to Dallas with her. That's when we met Francis."

Early that next morning Malone leaned back in his chair and steadily tapped the pencil on the desk. And while he waited at the precinct to receive the Austin P.D.'s faxed report, Annie was awakening to the smell of coffee brewing. Moments later David walked into the bedroom, carrying two cups of coffee.

"Explain this one to Taylor," she said, sitting up, brushing her hair back from her face with one hand, and reaching for the cup with the other.

"You know I've always been straight with Taylor," he said, standing by the side of the bed.

Annie looked at him over the rim of the cup. "Don't kid yourself, David. You've kept things from her. You've kept things from me; it's your nature."

David sat down on the side of the bed and Annie moved over to make room.

"Okay, Annie, if you want total honesty I'll give it to you straight," he said, placing his cup in the saucer on the night-stand and turning to face her. "I love you, Annie, and that, my dear, is the God's honest truth."

The room was quiet and Annie sat still before she spoke.

"David, I know I've hurt you, and I'm sorry. We've hurt each other through the years, but those were the choices we made. You made another choice when you married Taylor not so long ago and now you and I will do what we've always done and live with the choices we've made."

This time it was David who sat still.

"David, you know I'm right, don't you?"

David walked back to the living room and looked at the rumpled sofa where he had slept. His shoes were on the floor and he stared at the red book on the writing table. He picked it up like it belonged to him and slipped it back in his briefcase.

He heard Annie turn on the shower. He needed to get home. Home, where he was in control. He'd have lunch with Taylor.

———

In the meantime a uniformed clerk passed by Malone's desk and handed him the single-page fax.

Nothing there he hadn't been expecting, except one thing—David Matthews was at the Williams place when Luce and Chavez took her statement Saturday night.

So why the urgency for Matthews to get to her? There was a reference in the report to an overnight case so Malone was guessing David was still in Austin. If so, this might be a good time to make a house call.

———

When Taylor answered the door, Malone apologized for calling unexpectedly. When she told him David was out of town "on business," he offered to come back another time.

"Detective Malone, please, I just put coffee on," she said, and without waiting for an answer Taylor led the way down the hall.

Malone pulled out a chair at the kitchen table.

"I'm glad you came out this morning, Detective. I'm curious, how's the investigation going?"

"Mrs. Matthews, I don't have all the facts together and there's a lot we don't know yet, but make no mistake about it you *were* at the wrong place at the wrong time. Your prints are going to be all over that office and we have witnesses as well."

"Witnesses?"

"Remember now there's the security guard that night that had a conversation with you and you may not remember this, but I'm the same cop that pulled you over on Central on that night when you were in such an all fired-up hurry. Also, I recognized your car heading back on that same expressway about midnight."

"But why would I kill her? I hardly knew the woman," Taylor said, reaching across the table for the sugar bowl.

"It's easy to make motive out of jealousy, or maybe you got caught up in something unexpected that night at your husband's office."

"You think I murdered that woman in some kind of a jealous rage?"

"No, ma'am, I don't think you killed that woman, but you're going to have to trust me. Things don't look good for you the way they are."

Taylor was holding the spoonful of sugar and with that said her hand trembled.

"I've got an idea"—Malone reached out and stopped her hand—"I drove past an IHOP on the corner a few blocks up and the rain seems to have let up." Malone leaned back in his chair and looked through the glass doors to the patio. "I could use a stretch. You could too. Come on, Mrs. Matthews, let's get a bite to eat, it's on me. What do you say we take a walk?"

After breakfast they started down the tree-lined sidewalk to the Matthews home. Even with a jacket, Taylor was cold. As they hurried up the walk to the front porch, the rain started again. Taylor reached into her sweater pocket for the key, unlatched the door, and stepped inside.

Under the porch Malone took off his St. Louis Cardinals' jacket and the dark blue cap that bore the red letter M and shook the water from them before he entered the house. Once inside Taylor hung them in the closet by the front door.

"Which is it, Malone, you a St. Louie or a Twins fan?"

"First one and then the other." Malone shrugged. "These days, I'm an avid 'Stros fan. You like baseball?"

"I'm a die-hard Rangers fan myself." Taylor shivered.

"Why don't I start a fire here in the den and we can dry out. We can talk about you for a change . . . St. Louie, huh?"

———

When she walked out of the bedroom Annie knew David would be gone, but she hadn't expected to miss him—not this much—and the sudden loneliness, the emptiness, was overwhelming.

PART THREE

THE ALLIANCE

16

By the time David returned to Dallas he'd changed his mind about lunch with Taylor and instead drove to the office. He'd call her from there and let her know he was back in town.

Several hours had passed and Malone had left before Taylor noticed the flashing light on the answering machine. She listened to the message: "Hi, honey, just wanted to let you know I'm back and stopped in at the office. I need to go over a few things here for a while. Call me when you get this message." The message registered at twelve-fifteen.

This time David could wait.

David leaned back in the desk chair. The briefs had piled on his desk. For several months he'd been considering expanding the firm. Now it was time and he would get Liz started on the clerical applicants right away. He'd see to the interns personally. He had a couple in mind—one in particular.

He looked through the handful of phone messages. He'd work on those tomorrow. Annie's journal was in his open briefcase on the table by the coatrack. David picked it up and put it away in the desk drawer.

Annie wanted to forget about what David had said—the part about loving her—at least for now, but his overnight visit continued to dominate her thoughts the remainder of the day.

Taylor didn't hear David's car pull into the garage. It was seven P.M. and when she turned from the sink he was standing in the doorway.

"Jesus Christ, David, why don't you make a little noise when you come in?" she gasped. "You scared me to death!"

"Taylor—Taylor, I'm sorry. I want to explain . . ."

"Not now, David, for now let's just try and get through the next few days—the next few hours for starters—and see what happens."

"You're right, Taylor, I'll take it slow. Why don't we go outside on the patio and get some fresh air?"

It was a cool evening and for the first time in more than a week it seemed like the skies might clear. When they returned to the house David rekindled the fire in the den.

"How was your day?" he asked in an effort to at least sound comfortable.

"It rained most of the day so I stayed inside. I read a little—and Detective Malone came by earlier looking for you."

"Did he say what he wanted?"

"Just that he had a couple of questions and that he'd be in touch."

"Did you tell him where I was?"

"I didn't really *know* where you were," she answered.

"So how was the good detective?" David asked, shaking off a sudden chill. David had worked too many years with Dallas's so-called finest and knew most of them had very little going for them outside of their investigations. To that extent he had much in common with Malone.

He watched Taylor slip off her shoes, sit down on the sofa, and curl her long legs under her with a pillow in her lap to rest her arms. David wanted to sit close, but she had placed several small pillows between them. In spite of the barrier he felt himself begin to stir and wondered how a decent man, a reasonable man at any rate, could, in the same day, profess undying love to one woman and be aroused by another. What's worse, this was the second time in as many days that he was in this impossible situation.

"So, David"—she turned to look at him—"tell me just where were you last night? I'm listening now and you've got some listening to do, too. No reason to pretend and no sense putting this off any longer."

"You're right, Taylor, we can't pretend there hasn't been a problem here, but we can get past this, I know we can, if we want to."

"I don't know if we can—and I'm not sure I'm willing to try, David."

David tried getting closer, but Taylor said she was going to bed and when she went upstairs David left the house.

———

Sunday nights were usually slow in the detective division and once again Jake sat tapping his pencil on his desk on a near empty floor at the precinct.

Finally, he told himself, he'd call it a day and go home.

Home to what? He shrugged off the unwanted question that crept into his thoughts and reminded himself he liked his life just fine the way it was—uncomplicated. Malone got up, lifted his baseball jacket from the back of the desk chair, and headed for the door.

As he made the corner on the way to the parking lot he collided with the medical examiner who was in a hurry and on his way into the building.

"Whoa there, B. J., what's up? Why the rush this late at night?"

"Good—you're still here." B. J. grabbed Malone by the arm. "Let's go over to the Elm and grab a bite. I know you want to hear some of this. It's about the Duplissey murder."

———

The forensic investigation on the Jane began Friday afternoon right after lunch. The fully clothed body had been taken to the morgue directly from the crime scene and kept in the cold-storage drawer until the autopsy could begin. The toe tag was verified and corresponded with the case study number.

Wearing scrub greens with a tiny microphone clipped onto

the shirtfront, the pathologist had spoken aloud as he began the procedure.

"April twenty-third, case study number 34726, female, white Caucasian, late thirties, early forties, appears to have died from a single bullet wound to the chest."

Pierce took the Polaroid from the shelf and snapped a series of pictures of the fully clothed body with particular attention to the hands and face of the victim. All photos would be compared with those taken at the crime scene.

The handpicked forensic team began arriving, each one a clone of Pierce, each dressed in green, each tying a mask across their face as the they entered, each wearing a tiny clip-on microphone, and each snapping on a pair of disposable latex gloves with regimented flair.

"Good afternoon, Doctors," he greeted them jovially. "Shall we begin?"

The body was disrobed and each article of clothing, as well as rings, earrings, and a wristwatch, were placed in individual bags. Each bag was marked with the date and case number 34726.

The cadaver was photographed again. Closeups were taken of tiny moles, freckles, blemishes, scars, contusions, scratches, cuts, and any and all other marks on the body. The process was repeated for the right and left sides of the body and again for the backside.

Placed on a stainless-steel tray the body was transferred, tray and all, from the table in the center of the room to a gurney and wheeled into an adjoining room where it was X-rayed from various angles. The cadaver weighed one hundred and three pounds and measured five feet two inches.

The microphones remained on throughout the procedure.

Any of the voice-activated findings were available as evidence if needed. No remarks were censored or edited from the recordings.

While these preliminary forensic procedures began, surgical instruments were being unwrapped from sterilized bags and laid in proper order on a towel-draped cart. A small power saw was retrieved from the cabinet and plugged into the island's electrical outlet.

If one word could describe the aura of the events that take place in the morgue laboratory that word would be *cold*—stainless steel, frigid, rigid—deathly cold.

An inert liquid was injected in the femoral artery to force the blood from the body. Urine was collected from the bladder. Fluids helped determine the presence of any poisons, alcohol, or other drugs in the body at the time of death and once they were collected in containers a member of the team began the laboratory toxicology tests at a standing desk mounted with a precision microscope under high-intensity lighting.

The entire room was bright and the workstation, the center surgical table, was made even brighter when Pierce pulled the overhead lamps closer to the subject.

From the sterile tray Pierce picked up the surgical scalpel and made the initial incision just below and to the inside of the left shoulder. From there he cut a downward angle to the top of the rib cage and back up at the same angle to the right shoulder. He continued the classic Y incision by drawing the knife from where the angles met straight down across the thorax, past the abdomen, and to the pubic region. The head would be examined last.

The corpse lay open.

The ribs and cartilage were cut to expose the heart and

lungs. The pericardium sac was opened and blood samples were taken from the heart before the smooth organ was removed. Each organ—the lungs, the kidney, spleen, stomach, bladder, and liver—were subsequently removed and each placed separately and duly noted in a stainless receptacle.

A .38-caliber slug had passed through the heart and the bullet was found lodged in the spine. The bullet was then photographed, removed, bagged, and hand-carried to ballistics where department specialists would run their own autopsy on the projectile. Their report would be incorporated in the final analysis.

By the time ballistics got started, the forensic team was well into their task and various members of the skilled team were already doing cross-sections of the organs. The skull was examined next for fractures and punctures.

Pierce picked up another sterile scalpel from the tray and drew an intermastoid incision, starting just behind the right ear and extending to the left ear laterally across the top of the head. The skin was pulled forward to expose the front of the skull. He stood back as the young Korean doctor moved in with the small disc blade. In less than a minute the wedge of skull was removed exposing the brain and Pierce stepped back into position and skillfully detached it from the vessels and placed it into a sterile pan. After it was weighed, a member of the team began the cross-sectioning for microscopic review.

That was Friday afternoon and by Sunday night the medical examiner had his findings. Malone held the door open and he and Pierce stepped inside.

On most any night except Sunday the Elm Street Bar & Grill was a noisy, lively spot where police officers, detectives, attorneys, and clerks could grab a quick hot sandwich, a cold beer, or just hang out, and where trial lawyers often awaited an unpredictable jury's verdict. And it was here at the Elm where cases were hammered out at the bar of a different kind and where more than a few deals took place in the corner booths.

The lighting in the Elm was dim and left most patrons shrouded in a veil of obscurity. Malone and Pierce didn't have that kind of anonymity and when either man walked into the Elm they were easily recognized. A couple of cops waved them over. Jake waved back, but it was back to the business as usual and he and B. J. headed for a booth at the back of the room.

———

Wearing a white blouse tucked into tight-fitting jeans cinched with a silver concho belt and big hoopy earrings the middle-aged waitress was attractive in a hard-bitten sort of way. She was standing behind the bar and when she saw them walk in she turned and pulled two longnecks out of the cooler, put them on the tray, and followed them to the table.

"Hi, fellas, that'll get you started. What else?"

"Hello, Ruthie. Anybody in back cooking tonight?" Malone asked.

"You're looking at her," Ruthie answered, smacking on a fresh stick of Juicy Fruit. "It'll be slim pickin's, but I'll do my best for ya. What'll it be, Jake?"

"How 'bout a big roast beef sandwich on one of those soft buns with those little seeds on top with a little horsey-sauce on the side and maybe some fried potatoes if that grease bucket's still fired up."

"You bet. How 'bout you B. J?"

"Better make me one of those sandwiches too. And if

you've got any soup back there, darlin', I've got a chill that goes clear to the bone and could use a warming from the inside out." B. J. slid into the booth, but kept his flight jacket snapped to the throat.

A uniformed desk clerk walked in and moments later a motorcycle cop stepped inside and joined her at a table, placing his white helmet in an empty chair. "Be right with you," Ruthie called to them and left the two veterans in the booth to talk.

"So what'a you got for me, B. J.? I have to tell you, I don't believe the Matthews woman has anything to do with the Duplissey case. I think she's in a tough situation, but it's not murder."

"The killer could've been a woman. Duplissey was in pretty good physical shape, worked out regular I'd say. Do you think the Matthews woman is in that kind of shape? Whoever killed her had to struggle to do it—might of even lost if they hadn't shot her when they did. Couple of things missing here though."

"Like what?"

"Well, fingerprints for one. There aren't any that aren't supposed to have been there. We're missing prints that would have been left by whoever else was in the office when the lady Matthews came in looking for her husband. That's what she was doing, isn't it? Looking for her husband that rainy night?"

"The killer could have been wearing gloves, B. J.," Jake responded.

"You bet, could have been," he answered. "But not too many people wear gloves in April—not unless they were prepared ahead of time."

"So what's your call?"

"Well, the mechanics of death included a condition within the body in which the pericardium had been penetrated by a .38-caliber hollow-point projectile rupturing upon impact, causing massive and irreparable damage within the heart cavity."

"Like we thought then."

"Yep, like we thought."

"And . . . ?"

"And as the manner, we're ruling it homicide."

Malone was finishing the first beer when he saw David come through the door.

"Whaddya say, we invite him to join us?" Malone asked and Pierce turned to see who it was.

"Let's do it," Pierce agreed and unsnapped his jacket.

Malone slid out of the booth and walked toward the bar where David was about to take a seat. "Matthews," he said, approaching, "what brings you downtown tonight?" David turned and Malone offered a handshake. "Come on over and have a beer with me and B. J."

In spite of his dark mood, he followed Malone over to the booth. David grabbed a chair from an empty table and straddled it at the end of the booth.

David and the medical examiner were not strangers and had conferred on many cases in the past. While David had been with the D.A.'s office they'd had a good working relationship, but once he'd gone into private practice the two men were often at odds with each other.

"We were just talking about the Duplissey case. You sure do have some interesting clients," Pierce said, reaching across to shake hands.

"I have to admit it, Pierce, I do have colorful clients, but

Duplissey wasn't one of them." He turned then to Malone. "My wife tells me you came by this morning, Malone. Any leads on who shot Duplissey?"

"Don't really have much to tell you, Matthews, I'm still waiting on B. J. here to get caught up down there in the morgue."

Pierce kept his surprise in check long enough for Malone to brush over any details David might ask about, and Ruthie arrived just in time with another round of beer for Jake and B. J. and one for David.

When Ruthie returned next time she came from the direction of the kitchen and was carrying a large tray with the soup and sandwiches. Pierce and Malone unrolled the fighting gear from the napkins and as soon as the seasoned waitress unloaded the tray, David stood. "It's been a long week, fellas, and I'm going to head on home." He reached for his wallet and Malone told him, "It's on me tonight."

Pierce and Malone watched David walk out of the Elm before either spoke.

"So, B. J., what else have you got on the Duplissey woman?"

"Well, cloth fragments gathered in the wound and the burn hole in the dress indicate the gun was fired at point-blank range. The angle of the bullet at point of entry and through the body indicates that the shooter probably stood at eye level. Whoever it was wasn't much over five feet tall, five and a half at the most. And the contusions indicate a person with a small handgrip. The struggle was intense, so whoever did this probably didn't leave without some marks as well."

"You're sure about the struggle?" Malone asked.

"Oh, yeah, contusions covered about twenty percent of her

body. There was trauma around the mouth as well, probably trying to muffle her cries. Again, small hands—but strong hands. Also the killer fired holding the gun in the left hand.

"We've lifted trace scrapings under the nails but haven't found a match yet. So far we've got nada, zip, nothing there. There was a sizable collection of semen in the vagina, so the victim had intercourse not long before she was killed."

"Rape?"

"No, I don't think it was rape, no evidence of tearing and her clothes didn't appear to have been removed, not forcibly anyway. No, rape wasn't the case here. But she did have sex earlier, probably consenting but not much more than an hour—hour and a half max—before her death. Any idea who she might have been out with that evening?"

"No, but you seem to think she struggled with a woman."

"I said it's possible."

"So it could have been a man?"

"Of course, it could have been. I'm just laying out the possibilities for you."

"And you say she was with a man earlier?"

"What's up, Malone, are you going stupid on me?"

"No, I'm at a loss here, there's one big missing piece of puzzle to this and I have the damnedest feeling I'm barking at the wrong tree."

"Ballistics had their report yesterday," Pierce continued. "I'd have thought you'd have a report of that by now. I have one back in the office; I can make you a copy when we go back. Not much to help you there though. Ballistics obtained the Matthews gun for comparison. It doesn't match with the markings on the bullet removed from the victim."

"So what we have here is a missing murder weapon and not much else to go with."

"Not yet, but let me ask you something."

"Ask away."

"I know how Matthews operates and believe me, he's always had more than one gal in the wings. He doesn't know any other way."

"I can buy that. What's your question?"

"The locks on the front door weren't tampered with and it's not likely the door was left open. So, Duplissey had a key or somebody let her in. If not David, who else might she have been intimate with earlier that evening? Suppose the victim leaves her mystery lover to meet Matthews. She gets there first and is waiting in the hall when his wife shows up. The wife lets them both into the office where they argue, struggle, and the wife shoots her. Matthews arrives, realizes what happened, and now he's covering for the wife."

"Any other scenarios?"

"Or suppose Duplissey meets David later that evening at the office where they play out their sex game. David showers, cleans up, and splits, leaving Duplissey to lock up behind him. But the wife comes in and finds her there. They struggle, she shoots her, and splits."

Ruthie was behind the bar and Jake held up the empty bottle to get her attention.

"You're right, about Matthews's girlfriends," Malone responded. "Matthews had supper with a woman named Williams that evening, but after supper he took her back to the hotel. The doorman saw them come in and he saw David leave. The bartender at the hotel says Williams came into the bar about ten and ordered a drink. The cash register prints out a tab with the date and time on it; she charged it to her room and signed the tab. Since she did not have a car there, she would have had to take a cab or somebody would have had to pick her up if she left the hotel, or she would have had to walk out in the rain that night.

"The doorman is ready to swear she did not leave by the front door. He was on duty until eleven and he's certain he would have remembered. His replacement did not recognize her as one of the people he helped get cabs for later that night, although there was a wedding party at the hotel and there were quite a few people coming and going all evening—even with the rain.

"Her whereabouts after she signed the bar tab can't be confirmed, but there's no reason to doubt that she went to her room alone like she said she did. For now, nobody can prove it was any other way."

"But it is possible she left the hotel undetected."

"Right now anything's possible," Malone agreed.

"So how much do you know about Williams and Matthews?"

"According to both Matthews and his wife, David was at one time—maybe still is—in love with Anne Williams. She called David to tell him she was in town for the funeral of an old classmate of hers—Senator James Mitchell's wife."

"Mitchell was another one with a reputation for fooling around. And you say his late wife was a friend of Williams? What about David? Did he also know the senator's wife?"

"All these people knew one another well—except Taylor Matthews, David's current wife, but she had heard enough stories about the three women and of their relationships with her husband to be wary. At one time or the other he'd bedded each of these women."

"Were the ladies all friends?"

"Not really, but of those four women the only two I think were capable of murder are the two that are already dead."

"Are you saying Senator's Mitchell's wife was capable?"

"With the right provocation, yes. The problem with the two suspects I'm left with is that they both had opportunity, but neither seems capable of the crime."

"Yes, but only one has both opportunity *and* motive, and, under the right circumstances, Malone, anybody's capable of murder. Deep down you know it."

17

Malone caught the flight from Dallas Love Field, and within minutes of landing in Austin he picked up the midsize rental and headed north onto the freeway.

Anne Williams was preparing to leave for her office when Malone rang the front bell.

"Ms. Williams, I'm Detective Jake Malone from the Dallas Police Department." Malone showed Annie his photo ID. "I know it's early, ma'am, but I have a few more questions I need answers for. I won't take up too much of your time."

"I already spoke with your men—about Butter, isn't it?" she said, stepping aside to allow him to enter. Malone followed her down the hall to the kitchen where she invited him to sit down at the small table by the window. "Can I offer you a cup of coffee, Detective?"

"Yes, ma'am, coffee would be fine. It's an early call I know, and I don't want to keep you long. I just need to make sure all the *i*'s are dotted, you understand."

"And the *t*'s crossed? What is it that you really want to know, Detective?"

"Ms. Williams, I don't want to put you in an embarrassing position here, that's why I came all the way out personally this morning, but I need to know about your relationship with David Matthews."

"With David? We really don't have a relationship, Detective. David and I are old friends but I seldom see him these days and, for that matter, I haven't seen much of him for several years."

"But he was here over the weekend wasn't he?"

"Yes, David was here Saturday night—but you knew that didn't you, Detective?"

"Yes, ma'am, I did—and I apologize—I don't mean to insult . . ."

"Apology accepted, Detective, what else do you want to know?"

"Ms. Williams, would you tell me about your activities last Thursday?"

"As you know, I was in Dallas. I'd arrived there on Tuesday and was staying at the Adolphus. On Thursday morning I slept in and I had breakfast in my room, you can verify that, Detective. That afternoon I took a cab from the hotel and attended Lindsey Mitchell's funeral service at Oak Hill. After the service I had coffee with David Matthews at some diner on Northwest Highway and later that evening we met again and I had supper with him. Like I told you, our friendship goes way back. He and Lindsey Mitchell and I had all gone to school together in Dallas many years ago—back in Junior High and High School."

"Was it just the two of you for supper?"

"Yes, just the two of us. David had made reservations at Las Palomas—just off McKinney Avenue, I think. After supper he dropped me back at the hotel, and I went to bed—alone."

"I just have one more question, Ms. Williams. When was the last time you saw your friend Lindsey Mitchell alive?"

She stood at the sink with her back to Malone and he had to wait for her response.

When she turned she repeated the same story she had given David about meeting Lindsey at a restaurant the day after Lindsey had changed her plans for dinner.

She told Malone about Lindsey's deteriorating relationship with the senator, but what she did not tell him was about Lindsey's relationship with Francis Zacchoias. Nobody should know about that.

Malone finished his coffee, thanked her for the information, apologized again for the intrusion, and left.

As the 737 took flight he went over the events of the last four days: simple events all of them, but the people involved were not simple. Their lifestyles, their personalities, their problems were complicated. In a strange way, he felt sympathy for all of them, one in particular.

By two p.m. Malone was back at his desk.

Most homicide cases were solved within twenty-four hours and Malone was beginning to feel the heat to wrap it up. Police Chief Oscar Truly claimed he was getting pressure from the mayor, and that information alone sent up a red flag for Malone. Both Chief Truly and Mayor Sam Lyons were ordinarily sticklers when it came to tying up loose ends. Truly was noted for his insistence that every lead, regardless of how far out in left field it might appear, be thoroughly investigated. Rushing investigations was not the norm for this department leader.

The mayor had handpicked Truly, and Lyons had never failed to back up the chief's judgment. So why was the mayor interfering in an investigation?

Malone held the directive in his hand and rocked back in the worn chair. The chief wanted him to tie up the Duplissey case by the end of the shift. If he couldn't manage it the chief would reassign it to another detective who would. Malone was reassigned to an early-morning drive-by shooting on lower East Grand Avenue.

The door to the chief's office was open. Malone rapped on the glass and walked in. In the past eight years that the chief had been the chief, the two men had worked well together.

"Chief, you never pulled me off in the middle of an investigation."

"Don't read anything into this, Malone, we need you on this drive-by. It's the second shooting in the last five days, probably gang-related. You know the neighborhood and we need somebody with some grit to handle it."

"I'd like to stay with the Duplissey case."

With narrowed eyes, Chief Truly stared at him a long time. "Forty-eight hours, Malone, but that's it."

Malone was already backing out of Truly's office.

"Forty-eight hours, Malone," he heard the chief yell after him as he headed for the stairwell down to the parking garage.

————

Malone turned the unmarked car right on Gaston Avenue. He drove by Baylor Hospital, and continued down Gaston to the choice spot where the Bar-B-Q Restaurant had operated for decades and where Gaston merges with the beginning of Garland Road. He passed by the site of the old Pig Stand where hardened waitresses once sold oceans of bottled beer to working-class drinkers six nights a week and then continued up Garland Road to the spillway and passed the used car lot where the now long-gone Hi-D-Ho once operated.

He slowed as he drove by the present-day Dallas Arboretum with its immaculate landscaped and manicured lawns. The azaleas, he noticed, starting to bloom a few weeks ago, were being beaten down by the heavy rains.

With the signal lights in his favor he continued without stopping to the never changing Casa Linda shopping center, turned left onto Buckner, cruised down the hill, turned left onto Lake Highlands Drive and again left onto Lawther Drive, known always as "the road around the lake," and the road that forever defined the White Rock Lake neighborhood.

For the past fifteen years White Rock Lake had been a favorite retreat for Malone. He drove up the hill and parked at the Dreyfus Club, where the view of the lake was as close to a religious experience as he had ever allowed himself to experience.

Today the lake below shimmered with sparkling lights reflecting from the afternoon sun.

There were several small sailboats making their way to the middle of the lake. For two weeks the rainstorms had kept the skiffs moored at the Dallas sailing club pier on the east shore of the lake and this afternoon the normally weekend-only sailors were anxious to let canvases unfurl for the few remaining hours before dark—even on a Monday.

Malone got out of the car and walked to the picnic table.

He sat on top of the table, his feet propped on the wooden bench, and admired the Dallas skyline across the water. White Rock Lake on a chilly April afternoon was a good place to be and the hill overlooking the lake was a good place to sort things out.

Malone was methodical and except for this lake, an occasional sunset, blooming azaleas, and one particular blonde, he saw life as black and white. He reached for the spiral pad from his inside jacket pocket and started by systematically writing down the names of all those involved in the case.

By Duplissey's name he simply wrote: *Shot in the heart. Thursday, ETD Eleven forty-five P.M. Victim struggled. Bruises to face, wrists, and upper left arm. Sex prior to murder.*

Next he wrote the name of David Matthews, noting that Matthews was a criminal attorney whose long list of clients included most of Dallas's most illustrious, if not notorious, so-called businessmen. Old friend of victim. Married to Taylor Matthews.

And so he continued to write, dedicating a page to each player.

He added another page for Lindsey Rose Mitchell, deceased wife of Senator James Mitchell. And on the last page he wrote in the name of James "Buddy" Mitchell, U.S. Senator and possible candidate for the Democratic Party's presidential nomination for the upcoming election. Widowers usually had Malone's sympathy but as for politicians there were few he trusted—none actually. Next were lawyers. And most politicians, he reminded himself, started their careers in law.

When Malone left the lake that afternoon he returned to town and parked in front of the *Dallas Morning News*. He wouldn't be there long. He needed copies of last Monday's, Tuesday's, Wednesday's, and Thursday's papers. What did the press have to say about the late Mrs. Mitchell? It didn't take long to locate what he was looking for. Interestingly enough, they didn't have much to say.

From there he returned to the station, took the stairs to Records, and asked to see the case file on the Mitchell death. That took longer. Once he filled out the required request form he waited for the clerk to produce the flimsy report. The newspaper reported Lindsey Mitchell had died on a Friday "following a brief illness," but according to the death certificate the manner was "accidental," mechanics of death was listed as a "blow to the head," and the cause was "tricyclics and alcohol."

Where was the corresponding information? Where were the photos? Where was the autopsy report? Only a lousy one-paragraph report from a detective that arbitrarily determined that no detailed investigation was necessary. *Not necessary,* after an accidental and lethal fall? No mention of any illness in the police records. How can a senator's wife die, under *any* circumstances, and there not be a full investigation? Who signed off on this one?

Malone did not recognize the signature. He did recognize a coverup.

18

Early the next morning Malone made the easy one-and-a-half-hour drive to Tyler. The director at the exclusive Piney Woods Care and Rehabilitation Center was friendly—almost to the point of being helpful—but Malone would have to either get a subpoena or permission from the trustee who held the medical power of attorney for access into the Duplissey files.

From Piney Woods he drove to the outskirts of Tyler where he next met the caretaker and his wife who lived on the Duplissey estate. By four forty-five P.M. he reluctantly declined the caretaker's invitation to stay for supper, thanked them for their help, pulled away from the curb, and headed for I-20 west toward Dallas.

From the car phone he called B. J.

Malone was leaning against the wall outside the coroner's office when B. J. arrived with his keys.

"Been meaning to tell ya, pal," Pierce said as he turned the lock, "you need to get yourself a life."

The two men entered the morgue and Pierce flipped the light switch.

The medical examiner's private office was just to the right of the front desk and the cold-storage drawers were in a room to the left. Most of the furnishings in the outer office and in B. J.'s office were a throwback to the forties, but the lab and the three examining rooms, extensions of the central lab, contained state-of-the-art equipment. B. J.'s office was the smallest area in the downtown basement morgue.

"You do know I gave the release for the Duplissey body, don't you? Her attorney called, said he was making the arrangements. Some fella in Tyler. Had all the credentials 'in the event of her death.' Nobody's been here yet though. Probably show up in the morning. So what is it you needed me down here for tonight?" B. J. unlocked the steel door to the cold-storage area and snapped on the ceiling lights.

Blue-white fluorescent light filled the dark room and Malone shielded his eyes from the sudden brightness. "Darkness just doesn't cut it down here. No shadows either," Pierce said as he pulled the drawer and slid the cadaver from the holding chamber. Toe tag still in place, the nude cadaver was covered in white sheeting. B. J. folded the cloth away from the head and both men stood looking at the once beautiful face. After the removal of the brain, the wedge of skull had been replaced and the peeled face had been rewrapped in place.

"Mortician's gonna have his work cut out for him on this one," Pierce said.

"I don't know that anybody will care. Her husband is in an

expensive nursing home in town there, been there since his first stroke rendered him paralyzed almost four years ago. His doctor there told me the old man's condition had worsened and round-the-clock nurses take care of him."

"Any other family?"

"As far as anyone there knows the old man has only one child, a daughter from a previous marriage, but grown now and living and working in some capacity with the Peace Corps somewhere in the jungles of Central America. Apparently, she's an independent woman who barely knew her father's second wife. The caretaker and his wife told me she had never visited since her father's wedding to this woman." Malone gave a slight tilt of his head indicating the cadaver.

"Years ago," he continued, "the old man established a trust for his only child. He had one drawn up for his first wife—for this one too—but the daughter apparently hasn't much use for the money, at least so far, and her funds have remained untouched—increasing in value with each passing year.

"A separate trust, managed by the old man's attorney and appointed trustee, was in place to keep this wife in a comfortable lifestyle as long as she remained married to him. In the event of a divorce, a settlement had been prearranged. If he died and they were still married at the time, she would continue to benefit from the trust throughout her lifetime. Roberta Duplissey had no children of her own, you confirmed that much already. The old man had been astute when it came to finances and taken all the loopholes out of his estate."

"And you got all this from—?"

"Most of my information came from visiting with the caretaker and his wife in Tyler. I drove out there this morning. Of course, I need verification on all this. A talk with the attorney in Tyler ought to help there, but I'll need a sub-poena to go forward."

"That's the way it works, pard."

"Most times, yes, but the problem here is the chief won't go along with it. He's pressing me to either wrap this one up now, like yesterday, or he's threatening to pull me off and put someone else on it who'll close it PDQ—or sooner."

"So why did you need me down here tonight?"

"I need a favor—a big one."

———

Lupe Ybarra had been Senator Mitchell's housekeeper and cook before he married Lindsey and she continued to main-tain her position in the senator's home for the years following the marriage. She was not inclined to gossip, but little that went on within the house went unnoticed by her.

The senator was seldom a happy man and Lupe Ybarra knew he took his discontent out on his wife. She also knew that Lindsey was unhappy; the senator was *muy difícil*. With the death of Señora Mitchell, Lupe would not stay working for the senator.

The boys, Lindsey's children, were in boarding school, and Lupe would have no trouble finding employment in another prestigious home. But tonight she was preparing supper for the senator when she heard the front bell ring.

"Evening, ma'am, is the senator in?" Malone showed the housekeeper his photo ID.

Lupe asked him to step inside the foyer. When she returned she asked Malone to follow her to the senator's study. The senator set his bourbon glass down when Malone walked in.

A handshake and a few words of courteous conversation exchanged between the two men gave each veteran ample time to evaluate their opponent's strengths or weaknesses. Politeness was never misunderstood for any career warrior. Politeness was a craft, a magnificent covert weapon, and both men had their skills honed for this impromptu meeting.

"Bourbon?" Mitchell asked as he dropped two clear ice cubes into the crystal bar glass.

"No thanks, Senator."

"What can I offer you, a beer?"

"Sure, beer's fine."

With that said, Lupe disappeared and returned quickly with a bottle of beer and a chilled pilsner on a small wooden tray. Malone took the bottled beer, nodded a thanks to the housekeeper, and Lupe returned to the kitchen.

"Senator, I hate to bother you at a time like this, I'm sorry about the death of Mrs. Mitchell, but there are a few questions I need you to answer for me."

The senator said he'd help any way he could but only on the condition that Malone would stay for supper. After the meal the two men returned to the study. The senator poured himself a glass of B&B and Malone accepted the coffee that Lupe poured for him.

Mitchell stood with his back to Malone and stared at the mantel over the fireplace. The logs had not been lit and the room was cold. There were several framed photographs on the mantel, pictures of the senator and his late wife, photos of the senator and his wife with the Carters and another with the Nixons. On a table in the corner, another collection of photographs was framed and displayed. There was a photo of the senator and Mickey Gilley, in Western hats and boots, standing outdoors in the parking lot outside Gilley's Dance Hall in Pasadena, and another photo with a young Mohammad Ali. The Ali photo was signed, *Regards, Cassius.*

Malone recognized a photo of Lindsey Mitchell and Farrah Fawcett. If it wasn't her, it was damn near her double. There was also a photo of the senator and the author James Michener, and a black-and-white glossy of the senator and L.B.J. standing by a cedar rail fence with Longhorn cattle in the background, depicting a lifestyle of Texas ranchers and their politics.

Off to one side was one small picture of two young boys with dark curly hair, about five and six or seven years of age, holding hands with a young woman who Malone guessed to be about sixteen years of age.

Malone had never met any of these people, never cared much for "celebrity" types and sure as hell didn't care for the political type, but the anecdotal stories the senator shared were entertaining. In fact, that night the senator seemed pretty ordinary to Malone except that the senator ran with a crowd that was anything but ordinary.

19

The following morning from the front porch of the stucco house by Stevens Park, Malone could hear the television blaring. The doorbell was taped over with a handwritten note above that said OUT OF ORDER. He knocked on the door and while he waited he recognized the familiar phrase "Come on down" from *The Price is Right*.

He knocked again, this time louder, and the sounds from the television went silent. He heard the latch *click* and the flimsy safety chain dangle against the doorjamb as it slid from the groove. Dena swung the door wide open.

"Morning, ma'am." Malone introduced himself and offered his photo identification for her assurance. She ignored the photo, but told him to follow her into the kitchen.

"Go ahead, grab yourself a cup of coffee," she offered gruffly. "Cups in the cupboard left of the sink. Pour me one too. I know how you cops live on coffee. I was married to one—a long time ago. His name was Cole, Cole Younger—like the outlaw. Ever hear of him?"

"Yes, ma'am, I've heard of them both, the outlaw and the cop."

"Did you know my husband, Detective?"

"No, ma'am. I never met him. But I've heard others, veterans down at the precinct, speak of him. They say he was a fine officer—none better."

"You got that right, he was a good man, Malone, and I still miss him, after all these years. Now, what brings you out here this morning? Here," she said as she tapped the seat back of the kitchen chair, "sit down."

Malone put the coffee on the table and sat down as he was told. He expressed his condolences on the death of her daughter and explained he wanted to tie up some loose ends on the report. "Strictly routine," he assured her.

As soon as he mentioned the senator's name he could see her disdain for the man, and it didn't take any coaxing for her to repeat the same stories she had told Annie, but the emotion he was expecting from the feisty old red-headed woman wasn't there when it came to Lindsey.

Dena stood up abruptly and asked the detective if there was anything else he needed to know. If not, she had plans. She was leaving town for a few weeks, maybe more. "A long vacation," she told him.

————

The memo was on his desk when he got back to the office just after lunch.

"You looking for me, Chief?" he asked, standing in the doorway of Truly's office.

"Damn straight, I'm looking for you."

"What's up?"

"Close the door behind you."

Malone stepped inside and closed the door.

"This time you've gone too far, Jake."

"Clue me in, Chief," Malone said with a puzzled look on his face.

"Where is it?"

"What?"

"The body."

"Whose body?"

"You know damn well whose body. The Duplissey woman, damn it, that's whose body."

"I don't know what you're talking about, Chief. As far as I know, it's still down at the morgue."

"Well, it's not anymore. Pierce signed off on it and I gave the go-ahead for the funeral home over in Tyler to come and get it. They sent a car for it this morning and it was nowhere to be found. So what do you know about it?"

"Not a clue, Chief. Did you talk to the clerk in the morgue about it? Cadavers don't walk on their own, not usually anyway."

"Yes, damn it, I talked to the clerk, and nobody down there knows anything about it. When they pulled the drawer, it was empty. I've had three phone calls on this already. The mayor wants to know what the hell's going on down there. Then when the funeral home boys got back to Tyler—without the body—things got fast and furious. I got one call already from a lawyer in Tyler that handles the Duplissey affairs and I'm telling you he's not just a little unhappy about this."

"Now look here, Chief, settle down, this is just a matter of a missing person. No reason for anybody to get all puckered up, I'm sure we can get to the bottom of this if everybody just calms down. I'll go down to the morgue myself and talk to Pierce. You stall Lyons. Tell him I'm investigating and to sit tight. By the way, who is the attorney in Tyler? Maybe you ought to call him back and tell him everything's under control."

"Like hell it is," the chief said as the phone started ringing.

Malone walked out of the office and out of the building.

———

David had been busy at the law office all morning and when Liz came back from lunch she brought him a deli sandwich from the coffee shop across the street. As soon as she took the phone lines off the automatic switchboard a call came in for David.

It was Senator Mitchell.

James "Buddy" Mitchell had been the ugly duckling of the Democratic Party. He'd been a successful corporate lawyer in Dallas for many years before he ran for political office. His reputation had always—before, during, and after his election—been one of being a big mouth, rude, ridiculously obnoxious, and very shrewd. With his election it was required that he stand down from his position at the law firm but, although he denied it, it was rumored he continued to maintain a select clientele.

"Hello, Senator."

"I have a little business matter I'd like you to take care of for me, Matthews. Can we get together this evening? I tell you what, why don't you meet me at the club and let's get in a round of golf, nine holes before dark, can you handle that? Then we'll have supper."

David was reluctant to meet with the senator, a man he

disliked for every reason he could think of, a man who had virtually no redeeming qualities, a loud offensive braggart.

"Okay, I can wrap it up here in a couple of hours and I'll meet you there at say about three-thirty."

By four-fifteen David drove off the first tee.

"Nice one," the senator commented on David's powerful drive.

David was pleased. It felt good to be back on the course. It would have felt better to be there with somebody else— anybody else—but David was curious as to what the senator had on his mind.

The senator withdrew the Ping driver from the slick tan-and-white cowhide bag and approached the boxes, set his tee, and placed the ball on top.

"Did you know," he said, examining the club head, "there was a time when I was thoroughly disgusted with the way the Democrats were running this country?" He took only one swing to get the kinks out and then stepped up to the waiting ball. "Oh, hell," he said without waiting for David to answer, "I had my heroes, Lyndon for one."

Wap! He drove the ball deep into the fairway.

"Now *there* was a man that knew how to get things done." The senator picked up the wooden tee, slipped the big driver back into the bag mounted on the cart, and sat down on the passenger side.

"No, sir," he continued as David advanced the cart, "Lyndon didn't care how things got done, as long as they did. His philosophy wasn't about the means; it was always about the ends. That's what was important. And that's what I based my campaign strategy on and to hell with anybody that stood in the way of my goals. I guess you could say, I've been a determined hardheaded son of a bitch." The senator snorted.

"When I first decided to run for office, everybody said I was 'unelectable,' that I was a smart-ass with a temper tantrum. But to hell with them. Once I made up my mind to get into politics, I didn't let any of those mealymouth sons of bitches stand in my way. You and I, David, are cut from the same cloth, wouldn't you say?"

"No, I wouldn't say that, Senator."

They finished the first hole and proceeded to the second tee box.

David looked at the dimpled white ball again balanced on the monogrammed tee. He waggled briefly and drew back for his swing.

"Perfect," the senator commented as David's next power stroke landed some three hundred yards away.

The senator's drive was equally impressive and the twin balls now rested in the fairway with not more than six feet of distance between them and only a seven iron shot from the green. David pitched the ball to the edge of the frog's hair and Mitchell's next shot landed on the green and rolled twenty feet from the hole. David decided to chip with his pitching wedge, put some left English on it, and the ball rolled within inches of the hole. The senator fell short of sinking the long putt. David sank the ball with his next shot and the senator followed suit and retrieved both balls from the hole. He tossed David his #1 Titleist and both men walked to the electric cart and moved to the next green. Two under and it was a tie game.

The ninth green took them back to the clubhouse where David showered and changed downstairs in the men's locker room. Obliged to buy the first round, he waited in the bar. The senator entered minutes later, having changed, and showered in a private locker room elsewhere in the exclusive private club. A couple of drinks later the maître d' showed them to a choice table in the middle of the near empty main dining room. After the meal the waiter brought over a bottle of B&B and set it on the table with two small snifters. The senator poured and offered David a cigar. David declined and Mitchell put both stogies back in his breast pocket.

"I owe you an apology, Senator," David said, leaning back for a comfortable position. "I wasn't sure this was such a good idea to get together with you, but I have to admit I enjoyed being on the course with you this afternoon and I think it was the tonic I needed to get me out of the rut I've been in lately."

"Why the rut, son?" the senator asked.

"Too much work, not enough play, I guess. That and the fact I fairly well fucked-up my life these past few years."

"Hold on there, son. Don't be so rough on yourself. You've got one of the best law practices in the state and you're a hell of a golfer."

"It's a personal matter, Senator. I guess my marriage is coming to a close and that makes number three. I apologize for bringing my personal problems up at a time like this."

"No need to apologize, David, the truth is, Lindsey and I were on the throes of divorce ourselves. It's a shame she had to die and all but to tell you the truth, son, she was a hell-bitch and probably the only one that could have—and would have—buried me politically—and she'd have done it gladly. I don't want to shock you, son, but her death, as much as it pained me a couple of days ago and as much as it pained the boys, her death was my political salvation. It couldn't have come at a better time."

"Son of a bitch," David said beneath his breath.

"Yeah, it's true, I am one bastardly son of a bitch, but look on the bright side, with Lindsey's demise *everybody* stopped being unhappy. Me for one, most everybody she knew, that Williams dame, and Lindsey herself is in a happier place— even you for that matter. I know about the relationship you had with Lindsey, and from what I know about you, you didn't grieve any over her passing either. No, let's get it all out on the table, her death was a blessing in disguise, for everybody right on down the line."

"Okay, Senator, so I didn't lose any sleep over her death. My concern has never been about Lindsey, only those that cared for her, those people she used."

"The Williams gal?"

"It doesn't matter now does it?"

"It might, but not right now. Right now let's get down to business."

20

The unmarked car was parked alongside the curb in front of the Matthews house in the clannish Highland Park Village neighborhood. Malone stood leaning against the door, waiting for her as she came around the corner on foot.

"Ma'am, I hate to bother you this early. Is your husband home?" Malone asked, approaching her on the sidewalk.

"No, Detective, David left early this morning. By now I assume he's either at his office or at the Criminal Courts Building. Liz Jamison, his assistant, would know where he is. Come in and I'll get her on the line for you." Taylor opened the front door.

"No, ma'am, that's not necessary. I'll track him down when I get to town. Like you say, he's either in his office or close by."

"Come on in anyway, Malone. I'll make us a cup of coffee, if you've got a minute, that is."

Malone followed Taylor to the kitchen and she filled the

percolator with fresh water, added the grounds, and plugged it into the wall socket. "Let's go out back," she said.

The backyard of the Matthews home was small but well arranged. Green shrubbery around the pool deck was trimmed and large clay containers filled with red and white geraniums flanked the sides of the cabana. A matching set of wrought-iron furniture was on the pebblestone deck around the pool and Taylor invited Malone to have a seat.

"Place looks nice," Malone commented.

"I spend a lot of time out here."

"I can see that," he said further appraising the well-kept yard. "Mrs. Matthews—Taylor," he began, "how are you really—I mean since that night on the expressway in the rain, the night I stopped you on your way into town? How are you dealing with all this? Are you okay?"

"I'll admit the events of these last few days have been unsettling, to say the least. But, in spite of how bad it seems—and as bad as it may get—I'm in a far better place today than I was before that night on the expressway when you pulled me over."

"How's that?"

"Well, until that night I had a solid life and both feet on the ground—at least I thought I did. I had convinced myself I was a happy woman with a good marriage and was satisfied with the direction my life was going since I'd married David. David had been the man of my dreams, my prince charming. But that night—the night of the murder—I realized I'd been kidding myself and that I was an outsider, maybe even an intruder, and never really fit into the grand scheme of his life.

"David is, was, and will probably always be, a very complex man. I think it goes back to when he was a child. Most children can depend on their parents or at least one of them to be there for them. David didn't have that security and he grew up on the defensive. It was his armor, but at some place in time, somewhere along the way, it also became his albatross. Unfortunately that's a character trait that has been as hard for him to bear as it has been for anyone else who gets close to him."

"Where are you going with this, Taylor?"

"David and I are separating. We're not angry with each other; it has nothing to do with anger. It has everything to do with being happy—for both of us."

"I'm sorry," Jake said.

"Don't be, Detective, this is the best way. David and I reached a crossroads and there are no bad feelings between us. We've both tried, in our own ways, and we've both gained from the experience. We had to go through what we did to get to this place, and now we can be better people for having gotten this far. Staying together any longer isn't good. We're lucky actually, lucky to be able to take action to remedy it as soon as possible."

"So you and David have talked this through?"

"He has plans to move out of the house soon. Any reluctance on his part had to do with his not wanting to fail again."

"You don't think he loves you?"

"No, I think he does love me, but he just doesn't love me enough to let go of another."

"Do you mean Anne Williams?"

"Yes, we've talked about her and about those feelings he's harbored for her all these years and probably will continue to harbor and repress all his life. The sad thing about it is that theirs is the kind of love that might not exist if either of them had been willing to act upon it. But these two people are like those old ships that bump around on rough seas in the night. Sadly they never quite get together. If they did, just for a short time, maybe each of them could get over it."

"Or maybe it would be that great love every man and woman seeks in life."

"Maybe, but whatever they do from here on out, I'm not going to be on the fringe of their affair."

"So that's the way it is with you and David?

"That's pretty much it."

"And you're okay?"

"I will be."

———

Malone was waiting in the lobby for the next elevator. When the door opened, David was standing there. "Matthews," Malone spoke first. "I was on my way up to your office. Got a minute?"

"More questions, Malone?" David asked, stepping off the elevator into the lobby.

"It won't take long, Where're you headed? I'll tag along."

"Sure, why not? I'm on my way to the morgue. So, yeah, come on down with me, it's your turf anyway. I guess you heard about the Duplissey woman's body? Maybe you can help straighten this one out."

"How come you're getting involved into the missing body case? I seem to recall you saying Duplissey wasn't a client of yours."

"You recall correct, Malone, she wasn't. Never has been. But, as I'm sure you know by now, her husband's health, mind and body, is failing, but his money and the influence and sway his wealth has in the corporate and political world is substantial and as strong as ever."

"So where do you fit in?"

"I'm doing a onetime favor for the attorney in Tyler that handles all the family's personal matters. He acts in the capacity of nothing more than an agent, merely for monthly bookkeeping purposes. Except for the predetermined expenses of maintaining the estate, the caretaker's salary, housekeeping, nursing home charges, and the late wife's allowance, automobiles, and whatnot, the real wealth behind the Duplissey fortune is controlled by a trustee in Dallas."

"Is there a chance you're going to tell me who that Dallas connection is?"

"Look, Malone." David and Jake stopped and waited for the green pedestrian walk light. "I hate to pull one of those client confidentiality phrases on you, but you know I can't tell you much more than I have already, and my client has strong feelings that his name be kept out of anything that has Duplissey's name on it. That's part of the reason he works through an agent in Tyler. So that he can remain anonymous and still remain effective handling the Duplissey fortune."

"How long have you known about this, Matthews?"

"Not long."

———

Pierce adjusted his tie and pulled on his flight jacket. He was the last to leave the basement office and as he made his way to the door he snapped off the overhead lights and reached for his keys. When Malone and Matthews arrived at the morgue they saw him at the foot of the stairs, fumbling with the lock.

"You coming or going?" Malone called down.

"Lunch," B. J. answered.

"Want some company?" Malone asked.

"You bet," B. J. said, never slowing on his way up.

———

Ruthie saw the three men enter and waved them to an open table in the middle of the crowded room.

"How's the investigation going, Malone?" Pierce asked at the same time he draped his jacket over the back of the chair.

"You haven't heard? Seems somebody in your department misplaced the body."

"Misplaced the body?" Pierce responded.

"Seems that way," David interjected. "The funeral home sent a car for Duplissey yesterday, I guess you weren't there at the time, but they couldn't find the body down at the morgue."

"I'll be damned. That's probably why the chief's been leaving messages for me all over the place," B. J. said. "I've been on overload these past few days and just haven't had a chance to get back with him. I'll call him as soon as I get back to the office and straighten this out."

"You know where the body is?" David asked.

"Indeed, I do," B. J. answered. "It occurred to me, woke me up the other night, that we might have overlooked something. I wanted to rerun some of the tests we did on the fluids. I had the body in the back lab and after that I got into some other work that I couldn't ignore. I'd planned to go back and finish the Duplissey reruns when I'd finished. I guess the boys from Tyler came while I was working and you know I always give my staff strict orders not to disturb me while we're in session."

"That's it?" David asked. "All the commotion over a small incident like that?"

"Beats all, don't it?" Malone remarked.

"So what did you discover when you reran the tests?" David asked.

"Nothing, we did it all right the first time."

Ruthie brought out the lunch plates and the three men went right to work on the fare in front of them.

"I had an interesting supper companion a couple of nights back," Malone said between bites of his usual roast beef sandwich. "Senator Mitchell," he added.

A surprised B. J. and an even more surprised David stopped eating and looked at Malone as he took a big bite of the sandwich.

"You don't say." B. J. was the only one to speak before he got back to the business on the plate in front of him.

David wiped his face with the napkin and reached for his iced tea glass.

"Yep," Malone said with a mouthful this time. "I went out there—paid a little social call on the senator—to extend my condolences and all, I told him, and then I told him I had a few questions I needed to ask him about his late wife's friend Butter Duplissey."

"Butter?" Pierce asked.

"Her friends called her Butter," David added.

"And the Duplissey woman and the senator were friends?" B. J.'s interest was piquing.

"Not with the senator," Malone said. "She was friends with the senator's wife."

"And what was Senator Mitchell's wife's name?"

"Lindsey, Lindsey Rose Mitchell," David answered.

"That's right," B. J. agreed, relishing the drawn-out drama with Matthews. "I remember reading something about that in the newspaper last week. How'd that happen anyway?"

"What do you mean, 'how'd that happen'? Don't *you* know? Didn't she go through your team?" David asked anxiously.

"That's the damndest thing," Pierce went on. "The Mitchell cadaver never made it this far. Now that you've refreshed my memory here, I remember expecting to be called in on the case, but apparently, no case was ever developed on this one. Who signed the death certificate?"

"I'd have to look that one up in Records," Malone said.

"And I'd be curious to know the answer to that one myself," David added before directing his next remark to Pierce. "Lindsey Mitchell, Duplissey, and I were all friends at one time in the very distant past."

"Don't forget the friend in Austin," Malone reminded him.

"Never."

"I'm here to serve," Jake replied with his mouth full.

"Knock it off, Jake," Pierce interrupted. "Go on, Matthews, tell me about these old friends of Lindsey Mitchell. Sounds to me like there might be more to all this than any of us was expecting."

"I suspect there's a lot more to all of this than any of us was expecting," Malone added sardonically.

"Jake," Pierce cautioned, "don't do it."

Malone backed off and David settled into retelling the history of the women and their relationships. To Malone's surprise David left out virtually nothing. Before he finished speaking he brought both men up-to-date on his current relationship with Taylor.

"I'm sorry to hear that, David," Pierce said. "I don't think I ever met your wife, but she sounds like a fine woman. Sometimes, though, nobody's to blame, things just don't work out the way we think they ought to."

"So, David, did you ever come up with any ideas as to why the Duplissey woman was in your office that night?" Malone asked.

"I've had a lot on my mind lately, Detective, but you can imagine that's been right up there on top. And, yes, I've got an idea of what she was doing in my office that night."

Jake and B. J. sat still and waited for him to continue.

"She was looking for something. A book."

"What kind of a book?" B. J. was the first to speak.

David never intended to tell either man about the diary. But now, in light of the recent turn of events and more specifically the realization that his marriage was over, along with any hopes he'd ever harbored about Annie, he would freely give up any information he had to be able to put this all in the past.

Malone agreed to meet David in his office at four-thirty that afternoon.

———

David left Malone and Pierce at the Elm, walked down Main and entered Neiman's. He walked through the floor level of the store and out the Commerce Street doors, turned right on Commerce and made the block to Akard Street where he turned right again and then back to Main and crossed at the light. David looked behind once to make sure he wasn't followed before he turned into the alcove. While David stood inside the café, waiting for his eyes to adjust to the change in light, Jake and B. J. were busy talking apple turnovers with Ruthie back at the Elm.

"David," a familiar voice called out.

David turned expecting to see the big Greek. Instead, it was Tomas standing with outstretched arms. When their hands clasped, David looked beyond Tomas toward the closed swinging doors.

"He's not ah here," Tomas said before David could ask, "and I dont'a expect him back either. Not for ah long time."

David looked puzzled.

"Been gone since last Thursday."

"Gone where?" David asked.

"Retired," Tomas answered. "I know, I can't ah believe it either, but he finally called it quits. He wouldn't say so, but Marcus and I both think it had ah something to do with ah Lindsey Mitchell's death. You know he and that ah woman were good friends for a while and it wasa the day of her funeral that Francis called me early thata morning and said he wasa going away for a long time."

"But where would he go? Everything he has is right here in Dallas. What about his wife—and work? He wouldn't just up and leave like that would he?"

"Hard to say. A few months ago, well longer than ah that, sometime late last summer, Francis started changing. He stopped ah working so hard—and he got a little happier . . ."

"Happier? Happier about what?"

"Come over here. Sit down, I'll get us ah something to drink." Tomas led the way to a table in the near empty café. He motioned for the waitress and when she came over he told her to bring them both a cup of coffee.

"So what did Francis get so all fired-up happy about?" David wanted to know.

"I'm not ah sure," Tomas began, "for years Francis had ah been working like a Trojan, not just here ata the café, he had all sorts of business dealings here in town. Investors were meeting with him day and night, wanting him to put ah money into new ventures. Francis was a wealthy man, you know. He didn't get that'a way just working here, he had 'other interests,' you understand?"

"Go on," David encouraged. "You mind if I smoke?"

Tomas shook his head and David pulled out a fresh pack and offered Tomas a cigarette.

"Like I said I noticed a change in Francis last summer. Then one ah morning he came into the café like he always did and his face was all red-like. I said something about it and he said it wasa sunburn. He'd been sailing the afternoon before out at White Rock Lake he told me."

"Sailing? That hardly sounds like Francis."

"That'sa what I thought too, but that'sa what he said, 'Sailing out at White Rock.' And when he left that day I asked him if he wasa going sailing again. Even though I asked I didn't expect him to say yes, but that'sa what he said. He was going out to the sailing club again."

"What else?"

"A few weeks later, maybe not that'a long, he took off for a week. Said he wasa going to Galveston on a business and pleasure trip. That'sa the first time in his ah life that Francis had any part of a 'pleasure' trip. I guess he had to make it a business and pleasure trip in order for him to let himself go. All these years he never took so much as a day off from work. Francis didn't have any life other than work. I don'ta think he wanted it that'a way, not in the beginning anyway. He used to ah talk about him and Ismini and the family time they would share, but that never happened. He and Ismini were never close and Francis wasa real private about the business. When we were young men and just starting out here in Dallas, we were partners. But it's no secret Francis wasa the real push behind the success both here in the café and with the other interests in town."

"What other interests are you talking about?"

"Oh, lots of things," Tomas started as the waitress brought the coffee to the table. He waited for her to leave and then continued speaking. "To begin with, a long time ago, he bought'a this building over the café."

"I knew about that," David said.

"And after that he joined with a capital venture group and invested in other downtown real estate, and other places, not just Dallas. And not just Texas either."

"Weren't you partners with him back then?"

"No, when I went back to the islands I give up all my interest in the café. I never had the ambition that'a Francis had, not even close.

"Until last week, I worked for my brother and when I lock up the door here in the afternoon and walk down that sidewalk I go home to a wife and family. Oh, Francis, he paid me real good and me and Rhoda always had more than what we ever dreamed of having, but Francis owned this place and controlled all the businesses. I used to think we'd go back to the islands one day, me and Rhoda, but now I don't know. Things sure change in a hurry."

"How so?"

"I mean it's mine now."

"It's yours?"

"All mine. Francis signed over the deed to the building here and all his interests in the café. I'm not sure what I'm going to do but for now, until I can figure it out, I'm just gonna keep on cooking and keeping this place open to the lunch crowd like I always have."

"And what about the other interests?"

"That I couldn't answer, I never knew what all Francis

had invested in. There's a lawyer here in Dallas that'a I think handles a lot of the dealings for the capital venture group."

"What's the name of this investment group?"

"I don't think I ever heard him say."

"Do you know who the lawyer is?"

"He never said."

"Back up for a minute. Tell me what you know about the trip to Galveston. What was the 'business' part of that trip?"

"I couldn't tell you that'a either, but I do know that Francis bought himself a boat, a real fancy boat. And not one for White Rock Lake either. A big boat, a seafaring boat. He call her *The Texas Rose*. Francis showed me pictures of her and she was ah beauty. He flew down to Galveston just about every Friday afternoon after that. I asked him to invite us down with him one weekend and he said he would'a sometime, but he never did. Still, he sure liked getting away on those long weekends in Galveston. I guess he got real good at sailing 'cause he almost never missed."

"Did Ismini go with him?"

"As far as I know, never. Not ah once. She and my Rhoda have remained friends all these years. Not close friends, but Ismini calls her every couple of days or my wife calls Ismini and they talk, mostly about the children."

"Okay, so Francis held the controlling interests in all these ventures. And you worked for him—here at the café —and now you *own* the café?"

"And the building overhead."

David lit another cigarette and the waitress refilled the cups. "Did Francis say how to get in touch with him?"

"That's a the tough part, we can't."

"You can't?"

"That's a right. He told me he wanted to get away, away from everybody, including Ismini. He said he'd get in touch with me in the fall. But not to worry, he wasa going sailing, he knew what'a he wasa doing."

"Surely his wife knows how to get in touch with him?" David asked.

"I doubt it. I think a man could disappear if he wanted to—if he needed to—at least a man like Francis."

David knew Tomas was right. Men like Francis could very well disappear, disappear in style, for as long as it took—maybe forever.

21

With each step there was an increasing sense of urgency as David walked the six town blocks to his office. Unfortunately, Malone was waiting for him when he came through the office door. David's hello sounded cool to Malone. It sounded irritated to Liz, and if David analyzed his own greeting he would have recognized it as resounding disappointment to Malone's presence.

David asked the detective to follow him into his private office and he asked Liz to shut the door and to hold the calls.

"Looks like work's backing up for you, Matthews," Jake commented on the stacked files balanced on one end of the desk. There were several messages under a clear paperweight near the telephone.

"No question about that," David said, easing up on the attitude and sitting in the chair behind his desk, "but I've got a graduating law student coming in for an interview in the morning and if it pans out like I expect I can work my way out from under all this pretty quick."

Reluctantly, David opened the center desk drawer, reached in the far back and withdrew Annie's diary. "Malone, there are some personal passages in Ms. Williams's journal," he said, placing it squarely on the desk in front of him, his hands still resting on the closed book.

"I expect so," Malone answered.

"There are things here that have no bearing whatsoever on the case. Private matters, things that she wrote down that are nobody's business but hers."

"And yours?"

"Some of them, yes. What I'm saying is that I want to help in this investigation and if by having any information contained here it will help put closure to this, by all means you should have it. But I want your word, Malone, that you'll be discreet with what you may learn and keep what doesn't absolutely have to be in the investigation *out* of the investigation."

"Contrary to what you may have heard, Matthews, I'm a decent sort of guy and believe it or not, I'm not out here to hurt anybody."

"And I appreciate that."

"I flew to Austin on Monday morning."

"Did you learn anything new about Butter's death?" David asked.

"No, nothing new, Ms. Williams confirmed everything we'd already discussed. She mentioned you'd been there over the weekend."

David did not respond.

"Matthews," Malone continued, "I need to know what's in that journal. Why was the Duplissey dame looking for it and what's in it worth dying for?"

"You'll have to discover that for yourself, Malone. I haven't read the entire book, don't want to, but from what I have read, it will give you perspective as to the real feelings of these three women, how they operated, and the men they almost loved."

"I hope so."

"Read the book, Detective," David said, finally handing it to the detective.

———

David started for home that evening with a resolve to make arrangements to move on. If this was the way things were going to be, he was just as anxious as Taylor to put it behind them as soon as possible. There would be no contesting this divorce. There wouldn't be any haggling over a settlement— he'd give her anything she wanted.

As he made the last left turn out of downtown, a call came in on his cell phone.

———

David pulled the car into the circle drive and sat behind the wheel with the engine idling. The car radio was on, but he wasn't listening. He could still drive away—away from the senator, away from the whole damn mess. All he needed to do was put the car in gear and his foot on the accelerator. Primal instinct screamed at him to flee.

David rang the bell and the senator opened the door.

———

"Boss, wake up."

"What time is it?" David grumbled.

"Seven-thirty," she answered, appraising the situation and stepping over his shoes in the middle of the room.

David rolled to a sitting position on the leather couch, took a deep breath, and arched his back as he tried to get the kinks out.

"Need coffee," he mumbled.

"Right."

David was standing in his stockinged feet, staring out the window when she returned.

"We have a window?" Liz remarked, setting the tray on the credenza. "All this time, who knew?"

"Yeah, who knew?" David barely answered and drew the drapes shut.

"What gives here, Boss?" Liz handed him the coffee mug. "Obviously you've been here all night."

"No, not all night. I left not long after you locked up, but before I got halfway out of town Senator Mitchell called me on my car phone."

"Jeez, we're not getting mixed up with that sleazeball, are we?"

"Too late for the admonition, Liz, I got involved with our esteemed senator days ago. Last night I stopped by his house for a chat, at his request. I'm not sure what kind of information he wants from me, but he's got something on his mind. After I left there I came back here to try and get some work done."

"I can see that," Liz said, gathering the empty old-fashioned glass from the table and replacing the cap on the bottle of Jack.

———

By this time Malone had been sitting on the picnic table for close to an hour. He'd watched the eastern skyline as gray clouds partially sliced the horizon and a thin line of soft pink light steadily lifted the darkness. As the clouds rose higher, an orange glow filled in below. An empty Starbucks cup sat on the table next to him.

He'd driven in on Mockingbird past the old Wilshire The- atre, and cut back to Lawther just before it intersected at Northwest Highway, not his favorite part of the lake but a good place to watch a Dallas sunrise.

The morning air cleared his thoughts. Last night's read had pulled the pieces of the puzzle together. Annie's journal lay on the seat of the unmarked official car.

His next step was strictly by the handbook.

———

David had showered, shaved, and was dressing when Liz in- formed him his nine A.M. appointment was waiting in the front office.

He repositioned the Rolex on his wrist, adjusted his tie, and took a quick glance at himself in the bathroom mirror.

Back to business.

———

"Mr. Matthews"—she extended her hand—"I'm Rose Marie—Rose Marie Abbott."

David looked up from his desk and stared at her.

"We had an appointment," she said, standing now directly in front of the desk, still offering her outstretched hand. "Is something wrong, Mr. Matthews?"

"No—no, nothing's wrong." He walked around the desk and clasped her small hand. "Thank you for coming in on such short notice, Ms. Abbott. When did you arrive? Last night?"

"No, sir, I drove in early this morning from Austin. After these past three years, and especially after the last three months, I wanted to get on the open road for a few hours."

Still mesmerized, David continued to stare at the woman.

"I have a convertible," she said. "I put the top down this morning and watched the sunrise driving in. It was exhilarating. First light and the Dallas skyline, almost a spiritual combination, hard to beat, don't you think?"

"Would you like a cup of coffee?" Liz asked from the doorway.

The dark-haired woman took her cue from David, who nodded his response.

"Yes, please," she turned and said.

"Thank you, Liz," he added.

The interview that followed went as David had expected and by the time Rose Marie left they had agreed she would start working in the law office the first week of June, right after graduation.

She told him she would be staying with friends in Dallas through the weekend and she would use the time to find a place to live—"something small, something close to town"—perhaps one of the new loft apartments developing in the renovated section of downtown Dallas, the West End.

After Rose left, Liz walked into his office and saw David standing at the window, staring at the street traffic ten stories below for the second time in the same day. For the second time ever, the drapes were open.

This can't be good, she thought. "Boss?"

"Did Rose Marie leave a number where she could be reached?" he asked, still looking out the window.

———

Malone decided to detour by the Matthews place on the way to the station. When he made the corner he saw Taylor ahead on the sidewalk. Seeing her was a wake-up call. He eased on the brake and pulled into the first driveway, backed out, and left the way he'd come.

In the rearview mirror, he watched her open the door and disappear.

———

When Malone returned to the precinct he read through the Mitchell file again and when he finished he went over in his mind the conversation he'd had with the senator at supper a few nights ago.

Mitchell had told him that Lindsey had died early that Friday morning and that he had been the one to discover the body. He'd been out of town overnight on business and had arrived home after lunch that day. Earlier that morning he had tried calling from his cell phone, but there was no answer. Lindsey played golf or tennis about three days a week, sometimes more, he told Malone, and he assumed she was at the club that morning, she usually had lunch with friends at the clubhouse.

When he arrived home the house was quiet. He'd entered through the back door by the service porte cochere. Lupe was not there and no one appeared to be either in the house or on the grounds, but after his trip he was grateful for the solitude.

The senator said he called out Lindsey's name, but admitted he did not expect an answer. He walked up the kitchen staircase to the second floor. The master bedroom was at the end of the hall and the bedroom door was shut.

When he walked into the room he saw Lindsey lying on the floor by the bed. He leaned down to touch her and as he rolled her over he knew instantly she was dead. He said he sat down on the carpet and held her in his arms. He knew she had been dead for several hours, perhaps all night. He saw the empty glass lying on the floor. The spilled whiskey had already dried and stained the carpet.

Lindsey took prescription drugs for depression; she had taken pills for years. He said he was ashamed to tell Malone, but Lindsey was chronically depressed and he never understood why.

Malone rocked back in his desk chair and tapped the pencil eraser on the closed file folder. *Why hadn't an autopsy been ordered?*

22

The phone rang persistently in the outer office at the morgue. As usual the forensic team had started their routine early. By midafternoon they'd wrapped up, cleaned up, locked up, and left. Except for the medical examiner no one was there to answer the phone.

The caller wasn't going to give up.

"Pierce here," he said, picking up at last.

"Good, you're there. I need to see you."

Pierce unlocked the entry door from the inside, returned to his desk, and went back to transcribing the recorded notes. Methodically, one case at a time, he dictated the information into the document files. Systematically he disclosed the description of the body, clothing, evidence of injury, laboratory test findings, and his conclusion. All this he stated in medical terminology, but followed with a summary in layman jargon. If a crime was suspected the information in the document file would be available to the grand jury and the medical examiner's professional opinion would become a critical part of the body of evidence. In about half the court cases the M.E. would be required to give testimony to findings contained in the report. No detail would ever be left to chance recall.

When Malone entered the outer office, he could hear Pierce speaking.

"Hate to interrupt," he said, pulling up a chair by the desk.

Pierce shushed him with open hand and finished recording his opinion.

"There's coffee in the lab," he told him when he pushed the Stop button.

"You'll have a cup?" Malone asked.

B. J. stood up and walked around the desk. "So what brings you down here today?" he asked, leaning against the counter.

"It's this damn Duplissey case."

"You *do* know the funeral home picked up Duplissey this morning?" Pierce asked.

"That's good."

"So what's on your mind?"

"I picked up a copy of the death certificate on Lindsey Mitchell, Senator Mitchell's wife, and to tell you the truth I'm more than surprised this one got by without coming through your office."

"Do you have it with you?"

Malone pulled it from his inside jacket pocket. "Do you know the physician that signed it?"

"I've heard of him, but he doesn't practice here. Keeps an office in Austin and one in San Marcos I think. He would have had to be Lindsey Mitchell's physician to sign on this one." Pierce squinted at the small print. "It's likely the senator would want to keep this quiet," he said, handing the death certificate back to Malone.

"The woman had a reputation for booze. That was already out of the bag. As for the drug addiction that goes along with the weak woman-strong man profile. Mitchell's wife was probably an okay sort of gal at one time and he raked her into a world of egocentric power-hungry politicians. It happens and if a gal isn't strong enough to pull herself out of that surreal world then she copes with booze and drugs. Sometimes you have to let go of these hunches, Malone."

"And you don't see anything unusual in the fact that a senator's wife dies 'accidentally' of a drug abuse and her body never comes in for an autopsy?"

"No, what I *said* is that it isn't *surprising* that it was kept upstairs. The senator has friends in high places and if he wanted to keep this low-keyed he wouldn't have to pull many strings."

"Whose string do you think he'd pull?"

"Off the top of my head, I'd say Chief Truly, or Mayor Lyons—Lyons most likely. Didn't you tell me the chief was getting hammered from our esteemed city official? So," Pierce continued with the hypothesis, "let's say all Mitchell wanted to do was keep his wife's unfortunate death from becoming paparazzi fodder. That he wanted to gloss it over. The death of a senator's wife by suicide or accidental overdose can't do the man any good politically. Or say all he wanted was to protect his career and his family. Didn't they have a couple of kids away at military school somewhere around Austin?"

"Oh, hell, that's the San Marcos connection. Mitchell was probably in San Marcos often enough to know a doctor there."

Jake said he'd get back with Pierce later and hurriedly left the morgue, taking the steps two at a time. He made the call from the car phone.

––––––––

"Taylor, it's Jake. I'd like to see you this afternoon. Will you be home?"

"Sure, come on over anytime. When do you think?"

"Actually, I'm already here."

Taylor looked out the front window and saw Malone pulling up in the unmarked car.

He snapped the car phone shut and started up the walk.

She opened the door as he stepped on the porch and he followed her into the kitchen.

"Taylor, how much," he asked as he followed her to the kitchen, "do you know about Lindsey Mitchell? She was an old friend of your husband, did you know that?"

"My husband had a lot of old girlfriends, Malone. Lindsey, as far as I ever knew, was just one of many. The only difference was she went back a ways. I've been wrong about a lot of things as far as David's concerned, but I didn't think he'd seen her in several years. I suspect she kept a busy social calendar and old boyfriends weren't a priority for her. The most I recall David say about her was when the conversation included Anne Williams. As I understand it," she said, turning to face Malone, "Anne and Lindsey were the best of friends— lifelong friends—right to the end."

"Anne Williams called your husband when she arrived in Dallas for the funeral. Do you know anything about that phone call?"

"Yes, she called here a couple of nights before the funeral. I knew it was her because as soon as David answered the phone his mannerism changed."

"How so?"

"He acts different when it involves Annie. He gets nervous and when he does he smokes."

"He doesn't ordinarily smoke?"

"No—and he doesn't usually get nervous."

"Did he tell you why she called?"

"No, and I didn't ask. It was late and I really didn't want to get into it. We were about to have supper."

"Go on," Jake encouraged.

"Well, like I said, she called, at least I assumed it was Annie. No, I take it back. David *told* me it was Annie. In fact he said, 'It's Annie,' and then he went upstairs to the bedroom to talk. I could smell the cigarette smoke. When he came down he didn't say any more about her—and neither did I. But the next day, late that afternoon, no, later than that, it was almost dark and I was expecting David any minute when she called again. She asked me to ask him to call her. She didn't leave a number just said he could reach her at Dena's. I assumed it was a club or a bar or a restaurant, someplace they both obviously knew. She also mentioned she had forgotten to tell him something at lunch that afternoon. So you see I knew he'd already met her earlier that day. He never mentioned they had arranged to meet, but then, after she called again, I realized he didn't tell me on purpose. I was afraid he was back to his old ways and back to keeping secrets about old girlfriends."

"Maybe he just didn't want you to worry."

"Maybe," she said doubtfully. "Anyway, good intentions aside, David called me right after that and said he was on his way home. I told him Annie had called and wanted him to call her.

"He seemed to know exactly where that was, but he came

on home after that and we didn't speak of it further. The funeral was the next day, I'd read about it in the paper. Lindsey
had two children and I don't know why I think this, but for
some reason I think she'd been married a number of times.
Have you asked David?"

"What else can you tell me about Anne Williams?" he
asked, ignoring her question.

"Now *that* I do know something about."

Taylor poured two cups of coffee and handed one to Jake.
"Anne Williams was David's one true love. They go way
back, back before Lindsey. If there hadn't been a Lindsey
there may still have been an Anne and David. What I've
learned since I met David, a long four and a half years ago, is
that he had been in love with Anne, but had an affair with
Lindsey—I *think* it was Lindsey. Anyway, exactly how Anne
found out about the affair, I don't know. David's not the con-
fessing kind and chances are Lindsey wouldn't have told her
either, but the news of the affair slipped out anyway. I imagine it was the cause of Anne and David breaking up, but I
don't know that for certain, and I don't have any of the details. I do know Anne went away to college that year.

"David was in Dallas at that time and didn't go away to
school for a couple of years after that. I doubt they saw each
other during that time. It's possible but I doubt it."

"What about Lindsey? Did he continue to see her?"

"I have no idea what happened or where Lindsey went.
The first time I ever knew anything about Lindsey Mitchell
was after she married Buddy Mitchell. I read something about
the loud senator and his gorgeous wife in the paper one
morning and mentioned it to David. That's when I learned
he'd gone to high school with her.

"The rest of the story about the affair with Lindsey came

out following that one conversation over breakfast. That was before David and I married. At that time we talked openly about most everything—everything except Anne Williams."

"And when did you first meet Anne Williams?"

"That's the thing, Jake, I've never met her. I think I know her well, but we've never actually met, in the flesh, face-to-face."

"And what about Lindsey Mitchell? Did you meet her?"

"No, I never had the chance to meet her. Everything I know about Lindsey I learned from David."

———

Malone had placed Annie William's book in the desk drawer at the station for safekeeping and when he returned to the office he reached for it, sat down in the swivel chair, and began to reread the passage.

———

It has to look like an accident. But this is the one chance I have to get Lindsey out of this once and for all. It's a good plan. I'll have to find a doctor, but that shouldn't be a problem—Lindsey has already opened that door. Now it's just a matter of closing it.

The boys are at the academy—they'll be fine. I'll see to it.

Money's no problem, for once anyway.

This has to work. What's done is done.

———

Bella Italy was opening for the supper crowd. From a table by the window in the small dining area Rose Marie waved David over. He had offered to pick her up, but she said she preferred to meet him at the restaurant.

"Sorry, I'm late," he offered as he sat down.

"Oh, you're not late, I'm early," she said, smiling at the same time the waiter appeared with a glass of wine for her. "I hope you don't mind I ordered a glass of wine while I waited for you."

"Good, I'll have one too—only make it bourbon, rocks," he instructed the waiter.

As the workday came to a close, a steady stream of patrons began entering the restuarant and soon the happy hour crowd overfilled the bar and was being seated in the dining area. David ordered another bourbon with rocks and asked the waiter to bring the menus.

Over drinks and supper they talked about certain headline criminal cases, past and present, and David confirmed in his mind what he already knew. Rose had an unusually sharp mind, a quick wit, and a near perfect recall for previous court decisions—and he was attracted to her.

As the waiter cleared the table he regretted he had not insisted on picking her up for supper. That way he would have had an excuse for spending more time with her when he returned her to wherever it was she was staying.

Or, if he wasn't so out of practice, he would have asked her to meet him at the office and they could have ridden out to Bella Italy together. From there they could have taken a cab from town and a cab back later that night.

You need a good junior partner, you idiot, he told himself. *Your personal life can wait, don't go screwing up another beautiful woman. Leave this one alone.*

———

It was dark outside and the overhead kitchen light was the only light on in the house. Taylor pulled leftovers from the refrigerator, warmed them in the microwave, and sat alone at the table. She stared at the food on the plate and the questions in her mind nagged. *What did David know about the murder of Roberta Duplissey? Who was the man hiding in her bedroom that night and what was he after?* The answers wouldn't change the decision she had made about letting go of the marriage, but the deaths of two intimate friends of David in the same week had to be more than mere coincidence.

23

Annie arrived home minutes before Taylor's cab pulled up to the curb. She was in the kitchen when she heard the doorbell.

Introductions were awkward, but once made Annie asked her to step inside and she led the way down the hall to the kitchen.

"I confess, I've been curious to meet you," Annie was the first to speak. "David seems happier now with you in his life."

"Well, unfortunately, or maybe not, David and I have agreed to go our separate ways."

Annie was silent.

"It wasn't an easy decision for either of us," Taylor continued without coaxing. "We both care a great deal about each other but given David's history—and the baggage he carries—it was the best decision for both of us."

"Where is David now?"

"For now he's still staying at the house, but I suspect he's arranged for a place of his own and will be moving out in the next few days. But that's not why I'm here, Annie. I wanted to meet with you," Taylor went on, "to talk about your friendships with Roberta Duplissey and Lindsey Mitchell."

"There's not much to talk about there."

"But the three of you were the best of friends at one time. David's told me quite a bit about all of you."

"Well, Lindsey, Butter and I were friends all right—David too."

"You called her Butter?" Taylor interrupted. "You *are* talking about Roberta, aren't you?"

"Yes, Butter was a pet name, and as I recall David was the one that started us all calling her that. Butter, Roberta, had naturally curly hair and the color of sweet cream butter— very beautiful and very unusual."

"Please, go on," Taylor encouraged.

"Well, like I said, we were all friends back then, but through the years things changed—we changed—and in time we each went our separate ways. After a while I rarely saw either Lindsey or Butter very often—David either for that matter. In later years I stayed in touch with Lindsey more than I stayed in touch with Butter, certainly more than David, but the truth was we had very little in common with each other after high school."

"I thought you and Lindsey had stayed on good terms even through college?"

"Did David tell you that?"

"He did," she lied.

"Well, Lindsey and I did stay close and in fact we were all on good terms but we—Lindsey and I—didn't socialize with the others much, or at all for that matter, after we left high school."

"Because you went to different colleges?"

"Of course, that was part of it. Lindsey and I went to the same college in North Texas. Butter went to an all-girls' school in the East. Her family had more money than most of the families in the neighborhood and that's where they wanted her to go for her education. Eventually she married 'old money' and that's where her start for real wealth came from. Frankly, neither Lindsey or I had much in common with Butter once she left Dallas. David stayed back in Dallas and we didn't hear from him at all after we went away to college."

"So what do you mean Butter married 'old money'?"

"It's a bizarre story and, believe me, it could only happen where Butter's involved. One of her professors—one she was making the moves on that semester—had a friend who had a son, a student at nearby Harvard. And *nobody* goes to Harvard without old money—old wealthy family money—behind them."

"Right."

"Well, according to Butter, this guy, the son of the friend, fell in love with her and they eloped just days before Christmas in their junior year. Butter's parents were okay with the marriage; in fact, they were probably overjoyed with the acquisition of a son-in-law from an aristocratic family—real bluebloods. On the other hand, *his* parents were beside themselves with disappointment. According to Butter, they believed her family lacked the credentials necessary for their son's complete career success and Butter didn't have anything to offer in that regard—not in terms of class, education, breeding, brains, talent, or social skills. She was, in fact, what they considered a liability—a serious liability."

"I thought that just happened in old Elizabeth Taylor movies."

"No, it happened, but her new in-laws were wrong." Annie went to the cabinet, found a bottle of Merlot, and set two wineglasses on the table. She continued the story as she uncorked the bottle. "Butter may have been deficient in some crucial areas, areas her in-laws deemed important, but she had talents they couldn't dream of, and while she may not have been as gifted in the social graces as they wished, she was however *very* clever and they seriously underestimated her motives—and her determination.

"The boy's family wasn't prepared for the sweet-cream-buttery blonde from Dallas and the initial payoff was tremendous—and from there it just got better."

"You mean the marriage was a *scheme* on Butter's part?"

"Sure it was a scheme, but not just Butter's."

"The boy's?"

"No, he was an innocent in all this. Remember I said it was the professor that had the friend with the son?"

"The professor at the all-girls' university?"

"Yes, the professor arranged for Butter to meet the son of his friend. As it happened the friendship between the professor and the boy's dad was not what it seemed. They had been friends all right at some time in the past, when they were young men and college students and *both* of them were in love with the same woman. Problem was this woman had already agreed to marry the then would-be-professor, but along comes his friend and sweeps the love of his life off her feet. She broke the engagement with the would-be professor and became engaged to the would-be rich man. The professor held a grudge all those years while pretending to remain friends with his college roommate. Apparently when Butter came along and put the moves on the now older professor they, Butter and her professor, conspired to put their plan into action.

"Butter never loved the boy but she confessed she did have genuine feelings for the professor. It would be a sacrifice on both their parts, the professor's and Butter's, for her to marry the boy but, after the calculated payoff, Butter and the professor planned to reunite and share the spoils."

"What a piece of work."

"Oh, you don't know the half of it."

"There's more?"

"That was just the beginning," Annie said, pouring the wine. "The payoff was huge. Butter took it and agreed to the annulment. What nobody knew at the time—even Butter—was that she was pregnant. The dissolution of the marriage wasn't yet final when the cat was out of the bag. The professor didn't like the news of the pregnancy and, of course, neither did Butter. The boy's wealthy family wasn't happy with the news, but if there was to be a child they sure as hell would fight to keep the heir with them."

"So what then? Did they call off the annulment?"

"No, they offered to buy the child."

"And what about the father? Did he go along with the proposal?"

"His parents were very controlling and they kept that little bit of information from him. Butter didn't really care for the boy she married, like I said, it was just a scheme concocted by the professor and put into place by Butter, so she went along with keeping the boy out of the loop. Butter, you will remember, had all the credentials for this ruse: beauty, wit, charm, and a milewide evil streak. All in all, Butter lacked any kind of integrity."

"So did she have the baby and sell it back to the grandparents?"

"She said she would. The family upped the ante and this time the payoff was one million dollars."

"Jeeezus."

"So Butter took the first installment of the baby fee, somewhere around a half a mil, and left town. The family put her up in a posh resort on the Cape to await the birth of the child, but no sooner did she get out of town than she changed her mind. Butter was the vainest woman on the planet and she decided a pregnancy to full term would be too detrimental to her figure. So the professor joined her on the Cape and together they arranged for a safe abortion, but never told the family. For another few months Butter accepted cashier checks for the remaining installments. Eventually, she had to break the sad news to the family, news that included a story about her falling on the stairs and losing the baby. Heartbreaking for everybody of course."

"Of course."

"Everybody except Butter and her live-in professor."

"But people with that kind of money, couldn't they keep closer tabs on Butter?" Taylor asked. "What about the doctor, wouldn't the grandparents have wanted medical records, and the like? They couldn't have been that stupid, to trust the likes of Butter? To take her word for what happened?"

"I know, and as amazing as it seems she got away with it and collected the money. All except the last installment that is, but all in all, the take—the payoff for the divorce and the price of the unborn child—was well more than a million when it was tallied up. As far as medical records, with that kind of cash money available, finding a doctor willing to do the abortion and falsify miscarriage documentation was never a problem. The would-have-been grandparents never felt the financial loss and grieved quietly to themselves over the loss of the baby. No legal action could ever be brought against Butter because the scandal would have been more devastating to the old money family than the loss of the million plus."

"So what happened to the professor?"

"You see, there is a God. With all that money in her hands, Butter changed the 'arrangement' with the professor. In a matter of weeks, she left him high and dry. He was furious and threatened to kill her the first chance he got. I guess he put the fear in her, because for a while she felt the need to hire a bodyguard. But the professor proved to be a willy-nilly sort of fella and it wasn't too long before he gave up on getting revenge or any money out of Butter. Her own mother and dad died not too long after that."

"So did she come back to Dallas?"

"Briefly, to settle her folks' estate. She contacted a lawyer in Dallas—"

"David?" Taylor interrupted.

"No, not David. She contacted a lawyer from the large firm that had drawn up the wills for her mother and dad. The wills specified that whichever of the parents died first, the other would be the sole beneficiary. At the death of the surviving spouse then Butter would be the beneficiary. As it happened her folks died within months of each other. Since Butter was an only child the disposition of the estate was fairly cut-and-dry."

"Financially, it sounds like Butter was set for the rest of her life. How'd she get involved with Duplissey?"

"Butter always had to have a man, and not just any man either. She was bored most of the time and went out of her way to amuse herself. If a man was married, she'd set her mind to have him for that reason alone, if he was a powerful man she'd want to be seen on his arm. Operating like that she moved around from man to man for a couple of years. Then she met a man that met all her requirements. He was powerful in the business world, he was smart, he was handsome, he was much older than Butter, and he was married."

"Duplissey?"

"Right, but she had her work cut out for her. And better yet, he was just as manipulative—and he had his own plans for Butter. For the first time, Butter had met her equal in terms of immoral opponents and when the time was right, he arranged for a divorce from his wife. I think she was the only one to benefit from the relationship between Butter and her husband. I doubt he would have ever agreed to a divorce unless it was his idea and on his terms. The wife saw her opportunity and ran with it. Butter told me once that he had been generous with the terms of the divorce with the first wife and continued to take care of her expenses for as long as she lived—as long as she remained unmarried. That was okay with Duplissey's first wife, apparently she'd had enough marriage to last a lifetime, but Butter didn't want the ex to have any benefit from the marriage. Butter was completely selfish, but couldn't do anything about it this time."

"So did Butter love this man?"

"Butter didn't know how to love anybody. There was something missing in her genes. She went through relationships without genuine feelings. The sad thing about Butter is she never knew any difference. Caring or loving anybody but herself just never existed."

"So why did she marry him?"

"He could give her things she couldn't have otherwise."

"But she had her own money and from what I gather she had a host of boyfriends, what else did she want?"

"Status. She wanted to *be* somebody, and she wanted respect. Somehow she believed if she was Mrs. Duplissey, wife of the illustrious industrialist, she would have the respect she sought."

"And? Did it work?"

"Not by a long shot. She was delusional—any respect she imagined came from the fact she was married to a man that most people feared. The Duplissey family came from the southern region of France and the truth was the Duplissey fortune was created from mob dealings both in Europe and the United States. Even Butter was out of her league when she got involved with Duplissey."

"How did she meet him?"

"At the law firm when she was settling her parents' estate. Or through a lawyer there anyway. At that time I think the lawyer was a partner, but then he left the firm and went into politics."

"Surely not . . ."

"Yep, was—is—one and the same—Senator Buddy Mitchell."

"You know, when we started this conversation you told me there wasn't much to tell. This is incredible. What else?"

"Not much else," Annie said, refilling the wineglasses. "I knew very little of this story until recently. Butter called me one afternoon a few weeks ago and said she was in town, wanted to get together. It's no secret I never cared much for Butter, but that day I guess she caught me at a weak moment and I said okay. Butter and her never-ending exploits could be entertaining and she came over that evening and we had a good visit. After all the years, that was the first time I ever had the full story told to me and I heard it directly from Butter."

"And you could believe her?"

"What did she have to gain by lying? Her nefarious husband had suffered a stroke and was no longer a threat to her. I doubt he even realizes that Butter is dead."

"So when did Lindsey come back into the picture?"

"I'll tell you about it, Taylor, but right now, I've got to get out of these shoes and these clothes and get comfortable. It's been a long day. Open another bottle for us and I'll be right back."

24

David had been in court that morning representing a regular client, a power player in the community. In the early afternoon he'd met briefly with two new billable clients and by three forty-five he was on the first tee box with three duffers from the club. It was game on and David was glad to be back on the links to unwind.

After a shower in the men's locker room and a few bourbons with rocks at the bar with his friends, he was feeling pretty good as he left the country club that night when the long black car swerved and skidded to a stop, barely missing him.

The back window whirred open.

"Senator?" he said, bending down. The driver opened the door and the senator slid over. David stepped inside, the door closed behind him, and in moments they were pulling out of the parking lot and turning onto Preston Road.

"How was your game?"

"Let's just say I didn't have to buy the first round," David answered.

The senator snorted a smoker's laugh and then his tone changed.

"David, I'm going to need a little more help from you. Did I mention how much I appreciated the way you handled the Duplissey body. The fella in Tyler, the lawyer there, the one I told you does some busywork for me now and again, called and confirmed the funeral home picked her up right after we spoke—very next day. Good work, son, I knew you were the man to get things done."

"When's the service?" David asked.

"No service, she was cremated that same day the funeral home picked her up."

"No service at all?"

"None, there wasn't anybody around to hold any service for."

"So, what do you need from me now?" David asked, unable to hide the annoyance in his voice.

"Hold your horses, son, I'm going to pay you handsomely for this next one, but even if I wasn't you'd be chomping at the bit to do this favor for me."

"I can't see that happening, Senator."

"Settle down, son. You and me are going to be the best of friends before this is over."

"I *sure* as hell don't see that happening, Senator."

Mitchell pressed the intercom button and told the driver to take them into town, to the Davis Building on Main.

"Wouldn't it have been a hell of a lot easier to call for an appointment?" David asked.

"Maybe, but I wouldn't want to break protocol. And you wouldn't want to hear what I have to say during office hours—and I've got to be careful whom I'm seen keeping company with these days—after all, I do have my reputation to maintain," he answered and coughed out another phlegm-thickened laugh. "Besides, I wouldn't want you to get the impression this was any routine assignment." Again he snorted, coughed, reached in his coat pocket for a cigar. "Don't worry, I'll make it quick, almost painless."

The driver pulled into the underground parking garage and came to a smooth stop by the elevator doors. David and Senator Mitchell got out and the driver pulled the car to the side to await their return.

Smiley was watching a small black-and-white television set balanced on the corner of his desk in the lobby. Even with the rabbit ears pulled to their longest position and adjusted at irregular obtuse angles the reception was poor. But from his position at the desk the night watchman could see the elevators, the Main Street lobby door, and still keep up with the play-by-play baseball broadcast. It was a three and one count and a high fly hit into left field when they approached the desk.

This time Smiley was wide-awake.

"Eve'n, Mr. Matthews," he said, handing David the mandatory after-hours sign-in clipboard.

"We won't be here long, Smiley. Sounds like a good game," David commented.

"Yes, sir, Mr. Matthews, sur' nuff, them Rangers have themselves a mighty fine team this year. Now that Eddie Chiles done sold out to them new boys and George W. is handling things, I 'spects they's got the making of a real good team."

"You may be right, Smiley, enjoy the game." David initialed in, placed the time at something past eight, and handed the clipboard back to the affable smiling Johnny Johnson.

David and the senator took the first elevator to the tenth floor. David swiped the electronic key card through the slot on the office door.

"Nice touch," Mitchell commented. It was the first he'd spoken since they'd pulled in the garage.

David closed the door behind him and the automatic lock snapped into place. David proceeded across the room to his private office and unlocked it with the small key on his personal key ring. He held the door open and the senator passed ahead of him. David turned on the light and went directly to his desk and sat down.

"I can see business has been good for you," the senator said, making a quick appraisal of furnishings.

"Let's get down to business, Senator. It's getting late. What's the reason for this mysterious meeting?"

"Calm down, son, you'll thank me for this before it's over."

"This just keeps getting better, doesn't it, Senator?"

"Damn if it don't." Mitchell chuckled and David had a real bad feeling.

The senator wasn't playing this for a game. He wanted something and David was the way—apparently the only way—he could get it. Mitchell sat down on the leather chair in the corner.

"Son, I'm going to confide in you," Mitchell started. "You've got something I need."

"Not that I'm aware of, Senator." David felt relieved.

"I'm not saying you are aware of it, but you see, there's a book, a diary if you will, a personal accounting written by a friend of yours."

"Go on." David sat listening.

"Miss Anne Williams, a friend of yours—a very good friend of yours. Now do you know what I'm talking about?"

"Well, you know I know Ms. Williams. So what about this so-called diary?"

"Seems she wrote some things in her little book that she shouldn't have, things she didn't know enough about, and some things about my late wife that I wouldn't want to get out—made public, you know."

"And you think I have this diary?"

"Yes."

"How would I get it?"

"From your old friend, your old *girl*friend, Duplissey. Ring any bells?"

"You think Roberta Duplissey was my girlfriend?"

"I know it. I also know about you and the Williams dame—and I know about you and my wife, too, goddamn it."

"How could you know about any of us?"

"Hell, man, I was married to the goddamn queen of drama, the ringleader of your private sorority. Remember? Do you for a minute think we *never* talked about those things?"

"When was that, Senator?" David thought he had gained an edge on the man and now he pressed his opportunity.

But the senator did not answer. His gaze dropped to the floor and he slumped in the chair, his chin touching his chest.

"Senator? Are you okay?"

No response.

Concerned now, David stood and walked around the corner of the desk.

"I'm okay," Mitchell said barely audible, and slowly redirected his gaze upward to David standing before him.

"Can I get you something, Senator, a glass of water . . . a bourbon?"

"Make it a double," he said, taking a deep breath.

David opened the small refrigerator carefully disguised as

part of the credenza, reached inside and grabbed a large handful of ice cubes. He dropped two cubes in two glasses, tossed the rest of the ice back in the machine and reached for the bottle of Wild Turkey. He generously poured each glass and handed one to the senator.

"I suppose when you and Lindsey first married you were both in love?" David asked.

"Hell, no," Mitchell began. "I'm not sure when I fell in love with Lindsey, I'm not really sure I ever loved her at all, but I did love being around beautiful women and she was one of the most attractive gals I'd ever laid sore eyes on."

"We agree on that, go on."

"It was here in Dallas. She had contacted one of the lawyers at my firm about a divorce from her first husband. A no-good bum from what we were told. Never had a job more than a week or so and probably drank away more money than he earned. But Lindsey was the kind of gal that *needed* to be married, emotionally she couldn't make it on her own. And she needed help financially—what with those two little boys and all.

"Back then she was going to court reporter school, but when I walked down the hall that day and saw her sitting in that office with her legs crossed and her skirt up to here I knew she had a hell of lot more potential, and flat-out wasting her God-given talent with court stenography."

"Everybody felt that way about her, Senator," David said as he worked on the bourbon. "We were all hooked on Lindsey, at one time or another."

The senator nodded his head and took a hefty swallow. "I didn't waste any time finding out who she was, where she lived, with whom, and before the day was over had a complete dossier worked up on her. Her divorce was uncontested

and the husband simply left the picture. But I didn't approach Lindsey then. I was married at the time, but that
wasn't what slowed me down. What slowed me down was being about the busiest lawyer in town and I had just been made
a partner in the firm. Can you relate to that, son?"

"Go on, Senator."

"Several months went by, maybe a year, maybe not that
long, but I didn't forget about her, I purely just didn't have
the time to pursue the possibilities."

"And then you had time?"

"Hell, no, I never had time, not in those days. I was hungry, and I wanted to secure my reputation as a first-rate corporate attorney—the best. I couldn't accept anything less."

"As I recall, Senator, you managed to do just that. So why
did you leave the practice?"

"Well, like you said, I managed to do just that. The next
thing I knew I was representing some of the sharpest corporate minds in the country, most of them on the up-and-up,
and a few on the take."

"The 'take'?"

"Oh, come on now, Matthews, your client list isn't any different than mine was—or any other successful counselor. We
all know how to interpret the statutes to work the best deal
for preferred clients. And for the right money we can get the
right rulings. It's the nature of the beast, after all, we're all
lawyers—and when we think we can't get any better at what
we do, what do we do? Hell, we turn to politics."

"So you ran for political office, you told me that story, and
if memory serves here, you were the party's dark horse. Did I
miss something?"

"You got to learn to pay more attention, son. I told you I
was a hardheaded son of a bitch and I was determined to do

things my way. Well, my way included seeking a little advice from the A-Team, only this time I went to the big boys. You see, pay attention now, son, on a small scale I had been representing a client with more money than was legally possible—and damn if it wasn't. He was a pleasant-enough chap, a Frenchman, and part of a European cartel that was laundering drug money. So while I was seeking financial backing, this dandy and his confederates were, in fact, looking for something themselves—they wanted another man in place in Washington. It was all a matter of timing and a match made in heaven, ah, hell, forget heaven, heaven had nothing to do with this, son, it was better than that, it was a pact made with ole Lucifer—the devil himself.'"

"I'm assuming we're talking about Monsieur Duplissey now."

"See, what'd I tell you? Don't that just beat all? Always one step ahead of me. No doubt about it, son, you're the right fella for this job, a regular *pro-toe-gee*, you do me proud, son."

David caught a firey glint in the old man's political eyes. "I haven't agreed to anything, Senator."

"You will, son," the senator stated and, at that moment, David knew he'd been sucker punched.

Senator Mitchell stood and walked to the credenza. "Mind if I help myself?" he asked as he poured.

"Sure, help yourself, Senator. So when did you get hooked up with Lindsey?"

"Not until I was up for reelection. Several years had passed. My practice was very select and of course I had severed all my ties with the law firm before I ran again."

"You were *that* sure you'd win?"

"How could I not? By that time I was in bed with the whole damn lot of them, a real orgy. They could have had any man, but when they picked me from the talent pool it was a well-calculated selection and in the end I was the 'chosen one.' They backed me one hundred percent and I never once failed to deliver. The public election was a mere formality, a ceremony, something for the press, a pittance, a bone, nothing more. That first term I got a taste of how the 'real' system worked. I was the golden-haired child and caught on quick. Monsieur Duplissey was my mentor and sponsor and I was his right hand. Before long, he had me handling more and more of his personal business dealings as well. I was on my way to the top of the world."

"So when did Lindsey become a part of this 'top of the world' of yours?"

"I was in court one day, nothing of any consequence, I can't recall what it was about, but it was business as usual and that day the usual business had taken me before the bench where Lindsey was the court reporter. I recognized her at once, she'd matured in a sensuous way and damn if I couldn't keep my eyes off her. I made up my mind then and there, from that day forward, to get to know her."

"And of course, you did."

"Of course, I told you, I made up my mind, pay attention. Three weeks later we married in Vegas. And right away that's when the trouble started. Like I said I was up for reelection and nobody thought it was a good idea for me to run off and marry like I did.

"At the time, I didn't give a damn what anybody else thought. . . . I thought I was calling the shots, but it damn near cost me the election. I got a little crazy about how it could have gone, and Lindsey didn't love me enough to overlook my tantrums. That started the rift in our marriage and that rift was the beginning of the crater that would have ended in the divorce court, probably ended my political career as well. But you know the rest."

"There're still some glaring holes here, Senator. Why do you need me now? I can understand you needing to get Roberta Duplissey's body released and put that to rest for the sake of your client, but what's all the secrecy about now? Why are we here tonight?"

"It's about the Williams woman and her goddamn diary. I know you have it, David. Roberta told me she'd sent it to you the day before the funeral. She made a terrible mistake and if I don't get it back we're all going to regret it."

"I don't follow you, Senator."

"We're past playing games here, son. Did you read it?"

David stood up, crossed the room, and reached for the bourbon. He walked to the senator and topped off both glasses before he spoke.

"Yes, I read it, most of it—not all. But I don't recall anything that would have damaged you or your powerful clients, Senator. In fact, I don't remember reading anything about you at all in Ms. Williams's memoirs."

"Then you didn't read far enough."

"I read enough."

"Did you read about your daughter?"

"I did."

"And that didn't inspire you?"

"Inspire me, Senator? To do what?"

"To seek your rightful role?"

"A little late for that wouldn't you say? My daughter died when she was ten."

"Is that what you think? I know it's not what you read. Where's the book now, son?"

"Senator, were you here at the office looking for it earlier? The night Butter was killed?"

Buddy Mitchell straightened in his chair and David noticed a slight smirk coming across his face.

"Well, Senator," David said, his voice growing louder, "you're out of luck. I don't have it—not anymore.

"Calm down, son—"

"And, goddamn it, Mitchell, don't call me 'son.'"

"Okay, counselor, back up a minute—"

"And leave my daughter out of this."

"No can do, David, your daughter is a part of this and if you want to know where she is you'll come up with Williams's diary."

"What do you mean 'where she is'?"

"She's not dead, son, and for the life of me I can't figure why you say she is."

"Because her mother *told* me she died, goddamn it, *that's* why, and she's got a *hell* of a lot more credibility with me than you."

"You're wrong, boy. Your daughter is alive and if her mother told you different, well, hell, she out-and-out lied to you. Women *will* do that, you know."

The room went silent and David stood at the credenza with his hand gripped around the bottle of bourbon. Unexpectedly he turned and threw it across the room where it hit the wall and shattered, spewing glass shards halfway across the room and sending the amber liquid down the paneling and onto the floor.

"Feel better?" the senator asked, unaffected as he went through the motions of flecking a piece of glass from his pant leg.

"What do you care?"

"I don't, but I still need your help. Where's the diary?"

"I don't have it, not anymore."

"Where is it?"

"I turned it over to the detective investigating the murder," David answered, returning to his desk chair.

"Jesus Christ, man, why? What the hell were you thinking?" The senator was out of his chair and standing in front of David's desk.

"I wanted to get the investigation over with. Right now my wife is a prime suspect and if Malone can find any information in that damn book—information to take the heat off her—then I wanted him to have it. I had no more use for it— once I'd learned about my daughter. I asked her mother about it, I wanted to hear the story directly from her and not from some damn book. She told me the girl had died. Why would she lie to me?"

"That's a good question and one you should be taking up with her I'd say. As far as your wife is concerned, she didn't kill Roberta Duplissey. I can tell you that, son, and that's a fact, but you're going to have to prove it on your own."

"What do you know about Butter's death, Senator? Were you here?" David stood facing Mitchell and the questions hung in the air like a big net waiting to drop on both men.

"What do you want to know? Goddamn it, *I* did it, Counselor. I shot her. Shot her point-blank in the heart that night, right here—that very spot where you're standing."

David took a quick step back.

"I was here that night with Roberta, we'd come in to find the diary. I was furious with her for sending it to you. She'd always been a pretty smart dame until she sent you that damn book. Couldn't figure out why she'd go and do such a goddamn stupid thing. What was the point? But all she could tell me was she wanted to 'get *even* with the girls.' Girls, girls, girls. She held a mighty hard grudge all those years.

"She had no idea what that damn book could mean to me because all she was really interested in was exposing Anne Williams. And for *what*? *Revenge*? Some silly schoolgirl scheme to have the last laugh? To hell with the goddamn fallout. Well, son, that just wasn't going to happen.

"I didn't give a rat's ass about the Williams dame, or any of Lindsey's old friends for that matter, but the Williams dame made a mistake, a huge mistake by keeping that diary. Lindsey was already costing me a fortune and was about to cost me reelection and I sure as hell didn't need any busybody girlfriend of hers keeping a book exposing our private lives. I had to have that book back so I could destroy it."

"How'd you find out about the diary?"

"Roberta told me after the funeral service. Came up to hug me and whispered it in my ear as she was leaving—said she was going to your place for your reaction."

"She came by that afternoon," David confirmed, "gloating about the diary, but I didn't know why, not then. I ended up angry with her like I usually am, and she left."

"And that's when I caught up with her. I was on my way to see you when I spotted her leaving your building," the senator said, advancing the scene. "We went back to my place for a while—she could be entertaining company when she wanted to be—and I kept her with me until later that night when we went back to your office and broke in."

"How difficult was that?"

"Not at all, you've met my driver, a gifted man. And that old black man downstairs? Sound asleep, never knew we passed by, not coming or going. After we had the lock open I sent my man back to the garage to wait in the car, just like he's doing now.

"Then this gal, I take it that was your wife, the one you're so worried about implicating in this, the one *divorcing* you," Mitchell continued, "came in while we were here. We heard her fumbling at the lock on the front door, turned off your desk lamp there, hid in your little bathroom, and watched her from around the corner. I couldn't trust Roberta to be still and had my hand over her mouth to keep her quiet. She struggled, but not *too* much. Tell you the truth, I think she was kind of enjoying the rough stuff, she'd already had a taste of it earlier that evening at my place and—"

"Keep with the story, Senator."

"Okay, so this wife of yours opened the door into your private office, but she didn't come in—not at first. She stood there for a minute. I could hear her breathing, but then she turned back and shut the door. I could hear her making a phone call from your secretary's desk, but she never said anything and I heard her put the phone down. Then I could hear her moving around out there for a couple of minutes, but we stayed in the bathroom. In a minute she opened your door for the second time, only this time she walked in, right to the front of your desk. With the light behind her from the other room I watched her reach up to turn that desk lamp on, but she never did. I don't know what stopped her, she fiddled with it, but lucky for her she never turned it on. If she had she'd probably have noticed your desk drawer had been pried open. I don't have any idea what turned her around after going to all the trouble to break in and all, but then for the second time she stepped out of your office and shut the door behind her. In a couple of minutes, not long, we could hear her leaving. I kept my hand on Roberta's mouth to keep her from calling out and held her arm twisted behind her. We went out to the big room there and could hear the elevator doors open and close as your wife left. After that we went back into your office to look some more for the diary. That's when that crazy bitch started to fight back. I guess she realized this was serious business and got scared and damned if she didn't almost get the better of me. She was strong for a little woman. I grabbed her by the hair as she made for the door and at the same time I pulled the .38 from my jacket. I held her close and pressed the barrel under her left breast and squeezed the trigger. She stared up at me and kept her eyes on me as I let her slip to the floor. She never even cried out."

David took several steps back and lowered himself into his chair as he listened to the senator confess to the murder.

"Do you always carry a gun, Senator?"

"Not now, if you're worried, but I had recently acquired one."

"Where's the gun now?" David asked.

"Gave it to my driver that next day, told him get rid of it, to toss it in the Trinity."

"What about the man waiting for my wife when she returned to our house that night? Were you responsible for that too?" David managed the question as he tried to shake the image of Butter's body sprawling on the floor by his desk with her blood oozing onto her blue dress and her bright blue eyes staring at the obnoxious senator.

"He wasn't waiting for your wife, your wife had nothing to do with any of this, she just had the bad fortune to be there. I arranged for him to go over to your place and look for the damn book the first clear chance he got. He'd been watching the house since late that afternoon, and when she left that night he slipped in. She wasn't gone long enough though and I suppose he surprised her. I didn't know if you had the book at home or here at the office, and I couldn't waste any time—I needed it back immediately. That's all there was to that."

"Anne Williams is an art dealer, antiques and such. She doesn't give a damn about you or your dealings with the drug lords, her only concern has been for Lindsey's well-being."

"True enough. It was always about Lindsey—Lindsey's happiness, what Lindsey wanted—Lindsey, Lindsey, Lindsey, goddamn it it was *always* about Lindsey. Well, this time, Lindsey's out of the picture for good, once and for all, and your precious Anne Marie Williams knows a hell of a lot more about it than you could ever imagine, and she's going to regret it, I can promise you that."

"Hold on, Senator, what could she really know? She and Lindsey were good friends, that much we both know, we all knew that, even Roberta, and maybe Annie wasn't always square with me but that's up to me to decide, but *none* of that means she's involved in *any* of this."

"Can you be that sure? Obviously she's lied to you more than once. Don't try and defend her yet, Counselor. You'll have plenty of time for that. You and that cute young lawyer are going to have your hands full—and I can promise you that too."

25

Like a wild animal caged, Ismini paced back and forth across the bedroom in the Zacchoias mansion and kicked with her bare foot the papers scattered across the floor. The courier had delivered the legal documents the day after Lindsey's funeral and they had been on the floor where she'd thrown them ever since.

The instructions were simple. She had ninety days to vacate the premises and all her charge cards and money accounts had been frozen effective immediately. An irrevocable trust was established for her at the First National Bank in Dallas and money for her living expenses were already deposited in a newly established account.

For the first year her allowance was generous, after that it would decrease in semi-annual increments for the next four years and at that time the allotment was deemed to be reasonable and adequate. She would have to curb her outrageous spending habits—or find somebody else to support her.

There were no other stipulations, no other provisions, and no other options. Ismini Zacchoias was to have no rights to any of the Zacchoias fortune other than what was specifically set forth in the trust.

She could seek a divorce if she wanted, or not, it was entirely her call. Either way it no longer made any difference to Francis. His lawyer could handle any and all of his personal dealings as far as the marriage was concerned, and those mandates were clear. Francis was a powerful man, and his attorney had done his bidding for many years.

Fully staffed, the estate home would be available for Mama for as long as she wanted. After that, it would be perpetually staffed and maintained for the boys whenever they chose to come home. A trustee was designated through the bank's Trust Department to look after the children's interests.

Ismini was livid.

"Where the hell are you?" she screamed.

But there was no one left to answer.

The staff had left the day before as Ismini went through the house tearing the artwork from the walls, throwing vases from the tables, dishes from the cabinets, and pulling the heavy drapes from the windows where they lay in piles on the hardwood floors. She threatened to set fire to all the furnishings. For now, until things settled down, Mama was staying with Tomas and his family.

Ismini picked up the crumpled cover letter to the papers and attempted to smooth it out for the umpteenth time.

The attorney's letter informed her that Francis had left for an indefinite amount of time and there were no plans for a return. The boys, it was stated, had been transferred to a secured military school somewhere back in the East, or maybe it was somewhere in Texas. "His precious Texas, his precious sons." She spit on the paper. "What the hell do I care where those curly headed brats are? They're his kids, I geeve them to him like ah he wanted, and I wanta nothing more to do with them—or him—ever!"

This time she tore the paper into as many pieces as she could and threw them on the floor.

"He never care for anybody but his mama and his precious little Rosa—Rosa thisa, Lindsey thata—I'm glad she's ah dead. I wish him ah dead too. If I see him again, I'll kill him myself."

Ismini slung open the closet doors and began tearing through the endless array of expensive clothes. She took a crimson silk dress off the hanger, raised her arms, dropped it over her head and across her chemise where it fell past her slim hips and hung loosely at mid-calf. She stepped to the full-length mirror and pulled her dark hair up and away from her face and fastened it with an alabaster comb. She didn't need any makeup, her olive complexion was flawlessly cared for, her dark eyes blazed, and she looked radiant. She slipped her bare feet into a pair of Jesus shoes, and stormed out of the room.

Rage became her.

"May they all rot in hell," she said as she closed the door of her red sports car.

———

There were no lights on when she pulled into the circle drive at the senator's house.

But for this, she would wait. She killed the engine, switched the key to accessory, and turned up the volume on the CD player.

David had declined the senator's ride back to the country club, preferring instead to walk to the corner of Main and Field, take the short block to Commerce, and turn left to the Adolphus. If it took all night he would have preferred to walk the entire way to his house over accepting a ride with the senator.

Fortunately he had several other options.

The Hotel Adolphus had been built by Adolphus Busch when Dallas was emerging from a rough and rowdy boom-town to an up-and-coming first-class city. With its high-domed ceilings and magnificent chandeliers, rich tapestries, and murals, as well as the attentive staff, the grand hotel was once the preferred place for dignitaries, celebrities, and visiting royalty to stay. Early Dallas society had once claimed the Adolphus as the choice site for debutante balls, galas, and wedding receptions.

But like all things great and small, age and time took its toll. In the fifties the grand Hotel Adolphus became the headquarters for the traditional University of Texas and Oklahoma University feud, the Texas fans occupied the Baker Hotel across the street and the Oklahoma fans occupied the Adolphus. When the Longhorns beat Oklahoma after more than a decade of losing, the fans from both schools became a mob and hotel security was not enough to control the unruly crowd on that infamous Saturday night after the Cotton Bowl game during the State Fair in 1958.

David remembered it well. He and a few other young punks were in the midst of it all that night.

And as memory fast-forwarded he recalled the motorcade that had taken President and Mrs. Kennedy in that long black convertible down Main Street past the Adolphus that ill-fated morning in November. Along the parade route, protestors were passing out a wanted poster for acts of treason with Kennedy's picture on it and when the motorcade made the turn from Main at Houston Street to Elm and started downhill, the assassins found their target.

Downtown Dallas was in free fall and the old hotel was suffering a painful death. With its battle scars and beat-up furniture, tattered drapes, and worn carpets the deterioration couldn't get much worse. Old hallways that once led to fabulously appointed rooms where Presidents Roosevelt and Truman and Charles Lindbergh and Amelia Earhart and Rudolph Valentino had once stayed were boarded over and led to nowhere.

In 1979, the Hotel Adolphus locked its doors.

But tonight David stepped from the revolving door into the new Adolphus Hotel and couldn't help but smile briefly as he was showered with the bright lights reflecting off twin chandeliers.

"Evenin', Mr. Matthews." The hotel's evening doorman, Lew Little, knew David by sight and called him by name. Discreetly, he asked David if he'd be staying the night.

"Not tonight," David told him. Tonight he stopped by "to have a bite to eat in the dining room," and then he'd get Little to hail him a cab. He'd be going home shortly.

"Yes, sir, Mr. Matthews, I'll be waiting right here for you, get you a cab right away when you're ready to go, just you give me the sign, I'll be here all night."

David walked up the wide carpeted staircase, past the imposing ebony grand piano on the mezzanine, and got as far as the bar.

When the tuxedoed bartender saw him standing there, he turned and poured a bourbon on rocks and placed it on a cocktail napkin on the bar as David approached. It was the grand old days revisited and, like the grand old days, the service to faithful well-heeled customers was impeccable.

David admired the original mahogany bar, polished now to a glowing warm patina. He rubbed the smooth rounded edge with his hand, glanced at the polished glasses on the shelves, noticed the appointments around the room, and took a seat.

The house whiskey at the Adolphus was better than most call brands, it went down smooth, and David was grateful for the refuge he sought that night in the restored hotel.

The beer baron would have been proud. More than eighty million dollars later, the hotel glistened and if one took the time to remember, and to listen on a clear night such as this, one could hear the music of the big band drifting from the Century Room upward to the rooftop garden where dancers and romancers once cooled themselves with a gentle breeze blowing across the Trinity River.

———

There had been a string of luxury cars coming and going that evening on the streets along Turtle Creek—chauffeurs returning employers to their homes or taking them out for an engagement, staff leaving for the night, and a host of spoiled teenagers seeing and being seen in expensive SUVs. But when the Lincoln Town Car pulled into the circle drive in front of the senator's house, Ismini got out of her sports car and slammed the door shut. The chauffeur was holding the door open for the senator when she approached.

"Well, sweet Jesus, do tell to what do I owe this pleasant surprise?" he asked stepping out, ever the politician.

"You know who I am?"

"Of course, I know who you are, my dear, come in, come

in." The senator placed his hand in the small of her back and directed her to the front porch.

As they approached the porch, Lupe opened the door for the senator and the mystery guest. From a window Lupe had been keeping an eye on the lady since she had arrived. Lupe didn't like the way the woman waited outside in her car, she didn't like the way she walked with her hips swaying in exaggerated motion, she didn't like the cheap and tawdry way she was dressed, and Lupe didn't like the way the woman ignored her when she brushed by her with the senator.

Lupe shut the front door and followed them into the comfortable room. Earlier she had lit the fire in the fireplace and the ordinarily cold room had come to life with the glowing warmth. "Will you be having supper, Senator?" Lupe asked.

The senator looked at Ismini standing by the fireplace. "Have you eaten, my dear Mrs. Zacchoias?"

Ismini shook her head. The truth was she hadn't eaten in several days and she realized she was hungry—very hungry.

The senator turned to Lupe. "Yes, Lupe, thank you, we will be having supper. Mrs. Zacchoias will be joining me, and I think we'll eat here in the study—over there by the fireplace."

Lupe returned to the study twice. The first time to bring in a cloth for the small drop leaf table in the corner, napkins, china service for two, and silverware. The next time she entered she carried a large oval tray. The senator took it from her hands and put it on his desk.

Lupe had prepared a tureen of sweet potato soup drizzled with a ladle of hot heavy cream. The tomato bread, sliced into small wedges, was kept warm in a silver-plated wire basket and tucked with a linen napkin. For dessert, that morning she'd prepared a simple coffee flan, made with fresh whole coffee beans, chilled and inverted onto a deep platter with a rich caramel sauce pooling around it.

Lupe left the final decision on the wine to the senator, but earlier she had selected two bottles from the cellar for him to choose.

"No, no," neither would do for his guest, he told Lupe, while he kept his eyes, his gaze, and all of his attention on Ismini. "Wouldn't do at all, no, siree." He'd go to the cellar and select "something more appropriate for such a *special* lady."

No, Lupe didn't like this woman one bit.

When the senator returned with his special bottle he handed it off to Lupe and asked that she open it in the other room. When she returned she brought it on a tray with two crystal wine hocks.

"Thank you, Lupe," the senator said, graciously keeping his gaze on Ismini, "that will be all. Good night."

The fire in the fireplace was just Lupe's way of trying to do something nice, for Lindsey's sake. It galled her to have the senator share it with such a *puta*.

Lupe would be gone in the morning.

————

David came through the garage, up the back stairs to the kitchen entry, and called out for Taylor.

He walked down the hall and looked at his watch. It was later than he thought and he called out again. Returning to the kitchen he stared into the refrigerator as if that were the most logical place to start. He needed some downtime to consider what the senator had said—and he needed another bourbon.

The senator's confession had been a surprise, but the

reality of it was that it wasn't all that important to him. He was relieved to learn that Taylor's only role in this mess was as the innocent bystander, caught up in something she had nothing to do with. But primarily David was thinking of himself and how Annie had lied to him again—again and again.

He went to the desk in the study and looked up the phone number in his personal book and dialed.

———

"Taylor, could you answer the phone for me?" Annie called out from the bedroom.

"Too late, your machine picked it up."

Annie walked out of the bedroom wearing a pair of faded jeans and a pullover jersey. Barefooted, but carrying a pair of white socks and sneakers she headed for the sofa. "Just as well," she said and from the kitchen they both heard the message as it was being recorded.

"Annie, it's David. Call me when you get this—it's important. I'm at home."

———

The senator was snoring heavily when Ismini woke that morning. Her flimsy red dress lay on the floor covering her sandals. She sat on the side of the bed, her feet not quite touching the floor. She looked at the man and watched as a thin line of drool made its way from the corner of his open mouth, across his cheek, and soaked into the pillowcase. As she scooted to the edge of the bed he reached for her arm.

"Did I wake you?" she asked.

"Only because I wanted to be awake," he replied. "Come

back to bed, my dear. Here"—he lifted the sheet—"climb back under the covers with ole Buddy."

It was starting to rain and the little red convertible with the top down was still parked in the circle driveway.

26

When David awoke that morning his mind was groggy and his body was stiff. It was daylight and the house was quiet. While the coffee brewed he took a quick shower and called Liz as he poured himself a cup. "Damn," she heard him mutter when she answered.

"Boss?"

"Sorry about that," he said, "I just spilled more coffee on my hand than I poured into the cup."

"Where are you? Did you forget you have an eight-thirty with the men from upstairs?"

"I overslept. Are they there?"

"I can hear them in the hall now. You want me to reschedule?"

"No, I'll be there. Tell them I got caught up in traffic or something, tell them I'm on my way, just stall them a few minutes.

Get them some coffee and, hell, you know—doughnuts, something—anything. Do what you can. I'm on my way."

The office door opened and Liz continued to talk into the telephone after he'd hung up. "Oh, I'm sorry to hear that," she said, "so you're on your way? No, no problem, I'll tell them, they're here now. No, I'm sure they'll understand." She looked up and smiled at the two men dressed in dark suits and power ties. "I just spoke with Mr. Matthews," she told them as she stood, "he asked me to apologize to you for keeping you waiting. He was called over to the courts early this morning on an urgent matter, but he's on his way now. May I pour you a cup of coffee, gentlemen, while we wait?" she asked as she set up the cups.

Smooth as silk and as slick as she needed to be—whatever it took—Liz Jamison was the one person he could count on, through thick and thin, the good times and the bad—she'd take care of everything.

When David arrived it was clear that Liz had done another good job of keeping the business running smoothly. The men exchanged handshakes and David asked them to come into his office. Once inside they were ecstatic over the original Remington bronze David had on display. They were Eastern businessmen but they had not neglected their education for the Western arts.

Today's professionals were younger and healthier and had a broader appreciation for life. The client base was changing and many of those entering the corporate world were of Asian descent. David was paying attention.

The Far East was the future and, unlike earlier generations who spoke only through an interpreter and rarely traveled outside their country, today's educated generation spoke perfect English and traveled and studied abroad extensively. What's more, they spoke several other languages fluently and were prepared to do business on a worldwide basis. *America, wake up,* David thought.

It was late morning when the meeting broke up. Liz had prepared client contracts and by the time David asked her to step into his office, the men were eager to sign.

Their excitement was contagious and David was rejuvenated and while he knew he would be unable to take them all the way personally, he explained he had just the right lawyer in mind to get started.

When they left he asked Liz to get Rose Marie on the line for him and to call Southwest and get him a seat on the next plane to Austin.

And Taylor? Where was she? He dialed home and the machine picked up.

———

Annie and Taylor had stayed up all evening and talked through the night.

It started with the phone message from David. Annie tried to explain to his wife why he was calling her, but then admitted she didn't really have any explanations. It hurt to hear David's voice on the phone, but Taylor didn't blame Annie. Annie wasn't her rival. This Annie had never been her rival. Her rival had been the Annie that lived in David's mind: the other Annie, the untouchable Annie, the Annie on the pedestal. It wasn't this woman, the Annie wearing faded jeans with worn knees and tennis shoes. This was the warm, welcoming Annie that opened the door smiling when Taylor had come to face her nemesis. This Annie was healthy and bright and laughed freely. She was smart and interesting, and she listened attentively. Taylor admired her and a mutual respect began to grow as the evening progressed.

Annie told Taylor about Lindsey. She told her about meeting her in the ninth grade, how they'd been best friends all through high school and how they'd remained friends off and on throughout the years. She told her about the boyfriends, about Tommy Lee and the baby, and she told her about the hideous abortion.

They opened a third bottle of wine and Annie pulled out cheese and crackers and arranged a tray with nuts and fresh strawberries and carried it into the den.

Annie lit the fire in the fireplace. "Who says a woman can't have it all?" she asked smugly referring to the cheese, fruit, and crackling fire.

"A man, usually," Taylor said and both women laughed and fell back into the comfortable tell-all dialogue as only best girlfriends can do.

There was a trust between them—from the beginning.

Taylor told Annie about her first marriage when she had fallen in love with the high school quarterback. He said all the things a girl wants to hear and it wasn't too many Friday nights after the game before they were making love in the backseat of his car, twisting and turning to the mellow songs of Nat King Cole and the mournful wailing of Hank Williams on the car radio.

By the Christmas break she was more than seven weeks pregnant and they married before they went back to school after New Year's. She graduated from high school and had the baby in July. The marriage ended in August and she and the baby girl moved back to her parents to live.

Annie told Taylor about her first love—the one and only Tommy Lee—Lindsey's Tommy Lee. She told Taylor about her first date with the "tough guy" from back East and she remembered every detail—his dark hair, his black leather jacket, the way he looked at her, and the way the cigarette dangled in the corner of mouth. And she told her about his yellow convertible and about that first wet French kiss.

They both laughed when they started citing memorized passages from "the really good parts" of *Peyton Place.*

Taylor helped herself to the wine and refilled Annie's glass while she was at it. They pulled cushions from the sofa, sat on the floor, and leaned against the furniture while they warmed their stockinged feet by the fireplace.

Taylor told Annie about her second marriage. A man she'd met at the garage where her car had been towed after it broke down on the highway one hot summer afternoon in Louisiana. He was a mechanic and older than Taylor. "Mechanics make good lovers," she told Annie matter-of-factly.

"Unfortunately, as it turned out," Taylor continued, "except for the lovemaking, we didn't have anything in common. He'd been single too long and was already set in his ways—he had his garage buddies he liked to hang out with every weekend. I don't think we ever had a conversation that lasted more than five minutes and that was usually either about what was for supper or what was on the tube that night. He played cards every Friday night and I stayed home alone. At the time I didn't have anything but a high school diploma, a daughter still in diapers, and I was lonesome. I decided I could do better for myself."

"So you filed for divorce?"

"Not right away, I had lots of time alone to decide he wasn't the one for me. We're still friends, and he's been like a father to my daughter. Lord knows her own dad wasn't anywhere around for her. Never marry a handsome man, Annie. They're too hung up on themselves, or they're too busy looking around to see who else is out there, who's gaga over them."

"It's a curse. Pretty people, men and women, get hung up on pretty people, including themselves."

"And then there's David."

"Yes, and then there's David," Annie said. "Taylor, I want to tell you something I've never told anyone—not even Lindsey. I have loved David all my life."

Annie waited for a response, but Taylor sat quietly.

"I had his baby," she said quietly.

"When?" Taylor broke the silence.

"That first year after high school."

"David never told me."

"David never knew—not until last week."

"You told him?"

"Yes, but I'd never planned to tell him."

"Why? Didn't you think he'd want to know? Maybe you don't know David as well as you think. David would have made a wonderful father. A child of his own is the one thing he's been missing, it would have made all the difference to him. A child would have changed David's life—for the better—I'm sure of it."

"Perhaps, but the David I knew was not the kind of father I wanted for my daughter. But last week he found out about her and confronted me. He was, as you can well imagine, furious that I had kept her from him all those years."

"I can't say I blame him for that." Taylor poured more wine. "So have the two of them met?"

"He didn't tell you?"

"He didn't tell me about the child, no. The night he came home from Austin, and I'm assuming that's when you dropped that bomb on him, he wanted to tell me some things, wanted to talk, but I didn't give him a chance. Where is your daughter now?" Taylor asked.

Taylor listened while Annie repeated the story she had told David a few days ago—about the death of a daughter he never knew he had.

"I'm sorry that I didn't hear him out," Taylor said when she had finished. "He must have been hurting and I never gave him a chance that night. It doesn't seem like much of an excuse now, but that night I was dealing with my own feelings and I had reached a point where I just couldn't deal with any more of David's explanations."

"I understand—but David's a good man, and he means well," Annie said, "and he tries harder than any man alive to fit in and do the right thing. He does okay for a while and then something comes over him and he slips back into the old David ways—the nature of the beast, I suppose."

"I can't argue with that and I agree—he is a good man—and a damn good-looking one too.

"And, he's got money, don't forget that," Taylor added with a wink.

Annie and Taylor held their glasses high. "To David," Annie said.

"To David—a hell of a man," Taylor added.

Annie stood, arched her back, and stretched. "I haven't had a gab session like this in a long time. It feels good to talk to someone that I have so much in common with."

"By 'in common' do you mean like my husband and your boyfriend?"

"Yeah, that too." Annie smiled. "No, I mean it's just that lately I've been working with young interns at the gallery and to tell you the truth my patience has been wearing thin."

"That's understandable, but you're fortunate to have an interesting career. I imagine you get a chance to meet and mix with a stimulating group of people, people of culture and education, the elites, the upper echelon; it's got to be exciting. You've traveled to exotic cities, speak several languages, you have a wonderful life and, best of all, you're completely independent."

"And don't think I don't consider myself lucky. It's a world I created to my own specifications and most times I do enjoy it. And now, strange as it must seem, I think you and I could really be friends."

"Even with David between us?"

"Let's just accept it, Taylor—it's *because* of David we're friends."

They talked through the night and it was beginning to get light outside when they went to the kitchen for something to eat. Annie started a pot of coffee.

"I've got to get back to Dallas," Taylor said, "I left without telling anyone where I was going. David may be worrying about me."

"You want to give him a call?"

"No, not just yet. I'm going to try and grab the next plane out of here."

"Why don't you stay a few days, Taylor. You can get your things and come out here. I have a spare room and I'd love the company. There's a new exhibition opening at a gallery museum tomorrow and I'd like you to be my guest at a reception this evening. I think you'd enjoy it."

"It's tempting, but right now I need to get home. I haven't been completely honest with you, Annie. I don't want you to think badly of me, but there's somebody else."

"Really? Somebody else? Somebody besides David? Who?"

"Well, hold on to something, this is the shocker, remember the detective investigating Butter's death?"

"Yeah, go on."

"It's him."

"The cop?"

Taylor nodded her head and got up to get the coffee. "I know, I know," she said, "it surprises me too, but after all this mess with Butter's death I've gotten to know him pretty well. He always believed I was innocent and he's really a great guy, he's been a good friend and—we have a lot in common."

"Like *what?*"

"Like gardening . . . like pancakes for supper . . . and baseball games."

"Wow, all *that?* Sounds like the makings of the real thing to me—Taylor, you *can't* be serious?"

"I'm not serious about anything right now, but I do know I enjoy spending time with him. In the meantime I do need to get back to Dallas. I checked into the hotel by the airport when I arrived yesterday."

"Okay, I'll drive you to the hotel to get your stuff and then drop you off at the airport—but promise me you'll find time to get back here soon."

———

Malone sat at his desk that morning and reread the final passages from Anne's diary.

———

I've considered all the consequences, and calculated the risks.

I'll see to the details right down to the funeral services. I'll select her gown, see to the flowers, the music, and I'll keep a watch on the children. It will take a lot of money to make this happen.

There is no turning back—I will always miss her.

———

Annie answered the phone on the second ring.

"Ms. Williams?"

"Yes?"

"Ms. Williams, this is Detective Jake Malone, from the Dallas Police Department. I hate to bother you again, but there are a few more questions I'd like you to answer."

"What kind of questions, Detective? I've told you everything I could possibly think of about Butter—?"

"I'm driving to Austin this morning and I'd like to meet you there."

"I'm not sure I can. I have a busy morning and I'm already running late—"

"I'll be there by eleven," Malone interrupted. "Where can I find you?"

"Like I said, Detective, I have a busy morning, I'm not sure when I'll be able to see you—is it something we could talk about on the phone?"

"No, ma'am, it isn't. Like I said, I'll be there at eleven and I'll meet you at your house."

"I'll try."

"You do that, Ms. Williams, and I'll see you there at eleven."

"What was that all about?" Taylor asked when Annie hung up.

"It was your friend, Detective Malone, Taylor. He wants to see me—he's on his way to Austin."

"But why?"

"Beats me, but something tells me it's not just a friendly visit."

"Do you want me to be here?"

"I'd like that."

Annie smiled, knowing now that she and Taylor were going to be friends—best friends, just like Lindsey.

PART FOUR

THE TANGLED WEB

27

David barely made the no-frills, no meals, cheap seats, and capacity-filled plane, but by two P.M. the "peanut flight" landed in Austin with him aboard in a middle seat at the back of the plane. And in Dallas Liz stayed busy with the paper chase, scheduling, and the never-ending research. David's law library was extensive, but even with the convenience of it being in the adjoining conference room it was often necessary to trek over to the Criminal Courts Building once or twice a week.

David knew she was invaluable to him, the backbone of the business, but it went beyond that. Her reputation for loyalty, attention to the most insignificant detail, which often proved to be the most critical and significant to a case, her unwavering enthusiasm for the investigation, and the ability to read people was nearing legendary proportions.

She was the one legal secretary that could have named her

price and half the firms in Dallas would have offered double. A savvy woman, she was as comfortable having a cold one down at the Elm with the boys after a long session in front of the bench as she was having afternoon tea at the Adolphus with the wives of the city's elected officials.

Without Liz in his office, in his professional life, his business would not have been the success it was—and his golf game would have suffered noticeably. By now he considered golf a part of his routine, as much of a routine as going to a camp meeting on Sunday in Big D has been to many a civic-minded servant of the people.

But David steered clear of organized religion. For David, golf was his religion and the course his sanctuary. It was a place to think and sometimes it was a place *not* to think. Concentrating on his swing, on the rhythm, on the flight, the lay of the course, the lie of the ball, gave him the opportunity for situation assessment. Tested over time, his afternoons at the club were a critical part of his success. But there were exceptions and today was one of them.

David was the last passenger off the plane and Rose Marie met him at the gate.

Weeks Leonard was waiting for them when they arrived at his home. The professor hadn't seen Rose Marie in several months and they hugged when he opened the door. Weeks and David shook hands, but it was clear to Rose they would have been more comfortable taking jabs at each other's arms like the old days.

Shirley Leonard, a short and perpetually happy woman, wearing a white eyelet shirt, denim skirt, and Keds, came downstairs to greet their guests. After a few cordial minutes she and Weeks led their guests to the study and left them for their meeting behind closed doors.

David opened his briefcase and handed Rose Marie a thin file. As she opened it he explained that this was going to develop over the next year and a half, and that he wanted her in on it from the beginning. He told her this client had strong potential for a longtime relationship with the firm and that there would be traveling involved. A trip to Hong Kong would occur in the next few months. In the beginning, especially on this fact-finding trip, while she got a feel for working with the Asian partners, he'd be accompanying them to China as well.

Rose Marie processed the information and even though this wasn't a matter to be argued before the bench he assured her there were plenty of other cases—criminal cases—already backlogged and waiting. "I'm afraid you'll be working long into the nights for some time now," David said apologetically.

"That's not a problem," she told him and as far as the business trip to China was concerned she had several friends at the university that were of Asian descent and she had picked up some of the more informal conversational phrases.

She surprised him when she said she'd been to Shanghai twice in the last few years and to Hong Kong during a Christmas break only last year. The crowded cities held a fascination for her and she welcomed the chance to return to the Far East. In the meantime, she'd brush up on the language.

It was late afternoon when they finished and Shirley Leonard invited them to stay for supper. David insisted on taking them all out.

Weeks drove to a barbecue place that three of them knew well. Considering his supper companions of late, this was an about-face and a welcomed change and David realized how much he missed being with genuinely good people like Weeks and Shirley Leonard. And as for the young woman that sat next to him on the bench in the open air café with sawdust and peanut shells on the floor, she was witty and smart, pretty and . . . *If I were ten years younger, okay, so twenty years . . .*

That morning Anne drove Taylor to the Hyatt to get her things and check out.

The message light was blinking on the machine when they arrived back at Annie's just before eleven to await Malone's impending arrival. The first message was from David and this time when he asked Annie to return his call he said that he could be reached on his cell phone. He left the number. The second message was from Malone to say he'd been delayed by department business, but would be in Austin as soon as possible.

On the other side of town Weeks and Shirley returned to the house with David and Rose Marie. It was almost six P.M. when they parted company and David got in on the passenger side of Rose Marie's convertible.

"Where to now?" she asked.

David reached into his coat pocket and retrieved his cell phone. "Just give me a minute here to check my messages and then we'll see." He dialed in and listened. "Not too bad," he said lightheartedly, though he felt disappointed. "Now just one more call."

"Hello?" Taylor said.

"Taylor, I just got your message. Everything okay?"

"Not really, I need to talk to you—I'm in Austin . . ."

"You're in Austin?"

"Don't be upset, David, but, yes, I'm here—at Anne Williams's place—"

"What? Why would you be there, for Christ's sake?"

"Look, David, we can get into that later, right now, there's a bigger problem. Annie's in trouble here—and we need to help."

She needed only to mention next that Malone had driven in from Dallas and David said he'd be right there. "And tell her not to say anything—*anything*—do you understand, Taylor? Wait there. Tell her I'm on my way."

"David, where—" Taylor tried to ask, but David had hung up.

"So where to? Sounds important."

"Do you know the area north of Mopac?"

"Like the back of my hand," Rose Marie said as she accelerated.

In less than fifteen minutes, they turned off the highway and entered into the gated community. "What's the street?" Rose Marie asked.

She turned quickly and pulled up to the curb in back of two Austin squad cars.

David was halfway up the walk when the car door slammed shut behind him. He rang the bell as Rose Marie hurried to catch up with him. She pushed by him and was reaching for the door handle when Taylor opened the door.

"David, thank God you're here. Anne's in the back," Taylor said, leading the way.

Malone was with Annie in the backyard when David, Taylor, and Rose Marie approached them.

"Detective?"

"Matthews," he acknowledged. "Can't say I'm too surprised to see you here—though I *was* surprised to find your wife here this afternoon." Malone shot a glance in Taylor's direction. "I suppose you'll want to have a few words with Ms. Williams here. I'll let her explain it to you. Ladies, shall we give them some privacy?" Malone pulled the patio door back and Taylor and Rose Marie went ahead of him to the kitchen to wait.

"I'm Rose Marie Abbott. I work for Mr. Matthews's firm," she said to both Taylor and Malone.

"Since when?" Taylor asked.

"Actually, I'm just starting there."

"You must be the law graduate your boss was telling me about. This is Mrs. Matthews and I'm Malone, Detective Jake Malone. Homicide. Dallas P.D." Jake said, trying to defuse the situation, but Taylor had already moved away to watch Annie and David from the kitchen window.

"Can you tell me what this is about, Detective?" Rose Marie asked.

"No, ma'am, not yet. Better wait and let your boss fill you in."

Jake pulled out a chair and sat down at the kitchen table. "Taylor, you want to tell me what you're doing here? I remember you telling me you didn't know Anne Williams and next thing here you are at her house, so what's this all about? I thought you'd been straight with me. Am I losing my edge? Better fill me in here."

"No, Jake, you're not losing any edge." Taylor turned around to answer. "I have been straight with you. I didn't know Anne Williams. I only knew *about* her—only what David had told me—I never lied to you about that. But Annie's always been there between David and me and I decided the only way I was going to have any peace was to confront my mysterious neme-sis, face-to-face. I flew to Austin yesterday—I had questions of my own I needed answered—it was the only way I could put it to rest."

"And did you get the answers you were looking for?"

"Yes and no. I expected to meet a selfish woman, uncaring about anybody but herself, a woman with a cold heart, but instead I met a woman that was warm and thoughtful. We stayed up all night talking—and not just about David either. At first, of course, we talked about our relationship and our feelings for David, but after a while we talked very little about him. David's in the past for me"—Taylor glanced outside—"and I thought he was for Annie too, but now—now I don't know. But it doesn't matter"—she turned back to look at Jake. "What matters now is that Annie needs David—and she needs me too, Jake—so where do we go from here?"

Malone thought about the loaded question before he answered. "I'm taking Ms. Williams back to Dallas. You can ride along with us if you'd like."

"Ms. Abbott." Jake turned and directed his remarks now to Rose Marie.

"Yes, Detective?"

"Ms. Abbott, you look familiar. I know this sounds strange coming from an old warhorse like me, but, have we met?"

"I don't think so—I think I would remember meeting you, Detective, and I've lived here in Austin for almost fifteen years."

David and Annie stepped inside and David informed Malone they were ready to go. "Ms. Williams would like to get a few personal items together first, Detective, if that's okay. I don't consider her a flight risk, but if it would make you feel any better, I'm sure my wife wouldn't mind going with her to pack."

"That'll be fine." Jake turned and told the two uniformed officers to each stand at an outside door, one at the front and one at the back and then he remembered where he'd seen the younger woman.

"Ms. Abbott, I have another question for you . . ."

"Please, ask away, Detective Malone," Rose Marie said.

"I'm sure it isn't necessary to remind you, but it's important that you tell me the truth."

"Are you implying that I wouldn't tell you the truth, Detective? Because if you are, sir, you've misjudged me."

"And I apologize for implying anything along those lines, Ms. Abbott. I put that poorly, can we start over?"

"Of course, Detective, ask your question."

"Malone, I can't see any reason for you to question Ms. Abbott. She's starting to work in my office next month. Right now, she's still a student and this is of no concern to her. We were having supper and going over some details of her coming to work at the firm in Dallas when I got a call from Taylor."

Not certain whether to speak or not, Rose Marie was standing by the sink when Taylor and Annie came back into the room.

"Ready?" Malone asked.

"Yes, let's get this over with," Annie replied.

"I'll catch the next flight, Annie, and I'll be waiting for you in Dallas," David assured her. "And, Taylor, I think it best if you stay with her until I get there. Are you okay with that?"

He started to reach for Taylor, but she held her hand out to stop him. "We'll be fine. I'll stay with her. And we'll see you back in Dallas."

Rose Marie followed David down the hall and to the front walk. Before she caught up with him, she stopped, returned to Annie, and told her everything would be okay.

It was almost midnight, the station was quiet, and David was waiting in the hall inside police headquarters when Malone, Taylor, and Annie stepped off the station's garage parking elevator.

Under most circumstances Malone would have held Anne Williams for arraignment in the morning, but for now he still had it within his discretionary powers to make exceptions. Taylor asked him to release Annie into her custody.

The ride to the house was done in silence. When they were in the kitchen David said he wanted to talk to Annie alone for a few minutes.

Client privilege was not extended to Taylor and she knew that if and when Annie was brought to trial she could be subpoenaed to testify against her if the D.A. thought she had incriminating information. At this point Taylor knew there were things she wished she didn't know.

Taylor said she'd get the spare bedroom ready upstairs. When she turned from the linen closet, David was standing in the hall.

"I thought you were going to talk to Annie?" she said, brushing by him with her arms full.

"I will, but I wanted to see if you were okay."

"I'm fine."

"Taylor, if Annie confided in you about any of this, I need to know."

This time Taylor stopped and turned to answer David. "We talked a lot last night, about a lot of things, and yes, she did confide some things in me, David, but not about any murder. She told me about her longtime friendship with Lindsey—and about the four of you—"

"The four of us?" David interrupted.

"Lindsey, Annie, you, and Butter."

"Butter—how I'd like to forget her."

"We'd all like to forget Butter, but she may be the key to all this. Did you consider that? That Butter was more involved than we expected?"

"Yes, I've known that now for a while. Butter played a role in this from the beginning."

"So I'm not telling you anything you don't already know?"

"No, not yet. What else did you and Annie talk about last night?"

"Lots of things, David. Unfortunately nothing that will help Annie or you that much."

"Okay, Taylor, get some sleep. We'll talk in the morning." He turned and started for the staircase.

"David." Taylor caught up with him, reached out, and touched his arm. "David, I know about the baby."

David stopped, but said nothing.

"She told me about your daughter. I'm so sorry, David. I know that must have hurt a great deal—and I'm sorry I turned you away that night when you came back from Austin. . . ."

"You couldn't have known and I don't blame you for being angry with me. I treated you despicably and you deserve much better. We both know that, Taylor."

"You're a good man, David, and you deserve to be happier. You know I'll always love you."

"And a part of me will always love you, Taylor, but we've made the right decision, no sense fooling ourselves here, we have to move forward, we can't go back."

28

Malone stood on the porch with the morning edition under his left arm and rang the front bell for the second time.

He knocked loudly.

Still no answer.

He then walked along the driveway to the back of the house where he saw the senator's man coming down the outside stairs of the apartment over the six-car garage.

"Hello there," Malone called out.

"Hello yourself, what can I do for you, mister?" the muscular man with the Swedish accent asked the approaching Malone.

"Looking for the senator," he said as he presented his ID.

"Kinda early for the senator. He's not usually up before eight A.M., never has callers before ten."

"Well, it's not exactly a social call this morning, but I do need to speak with him so what say we go in and see about rousing him out of bed this morning?"

"He's not gonna be happy about it."

"He'll get over it," Malone said, following the chauffeur along the cobblestone path to the back entrance of the house with its ivy-covered stone walls. Built with oil money from wildcatter days, the Tudor-style house had aged gracefully for the better part of sixty years and Malone couldn't help but admire the stately house and the manicured gardens. "Beautiful out here in the spring," he commented.

"Ya, ya, but this year, not so good—too much rain."

The Swede opened the back door and went directly to the alarm keypad on the wall and disengaged the coded electronic device. "Boss, likes to keep real private here. The housekeeper left a couple of days ago and right now, he's got nobody here but me. I think a new gal may be coming in later today to clean maybe. Want some coffee?"

"Sure, coffee's fine. Where's the senator now?"

" 'Sleep."

"Do you want to go get him?"

"Not me, you can, but I have orders, and those orders are not to disturb him."

"Where's the phone?"

"Can't call him."

"Why not?"

"Turns the ringer off the bedroom phone."

"Well, let's put it this way, the senator left word with you he's not to be disturbed. You let me in the house. Who would he rather have knocking on his bedroom door, you or me? Either way, you lose, it's just a matter of how bad, think about it."

"Okay, Detective, so then I'll go up."

"You do that. I'll be waiting here—with my coffee."

In just a few minutes the Swede returned with news that the senator would be down shortly.

"Good work," Malone acknowledged as he scanned the morning headlines from the *Dallas Morning News*.

"Detective Malone," Senator Mitchell greeted him as he walked into the kitchen. "You're up and about mighty early, aren't you? What can I do for Dallas's finest this morning?"

"And you're in good spirits, Senator, here I thought you'd be madder 'n a sow bear having me wake you up and all."

"Not at all, my good man, I was already awake and going through some papers upstairs in my room. No rest for the wicked," he said, struggling to suppress a cough.

The Swede handed him a glass of tap water, but by then Mitchell's face was red and a mass of hair still wet from the water he'd combed through it settled on the side of his face. For the awkward minutes that followed, the pompous senator, clad only in a silk bathrobe and fur-lined house shoes, suffered through a smoker's morning coughing spasm while the veteran detective from homicide continued reading the paper, drinking his coffee, and quietly waited. Whatever composure the salty politician had lost, he struggled to regain.

"So, what can I do for you, Malone?" he asked, attempting to pour himself a cup of coffee while trying to clear his throat. "You'll have to excuse the informality here, my housekeeper decided to seek employment elsewhere."

"Lupe?"

The senator shook his head. "Hmm, seems she and my late wife were good friends and I think working here without Mrs. Mitchell was too painful for her, poor thing."

"I'll know you'll miss her cooking."

"That I will, Malone, that I will. Now, what is it you want from me this morning?"

Malone snapped the pages together, folded them, and laid the senator's newspaper on the table.

"Senator, I'd like to have a look around. Now you don't have to let me do that, you know, but it would be helpful if I could go back into your study for a few minutes."

"Exactly what is it you're looking for? Maybe I can save you the trouble."

"A photograph."

"Come on, bring your coffee with you, and let's go see if we can find you a picture that's so all fired-up important this morning."

The drapes had been left drawn and the only light was through the doors opening from the front foyer. The senator walked ahead and turned on the table lamp. It helped, but not much. Malone still could not see well enough to cross the room. The senator turned on another lamp. The oval tray and the dirty dishes were piled on the desk, wineglasses left on the coffee table.

"You see anything here? Most of the photos are over there on the mantel."

"Yes, this one," Malone said, reaching up for the small framed snapshot for a closer look. "Who are these people, Senator?"

"Those are Lindsey's boys, and the girl—I don't know her name, but she's the kid of my late wife's friend—Anne Williams, I think. Yes, Anne Williams—lives in Austin."

"You say she's her daughter?"

"That would be my guess, Detective, the two of them are always together—at least that's what Lindsey told me."

"I wonder, Senator, would you mind if I held on to this photo for a while? I'd like to show it to a fella I know."

"That'd be fine, Malone. Return it when you can. Now, is that it?"

"That's it. I'll be out of your way, Senator, thanks."

"Anytime, Detective."

———

Malone was waiting in his office when David and Annie arrived promptly at ten A.M. He'd taken the photograph out of the frame and laid the picture casually face up on his desk.

Annie saw it immediately.

"What's this, Detective?"

"Interesting picture don't you agree, Ms. Williams?"

David took it from her hand. "Who are the boys, Malone?"

"You recognize the girl?"

"Of course, she's a little younger, but I know who she is."

"And what about you, Ms. Williams, do you recognize the girl in the picture?"

"You know I do, Detective."

"What's this about? Malone, the girl is my new hire, Rose Marie Abbott, you met her last night."

Annie remained standing, but said nothing.

"That's right I did, but do you know who the boys are?"

"No, Detective, who are the boys and what has this snapshot got to do with anything?"

"You want to tell him, Ms. Williams?"

"Why? And spoil your surprise?"

Malone squared up, looked at David, and said nothing long enough to make him know Malone was about to drop a bomb.

"Cute aren't they?" Malone could turn a screw when he felt like it.

David did not flinch.

"They're Lindsey's children," Annie broke down and told David.

"Okay, obviously this was taken a few years ago, so why is Rose Marie in the picture with them?" David asked Annie.

"Look, Matthews," Malone said, "I've been insensitive here, let's start over. Ms. Williams, how 'bout a cup of coffee? Matthews, how 'bout you?" Malone walked to the coffeemaker where a fresh pot and not the usual dregs was ready to be poured. He took two ceramic mugs from the shelf, poured them to the brim, and brought them back to his desk, spilling a little on the way.

Annie took a sip and David tasted it only enough to know he needed sugar. "Over there in the cabinet," Malone said, pointing back to the coffee bar in the hall. David helped himself and when he returned Annie was back to being her old self again and the picture lay on the desk.

"The girl in the photo is Ms. Williams's daughter, Matthews," Malone said.

The room exploded and David's ears rang with the news. *Ms. Williams's daughter! That would be my daughter!* David wanted to scream the words—and shake the hell out of Annie.

"My *daughter*? I'm afraid you're wrong there, Detective," Annie said and directed her next remarks only to David. "David, Rose Marie is not my daughter," she told him firmly and redirected her attention back again to Malone. "She's *like* a daughter to me, but, no, Detective, she is *not* my daughter. Whoever told you that is playing a very cruel joke."

David sat in the wooden chair and somewhere in the aftermath of the mind explosion he heard Annie deny her own daughter's identity. *Of course she's Annie's daughter, why would she say otherwise, they resemble each other in every way, that's why I'm so attracted to her. She's Annie's daughter, she's my daughter—she has to be . . .*

"David, David, listen to me, she's *not* my daughter—she's

Caroline's daughter. She's my niece and sometimes, when she can, she stays with me. We've traveled together on breaks and we've been great friends. I love her dearly, David, and I suppose I love her like the daughter that I—that we—lost, but David, Rose Marie is *not* our daughter."

"How did you come by this photo, Malone?" Matthews spoke now for the first time. In that brief moment he'd been the father he wanted to be and then for the second time in the same week had his daughter taken from him. "Who said this was my daughter?"

"Now look, Matthews, I was told this was Ms. Williams's daughter and after last night's meeting in Austin it made sense."

"Who told you Malone?"

"The senator."

"Buddy Mitchell?" Annie said.

"One and the same," Malone answered.

"Why would he do that?" she asked.

"Because I think he believes it *is* your daughter, Ms. Williams. The picture was framed and on the mantel in the senator's study. Now I have to assume the picture was there because his late wife wanted it there. The senator doesn't strike me as the kind of fella to think enough of these sorts of things to keep them around."

"The senator is the kind of 'fella,' Detective Malone, that would indeed keep a photo framed and displayed," Annie said. "What he wouldn't keep around are the children themselves." She continued now for David's benefit, "I remember when Lindsey took that picture. She was in San Marcos visiting them at the Academy. It was just before the semester was over and she called me and told me she was driving down. Rose Marie was visiting me that afternoon and together we drove out there to meet her. We all had supper at the Springs and had gone for a long walk in the park and the boys played on the swings. So did Rose Marie. It was a wonderful day and Lindsey sent me a copy of that picture as a memento. I still have it somewhere in an album."

"But the senator *said* this is my daughter?" David looked to Malone for the answer.

"Mitchell said it was Ms. Williams's daughter," Malone said.

"Look, David," Annie said, ignoring Malone and reaching for David's hand, "the mind can do things to a person, make them believe something that isn't true if they let it, but, David, it's *not* true, our daughter died like I told you. Let it go, David, Rose Marie is Caroline's daughter."

"Detective, can we postpone this meeting until this afternoon?" David asked as he stood. "I think you owe me this one, Malone."

Annie stood and they left Malone sitting at the desk holding the snapshot. Without a word of conversation David and Annie walked up Main Street to the Davis Building and took the elevator to the tenth floor.

Liz was away from her desk but came around the corner from the supply room when she heard them come through the doors.

"Glad you're back, Boss," she greeted them. "How are you, Ms. Williams? In town for a little business—or is it pleasure this time?" she asked, handing David his phone messages.

"I'm afraid it's neither one," Annie answered. "The police are questioning me about the death of my friend."

"Wait here," David told Annie and went into his office and closed the door.

David looked up Weeks Leonard's phone number at the

university and dialed him direct. The phone rang several times. He was about to hang up when Weeks answered.

"Leonard here."

"Weeks, I'm glad I caught you . . ."

"David, are you still in town?"

"No, I caught a late flight and I'm back in Dallas, but I need you to answer a question for me."

"I'll try, lay it out there, what'd you need to know?"

"It's about Rose Marie—how long have you known her?"

"I've known her for a long time, David, she was in my class her freshman year here in Austin, she's a fine girl and I don't have to tell you she's got a brilliant mind."

"No, you don't have to tell me, I know she's smart, but what else do you know about her? Where does she come from?"

"She's lived here in Austin for as long as I can remember. I've known her mother ever since she moved here about fifteen years ago, a widow and a fine woman."

"Thanks, Weeks. I just needed to know."

"Is that it?"

"That's it. Thanks again for yesterday."

"Anytime."

When David walked out, Annie was looking out the window at Main Street below.

"I thought I'd take a drive out to Senator Mitchell's place," he told her. "Do you want to ride out there with me?"

"I really don't care if I ever see that man again, but if you need me to, or if you need to see him about that photograph— if I can help you get this behind you—then I'll go with you."

———

Passengers were still boarding the American Airlines 747 as the senator was being served a bourbon with a splash of branch in the first-class section of the plane. A long vacation was just the ticket he needed. His constituents would understand; he was still the grieving widower.

———

By the middle of the afternoon David and Annie returned to the police department where Malone was waiting.

Annie's journal lay in the middle of the detective's desk.

"I've read your book, Ms. Williams, and I'm sure I don't have to tell you that there are some things in there that implicate you in the death of Lindsey Mitchell." Annie did not reply and he continued. "What's more we've not been able to verify your whereabouts the night of Roberta Duplissey's death. You say you went back to the hotel that night and had a drink in the bar at about a quarter past ten, but it's only a five—easy eight—minute walk to the Davis Building from the Adolphus and that makes it possible to place you there at the time of the murder."

"Are you accusing my client of culpability in the Duplissey murder or did you call her in for questioning about the death of Lindsey Mitchell?"

"Well, both, Matthews. I think Ms. Williams here has knowledge about both incidents, isn't that right, Ms. Williams?"

"I can assure you, Detective, I did not murder anybody."

Malone opened the journal to the last entry and pushed the book across the desk for Anne and David to see what she had written.

"Would you care to tell me what that means, Ms. Williams?"

"Detective Malone, are you going to arrest Ms. Williams? If you are I suggest you read her the Miranda warning now, and if you're not, she will be taking the Fifth and we're leaving."

"You're free to exercise your constitutional rights, Ms. Williams, and since I'm not placing you under arrest for either of these deaths at this time, you don't need to hear the Miranda, but you are a person of interest in both of these cases, do you understand that?"

"Yes, Detective, I understand."

————————

David and Annie returned to the Main Street building and this time Annie followed him into his private office. David went to his desk and looked through the short stack of phone messages.

"The senator called," he told Annie.

"Why?"

"Just says he's leaving town for a while. I guess we already knew that, didn't we?"

"So where do we go from here?" Annie asked.

"You tell me, Annie, where *do* we go from here? And why does it sound like you had something to do with Lindsey's death? As far as Butter goes, I do know you didn't kill her, but you do realize Malone can make both motive and opportunity now?"

Annie nodded.

"Malone has enough now to make an arrest," David continued. "He'll probably go to the grand jury for an indictment in a few days."

"What about the senator? Did he play a role in his wife's death?" Liz asked, walking into the office.

"Can't he take the Fifth?" Annie asked before David could answer Liz.

"Well, no, since he's not a suspect, he can't refuse to answer. And if he lies and it comes out later, he'll be facing felony charges for perjury. That would be the end of his political career, but who knows, it might not affect his career at all, stranger things have happened in politics."

"I thought Mitchell had fairly well come to the end of the career rope anyway," Liz commented.

"Yes, until Lindsey died. One thing's for sure," David said, glancing at Annie, "I need to talk to him before Malone gets to him."

"He'll have to be back for the campaign, won't he?" Liz asked.

"Maybe, maybe not—he's pretty shrewd," David answered.

EPILOGUE

Taylor and Annie were asleep when David left for the office early that next morning. By the middle of the afternoon, about the time Annie arrived at the law offices, David approached the number three tee box and drew the big wood from his bag and thought about his next drive. Liz had assured Annie that David planned to return.

It was almost dark when David walked into his office and found Annie waiting.

The fax line rang from the supply room. "That's probably what you've been expecting," Liz said to Annie. "If it is I'll be right back, otherwise I'll leave you two to your troubles and see you in the morning, Boss."

Liz returned to David's office with a single sheet of paper for Annie.

Annie looked it over and handed it to David. "It's a copy of the death certificate," she told him. "I called the county clerk's office in Philly and asked that they send this on right away."

David held the page in his hand and read through it. Lauren Rose Matthews. Annie had given her child—their daughter—his name. David turned in his swivel chair and faced the covered window behind him while Annie sat quietly and waited. After a few minutes he stood, opened his briefcase, placed the document inside, snapped the lid shut, and leaned against his desk, his arms crossed on his chest.

"Annie, are you ready now to tell me what happened to Lindsey?"

"Yes, David, I'm ready, but you're not going to like what I have to say. I know you, David, and you have to promise me you'll let me get through this. If you stop me, I don't think I can do it again."

"Annie, I need to know what happened to Lindsey."

"Promise me, David."

"Just don't leave anything out. This time I need all the facts—the good, the bad, and the ugly."

When Annie had finished her story she sat quietly and waited for David to speak.

"Let's go home, Annie." He reached for her hand.

————

Taylor had left a note on the kitchen table along with a bottle of Merlot. She had decided to join friends for dinner and told Annie not to wait up, not to worry, she'd be out late. David was reading the note aloud when there was a knock at the front door. When he opened it Malone was standing on the porch. It was starting to rain again and the detective stepped inside.

"Come in," David offered and followed Malone down the hall to the kitchen.

"Ma'am." Malone took off his baseball jacket and hung it loosely over the back of the kitchen chair. "Here, let me give you a hand with that," he said, taking the bottle and corkscrew from a surprised Annie. Annie went to the cabinet for a third glass and while the detective poured she and David sat down at the table. Malone savored the first taste while Annie and David watched.

"What's this all about, Malone?" David asked.

"Well, you see, it's like this"—he looked directly at Annie—"substantiated by your diary, Ms. Williams, we've established enough circumstantial evidence to indict you for the murder of your old friend, Lindsey Mitchell. As for the death of Roberta Duplissey we believe that given your relationship with her we can establish enough of a motive to go for murder one. We already have opportunity nailed. What we don't have is the murder weapon, but, sooner or later, those things always turn up."

Malone reached for his jacket and pulled out a small cassette recorder. "I just came from your office, Matthews, I guess I left this there by *mistake* that afternoon I came by to get Ms. Williams's diary. It's a voice-activated little gadget."

Annie stared at Malone. He'd taped their whole meeting? Her mind raced, what had she told David?

Malone pressed the Play button and the story began to unwind.

"That day of the funeral—afterward when we went to the diner—remember you asked me when I last saw Lindsey?" Annie began. *"The truth was I had seen Lindsey several times that last year."*

Annie sat staring as the recorder played through the smoke.

"By that last year Lindsey was taking a lot of drugs. She'd seen

several doctors and every doctor she saw prescribed medications for her depression, for her headaches, for her nerves, for her insomnia, for just about anything she claimed bothered her. There was a pill for every reason. By their street names, you'd know them all, David, but she was addicted to legitimate prescribed drugs. Buddy knew it but he was no help, in fact, he was the reason she needed pills. He had an impressive schedule of social and political events to attend and he demanded she be perfect at all times—she was, after all, his biggest asset. Unfortunately by then she felt like hell most of the time—and was beginning to look like it, too."

Malone hit the Stop button and topped off Annie's glass as she began to elaborate. "There was one evening in particular Lindsey could hardly walk straight—I'm not sure if it was the drugs or the liquor, there was always plenty of both, but she bumped against the walls and furniture often enough so that she was always bruised somewhere, but that night somebody noticed. Next thing you know there was a rumor going around that the senator had hit her. It was common knowledge he was verbally abusive and when the tabloids painted him as a wife beater he was furious. Buddy Mitchell was scurrilous all right, but the truth was he never struck Lindsey; at least she said he hadn't, until that night. It must have felt good because he hit her again and again and again."

"And you know this because . . . ?" Malone asked.

"Because Lindsey told me—okay, she could have lied . . . but she didn't."

Again Malone pressed the Play button and Annie's story continued to unwind.

"Lindsey knew her lifestyle with the senator left a lot to be desired. The children were left with nannies most of the time. She also knew that the kids growing up in their neighborhood had lots

of money in their pockets and little supervision and she was smart enough to know she couldn't control the inevitable if they remained with her and Buddy in Dallas. She wanted the boys to have a fighting chance and enrolling them in the San Marcos Academy seemed like the best possibility."

"Wasn't it difficult to convince the senator? After all, the appearance of a family would have more political appeal?" she heard David's voice ask.

"Not really, Buddy saw the boarding school as the solution to several problematic situations. He needed a 'family' all right, that always had voter appeal, and with Lindsey he got his ready-made family. But he also needed an attractive doting wife on his arm at all times."

"All the trappings and none of the trouble," David said beneath his breath.

"Exactly—and Lindsey wanted to protect her sons," Annie snapped back as the recorder played forward.

"I realized that Lindsey needed to rid herself of Buddy once and for all. Without Buddy, Lindsey could move out of the house on Turtle Creek, the boys could move back with their mother, Dena would have her daughter back, the Democrats would no doubt recover, and I'd have my friend in my life again. As I saw it the senator would have to go—permanently."

The recorder stopped abruptly at the end of the tape.

"Permanently?" Malone asked.

"Very. I wanted him dead, Detective."

"You intended to murder the senator?" Malone asked while David opened another bottle of wine and Annie continued.

"Yes, Detective, I did. Lindsey knew Buddy's schedule that week and all in all it seemed simple enough. The senator had a new driver, "Swede" he called him, but Swede wasn't all that familiar with the routine just yet. We decided to make it look like a break in. Lindsey took a few things out of the house ahead of time and got rid of them—jewelry, that sort of thing—to make it look like a burglary.

"Then for the purpose of creating an alibi Lindsey planned to attend an event with friends that evening. Swede would drive her, wait, and return her to the house afterward. When they arrived home he would see her to the kitchen door and would hear her call out to the senator when she started toward the den. She planned to scream when she discovered the body. Swede would hear her and rush back inside.

"Late that afternoon," Annie continued telling Malone, "I drove into Dallas and straight to Lindsey's. By the time I arrived she had gone, and like I said, she'd already taken the items to make it look like a burglary, everything but the Rolex—I would take that off his wrist after I shot him. Lupe was away for the evening. I cut the headlights and pulled around to the back of the house. The side door was unlocked, Lindsey had seen to that too.

"I went through the kitchen door and could hear the senator in the study. When he looked up and saw me standing there I had the gun firmly in my hand. He stood up quickly when he saw me."

"I can imagine," Malone said.

"Lindsey came home as planned and had expected to find the senator dead, but our timing was off. I was pointing the gun at him when we heard Lindsey call out his name. When she came into the study he lunged at me, knocked the gun out of my hand, and it scooted across the floor. Lindsey grabbed it, not knowing what to do next. Buddy told her to give him the gun, but she just stood there pointing it at him. I told her to give it to me and she said she couldn't go through with it.

Buddy put it together pretty quick and realized we were in this together and he started to talk Lindsey into putting the gun down. He said they could work it out where nobody would have to die—that we should trust him.

"Lindsey put the gun on the desk, stepped back, and Buddy walked over to the bar and poured himself a drink. With both hands shaking now, he refilled his glass and this time poured each of us a shot. Buddy put the gun in his desk drawer and when it was out of sight we all started to breathe a little easier."

"So when was this exactly?" Malone asked.

"Back in February."

"And the senator's wife died in April, just two months later," Malone commented.

"Well, after we didn't shoot the senator, the three of us sat there all night talking about how everybody would be happier if Lindsey and the senator ceased to exist as a couple."

"I know it's not original but did the word *divorce* ever come into the conversation?" Malone asked.

"Yes, they'd both talked of divorce, but that was out of the question. Buddy had already been through one nasty tabloid divorce and a second one would be the end of his career and he wasn't going to have that happen. So as the night went on, death again became the most promising possibility. Only this time it would have to be Lindsey's death. We could fake the death and Lindsey would be free to disappear forever. Anywhere she wanted to go, but she could never return."

And while Annie told her version of the story to Malone, David replayed her tale in his mind. *"Ah, so the plot takes a turn,"* David remembered asking.

"Indeed, it took a big turn and here's where Francis comes into the picture."

"Francis? Francis Zacchoias? The Greek?"

"The Greek, as you so eloquently put it, and Lindsey loved each other and Francis had been unhappy for years with Ismini and eventually it became clear to him that Ismini was going to be a spiteful woman all her life. He was living in a hell that had no way out—until we told him there was a way out."

"But I was with you when he learned Lindsey had died. He was devastated when we told him that day down at the café."

"So it would seem—he even surprised me with the performance. But he was in on this from that very next day back in February when we tried to kill Buddy. We had to move fast, but Francis would do anything for Lindsey. He'd never stopped loving her and when Lindsey told him that she was going away forever he made up his mind right then to go with her. He'd give up everything and the best part of it all is he didn't have to give up anything. Francis is a very wealthy man and he had enough time to arrange a comfortable new life for them both—on the other side of the world. He could make all this happen and nobody would ever be the wiser. The truth was nobody would care if Lindsey or Francis lived or died and for them dead was the better choice."

"And Francis was going to handle all the arrangements?" David had asked.

"He was the only one that had the kind of money that couldn't be traced back. No one would suspect he had anything to do with this. You witnessed his reaction when we told him she was dead? You're a seasoned investigator and even you didn't suspect he was in on this?"

"The senator would go along with all of this"—David composed himself without anyone noticing and added to Annie's story to Malone—"because he stood to benefit as well. His political career had been on the skids and a wife's death would get him sympathy votes, and that's all that mattered to him."

"So how did Duplissey manage to get into this mess?" Malone asked. "I know for a fact she is one very dead woman."

"Butter came to see me a few weeks ago. I suspect she picked up my diary while she was visiting me in Austin. When she found out about the baby I'm certain she just intended to torment David. I doubt she read the whole book because she didn't have that kind of patience, but she made a huge mistake when she told the senator she knew all about 'it' and about Lindsey and me and that she had the diary that revealed all the little secrets. The senator assumed that Butter knew more than she did. He wanted the diary back so he could destroy it, but by then she'd given it to David. It wouldn't have mattered, it didn't say anything about the senator, or the night Lindsey and I tried to kill him, but by then the senator was a desperate man. If Butter hadn't been killed that night in David's office, Lindsey's death would never have been under investigation."

"Back up a minute and tell me about the body in the casket. If it wasn't Lindsey, then who?" Malone asked.

"Ever been to one of those wax museums?"

"You mean it was a wax replica?"

"*Yes, but we also had to have a real body,*" David remembered Annie saying. "*Since we were going to cremate we needed ashes so Francis arranged to have a body 'snatched' from the cemetery the night before the funeral. That was the final touch.*"

"Lindsey was there that afternoon, at the service," Annie told Malone.

"Wearing a dark blue coat?" Malone mused.

"She couldn't pass up the chance to attend her own funeral," David heard Annie calmly tell Malone as he realized she was still keeping secrets. His mind focused now on the rest of their previous conversation.

"The morning of the funeral I met Lindsey at the café. Francis had closed that day and nobody was there. The three of us said our good-byes. He and Lindsey were going to meet again that night in Galveston. Francis had it all arranged. From there they would sail into the Gulf of Mexico and after that who knows. They have no plans to ever return."

"Annie, you realize Malone is going to arrest you for the murder of Lindsey, don't you? At the very least he'll go after conspiracy charges. What's worse, Butter was shot with a .38-caliber gun and if that gun turns up and turns out to be the same gun belonging to you, he'll go after you again—for murder one." David had told her.

"Ms. Williams, your story's preposterous." Malone leaned in and spoke clearly, his eyes fixed on Annie. "No jury would ever believe it, and this tape is inadmissible and can't be used to substantiate your testimony even if they wanted to believe it. However, your diary, Ms. Williams, with all the implicating statements and innuendos therewith, is admissible as evidence. The diary says it all. The D.A.'ll see motive and opportunity. It's everything he'll want or need."

"Where's my book now?" Annie asked quietly.

Malone stood, took the dog-eared journal from the inside pocket of his jacket, walked to the liquor cabinet in the next room, and helped himself to a bottle of Jack. Annie and David followed him into the den. "I need a drink," he said while he rifled the pages of the diary and drenched them in the whiskey. Then he hurled the journal and the half-empty bottle of Jack into the fireplace, the soaked pages and the liquor exploding into flames on the hot coals.

Annie raised her glass.

"To Lindsey," David offered the toast.

"To love and death in Dallas," Malone mused with a shrug. "I could have ridden that diary all the way up the command chart."

"In Dallas County?" David said. "They'd make you commissioner."

"President," Annie added.

"Stranger things have happened in Dallas," Malone said, fixing Annie with a long hard stare.

———

The Swede sat in the limousine and watched from a distance as the international jumbo jet took flight from DFW Airport. He reached over and opened the glove compartment where he'd placed the .38-caliber pistol on the way to the banks of the Trinity River the morning after Butter was killed.

It was his secret and for now he'd hang on to it, it might come in handy sometime.

He started the car and turned east toward Dallas where his new woman—a tart thing, dark hair, slim hips, nice rags, and an expensive little red sports car—was waiting for him at the senator's house.

It was just the beginning . . .